This Charming Guest

By

Sharon Gartner

www.sharongartner.com

Angelwords Publications

IBSN 978-0-9873750-4-9

Cover Design
Libbi Reed
www.addlibbi.com.au

Editing Janine Ogden

Also Available by Sharon Gartner

This Charming Shack

This Charming Angel

www.sharongartner.com

For all the single ladies out there

Facebook Profile.

Lisa Collins.

Approaching 40.

Successful event planner, B&B owner, petting zoo operator.

Single.

About me: Well after almost getting married to Rick Crankshaw (when my cougar friend Neroli and her young fiancé Matt broke up on the day of their wedding leaving Rick making the suggestion that he and I get married instead) I have decided to concentrate on my career as an event planner. I am now a proud aunty to my best friend Millie's baby girl Amy, and have a fantastic business partnership with Daniel the local photographer and event merchandiser (used to be an obnoxious twat but not any more). I found I have a true gift, and that is to connect with ghosts (well just one ghost and he's not around now but I'm sure it's just like riding a bike; you'll never forget how).

Advisor for the Impulse Behaviour Group.

Spiritual adviser and dating expert.

****

New moon wishes for Lisa Collins <3 <3

1) I wish I could have a baby before I turn 40 otherwise I will miss my chance.

2) I wish to meet nice men who are interested in having babies.

3) I wish Millie would let me take Amy to single parent support groups so I can meet nice men who are interested in having more babies.

****

1

Eve of 39th birthday, 11.23pm.

Ugly bald guy is really starting to piss me off; I mean he really isn't appealing at all so why is he trying to convince me he is Brad Pitt?

Really need to log off dating site but cannot sleep because tomorrow is my birthday which means I only have one year left to find a man and have babies before I shrivel up.

Oh god now ugly bald guy wants to show me something via Skype.

Think it's definitely time to log off.

Unless…

No better log off.

It's so unfair; since Millie had Amy I have been sooo clucky and since Rick and I split up almost a year ago I haven't been on a single date and am starting to feel like a crazy cat lady.

Except I don't have a cat.

Just a crazy dog called Monty that I got given by an equally crazy Italian man and his out-of-control wife (who insisted I was trying to proposition her husband because he fed me olive oil with a teaspoon). So cannot really blame dog for his psychotic behaviour.

"You still trawling the 'net?" asked Millie in a quiet voice, supporting a sleepy Amy on her shoulder.

Amy is almost five months old now and is the cutest little thing you ever did meet; I'm teaching her to say *'Lisa Collins Event Planner'* using flashcards.

I had seen on an infomercial that any child can read before the age of two if you start the brain early, so instead of buying 'Phonics is Fun' educational set for 3 easy payments of $39.95 (plus postage and handling) I decided to make my own flashcards so when Amy does mutter her first words then at least she will drum up a bit of business for me with all her cuteness. (Even though Millie ripped up the first three flashcards I made saying she does not buy into this crap and stop using her daughter to pick up clients).

Millie has gone back to work and Sid is now a stay-at-home-Dad (well in-between running the B&B).

He is sooo good at it, being a father I mean.

Oh did I mention the attic is now a Bed & Breakfast?

"Can't sleep," I moaned, closing my laptop and putting my pity face on.

Millie sighed as she gingerly sat down on the chair next to me so as not to disturb an almost asleep baby and a passed out Monty who is curled up on the sofa beside me.

"Why don't you just take the plunge and ask Daniel out?" Millie said for about the millionth time this year, "got nothing to lose," she yawned.

"Um because that would be just too awkward," I said in my 'is this getting through to you' voice.

Daniel and I have joined forces and are now called '*Cannon and Collins. Photography, Event Planning and Supplies*'. Daniel still does his photography and I do my event planning as well as running the shop with the event merchandise. Daniel is Rick's best friend and we met when Rick and I were dating. After a rocky start to our meeting by me flashing half-naked self at him and then hiring his old family church; during which time my ghost friend Larry informed police of a dead body under the stairs, which didn't really matter because Neroli and Matt ended up breaking up on their wedding day anyway; we have become great business partners.

Oh did I mention the ghost I used to see was called Larry?

Daniel is really nice and I'm convinced he is really into me, it's just the vibe I get from him, and Millie has even noticed the way he is around me, she said I should just shag him and get it over with but it's okay for her she doesn't have to work with him.

Okay secretly I wouldn't mind shagging Daniel but I know if I go there it would be too awkward us working together and that part of it is going really really well.

And besides Daniel would have to make the first move and considering he has already been on about a dozen dates so far (some are even second and third dates) he's probably not that horny.

Although I was secretly pleased when he slammed the phone down on his last date and spent the afternoon at a photo shoot complaining about her.

But still no proposition of a shag for me.

"Well, whatever," Millie yawned and checked over her shoulder to see if Amy had fallen asleep, "sometimes I think you're too picky, what about the guy you were chatting to on the internet? He seemed nice."

"He was bisexual and asked if I was into threesomes, then ran a mile when I said I'd consider it as long as he was up for having children. I mean it's okay for you Millie you're married, even if it is to Sid. You don't know what it's like to be single and desperate," I whinged.

"Maybe that's your issue," said Millie in her 'I know what's best for you' voice, "you're too desperate, maybe you should stop being so pushy and let things flow. Go on a couple of dates and see how things go."

Not going to answer as I can see she is in her motherly ranting mood. Which is coming off sooo annoying.

"Well as I said, whatever; I'm off to bed," Millie said, carefully negotiating herself off her chair with baby in arms. She leaned down as she passed me so I could give Amy a goodnight kiss. "And if that doesn't work, there's a lot of sperm donors out there," she chuckled.

I watch her exit the room and now I do feel really desperate, I mean I know Millie was joking and all, but sperm donors, is that what I have to consider?

Great, can just see headstone now; *Lisa Collins, crazy dog lady, will be dearly missed by those at the local sperm bank.*

Just thinking about going to bed when I heard a car pull up outside, I really should get Sid as sometimes we have late arrivals at night looking for accommodation even though the sign out front says 'no enquiries after 8pm', but Sid's too soft on guests and doesn't even care if they are rude to him, which is great for business; I mean if it was Millie having to deal with the guests, we would be bankrupt by now.

Oh, it's not a potential guest, just Matt.

"Sup?" he greeted, sauntering in and planting his youthful butt on the sofa.

Matt and Neroli broke up on the day they were supposed to be getting married and Neroli took Baby Bailey and Tom back to be near her parents in Perth, leaving me looking silly as I was the one organising the wedding. He has only recently been game enough to be in the same room as me without protection.

"It's Friday night, what are you doing here, it's almost midnight?" I asked like an old person.

"Yeah well we were at this party and then Munta hooked up with this chick and Damo had a bong so he's trashed and passed out in my car, and I'm bored as, so thought I'd come and say hey."

"What about your girlfriend Melanie?" I asked.

"That's who Munta's hooked up wif," he said as he flicked though the TV channels.

"And does that bother you?"

"What? Yeah, I mean he better not spew in my car or nuffing."

"No, does it bother you that Munta has hooked up with your girlfriend?"

"Oh that, um, nah not really, going off her anyway."

Man, youth romance is so uncomplicated.

I don't feel tired so I sit with Matt for a while as he watches some stupid TV program about extreme motorcycles and I am so ignoring the fact it's just ticked past midnight and I am now officially in the last year of my thirties.

God maybe *I* need to suck down a bong and pass out in Matt's car.

Doesn't help that it's my time of the month, I always seem to get it on every birthday which makes getting older seem so much worse.

"You don't look right," Matt said like he has suddenly noticed I'm still here, "you look like, I duno, depressed or somefing."

Great, even drunken youth is telling me I look terrible.

"Hey fuck it's your birthday tomorrow," said Matt, suddenly realising.

"Actually it's today," I corrected, pointing to my watch.

"Oh cool, happy birthday. Why do you look fucked off about it?"

I don't really want to tell Matt why; I mean Millie's okay, but when you go to tell a guy that your biological clock is ticking and you feel like your woman parts are going to stop working due to lack of interest it kinda sounds… well…

"Is it because you're 40?" Matt said trying on a sympathetic look.

"I'm 39!!"

"Oh."

"And no, it's not just that Matt, it's well, oh never mind."

"Okay," he shrugged, going back to his TV program.

"All right, it's like this," I continued, "I'm a year off turning 40 and if I don't find someone to have a baby with soon then that's it for me, may as well forget about having a family, I mean who's going to look after me in my old age?" oh god I'm nearly crying.

"Oh come on now," Matt sympathised, "I mean you're a nice looking chick I bet lots of guys want to shag you, Damo fancies you, he'll shag ya."

"But what if I don't have a baby Matt?"

"Then have one anyway, just get someone to shag you."

"And bring a baby into this world a single mother; yeah that's really healthy Matt."

"Unhealthy if you're wif the wrong guy just because you want a baby."

Surprised at youth's very mature statement.

"And besides any kid of yours will have lots of dads, I mean I'd be a kind-of dad to it you know, I love kids."

Very touched by Matt's statement but still feel like shit.

"I know what you need," said Matt, "you need a birthday bong."

"No I don't."

16

"Awwww why not?"

"Because this is a place of business Matt, we can't be having bong parties here, guests or no guests; and besides I don't do that."

"Yeah well maybe you need to start 'cause you're being such a nana."

"I am not being a nana."

"Are too."

"Are not, just because I choose not to spend the first few hours of my birthday frying my brain with illegal substances, not to mention what side effects are inflicted on your body, does not make me a nana."

"Whatever… nana."

Not going to bite at rude statement made by youth half my age.

Oh my god, youth half my age just called me a granny.

Okay not to panic, I mean there is 19 years difference in age. When I was 20 I'm sure I thought anyone almost turning 40 was ancient.

Matt's just annoyed because I won't smoke pot with him.

Besides I'm not the one sitting at home on a Friday night, sipping tea, watching TV with a woman who is twice my age.

Pff, I think we all know who the 'nana' is here.

2

7 hours into 39th birthday.

Think someone is knocking on the door but cannot be sure as cannot lift eyelids open.

And sun must be up 'cause it's burning my face.

There goes that knocking again.

I'm sure Millie will be up by now so she can answer it, anyway, too early, so must be guest for accommodation.

Which is great 'cause it means Sid can deal with it and I can go back to sleep and not worry.

Ow, something just wacked me in the face.

And it stinks.

Must be Monty wanting his breakfast. Well he's a dog he can go hunt his own. Not running a B&B here.

Well I am, but not for dogs.

God there goes that knocking again, is anyone going to answer the fricken door?

I really need water as my mouth feels like someone emptied an ashtray into it and it's like 100 degrees in here, it must be around mid morning. Which is perfect as I'm trying to ignore the fact it's my birthday but I know what Millie would say if she knew I was sulking.

I decided after Matt's nana rant that the best way to avoid depression is to cancel my birthday so am going to stay asleep until tomorrow.

Well that would be the plan if this bloody knocking would stop.

Actually that knocking sounds really loud.

Right, new plan, really need water and to open a window because the air in here is almost suffocating.

Also need to pee.

I'll get up, sneak into the bathroom via passageway to avoid kitchen where Millie is bound to be with Amy, and use the rinse glass in the bathroom to carry water back to bedroom; open window and go back to bed, avoiding contact with housemates.

Also hoping Sid will answer the fecken door soon.

Okay, 1… 2…

Argghhh!!!

What the…??

"Ow!"

"Sorry, my bad," said Matt, removing his smelly foot from my eye socket.

It also appears someone is lying on my legs and it's neither Matt nor Monty.

Why does it appear I have woken up in a game of twister?

"Someone put down the window," said a voice that sounded an awful lot like Matt's stoner mate Damo.

"You're in the front, turn the key on," said Matt.

"Can't, no keys, you must have 'em."

"Open the door then."

"It's locked."

"Then unlock it, ya muppet."

Okay, why does it appear I have woken up in a game of twister in the back seat of a car with two youths?

Arghh, and who is that?

"Are you alright in there?" called a strange gentleman through the glass, "you need to unlock the door."

My god, where are we, in some car park somewhere?

My god this car stinks of…

Oh no.

It appears I did suck down a bong last night and pass out in Matt's car with Damo; and now a strange man has appeared to perve at us passed out in car with a bong and what appear to be discarded potato chip bags.

Oh my god I hope he isn't a cop.

I so don't want to go to jail.

Grrrr, why oh why did I let Matt talk me in to this? Why can't I just go back to sitting on the sofa in my PJ's, sipping tea on a Friday night like a nana?

Shit here comes Millie.

Well at least we are at home.

"What are you doing?" she hissed as the car door flings open.

Millie is looking mortified as the strange young man explained he was here to check into the accommodation and got quite concerned when he spotted us sound asleep in the car in the baking hot sun and could not rouse us.

Phew, thank god he isn't a cop.

Monty has now appeared and is jumping all over Damo who has passed out again.

I could hear Millie explaining that we must have forgotten our keys after coming home from a night out as she coaxed the strange man towards the house, shooting us a glare over her shoulder as she goes.

She looks embarrassed and angry.

Okay I really need to cancel my birthday now; no-one embarrasses Millie and gets away with it.

Shit now Damo has thrown up all over Monty.

In kitchen.

Monty and Damo are all cleaned up after I took the hose to both of them and now he and Matt are cooking breakfast for everyone.

Haven't seen Millie again but we thought if we cooked her breakfast it would be less likely she would tear us to shreds on a full stomach. We have seen Sid however, not that Sid has the ability to tear us to shreds, but he did express how very disappointed he was with us all as this is a place of business, and not that he has anything against us having a bit of fun but it looks very very bad.

So now we feel like naughty kids needing to get on the good side of our parents.

Also trying to pretend there's no birthday happening.

"There ya go, happy birthday," said Matt placing a plate full of overcooked eggs, burnt sausages, and toast in front of me.

Did I mention I'm now a vegetarian?

Daniel put me up to it.

"Err thanks but I'm still mortified you talked me into our little 'party' last night Matt."

"I didn't talk you into it, you wanted to, not my fault you're feeling old and wanted to get off your tits."

"Yeah 'cause you were calling me a nana, not a good thing to say to a person on edge Matt."

"Aww don't be so sensitive, I was just messing wif ya, besides you were a crack-up last night, oh man you should have seen ya face, you were so out-of-it."

Damo chuckled in agreement.

Not that he would know, he could barely see.

Cringing as memories of sitting in the back seat of Matt's car in my pajamas in a smoky haze comes flooding back.

Although it did make me forget I was 39.

Also made me a very very boring person as I think I spent the night talking to youths about the effects of potato chip oil on car upholstery.

Not that they were really listening. Too busy eating potato chips.

But anyway, didn't solve anything because now I'm back on planet earth and I'm still one year off being 40 and have no man or babies.

Matt has now called Millie and Sid to the kitchen and I am embracing myself for the 'Millie' lecture. But turns out there isn't one. In fact, apart from 'happy birthday' and presenting me with a beautiful gift of a Milche bag and matching wallet that I had hinted for, she hasn't said a word.

Which means she's saving it up for my mother's next visit.

We're all seated around the table now and after Matt insisted we raise our mugs of coffee to toast my birthday, the conversation seems to be a bit mundane, which is great as I can still pretend it's not my birthday.

Ohh just got a birthday text from Daniel; it's a long one as well, followed by an *x*.

Just got goose bumps, think I'll read it again.

"Why don't you just shag him?" said Matt through a mouthful of eggs.

Mumbles of agreement all round.

"Did I say something out loud?"

"Nah, could tell by the silly grin on your face."

Mumbles of agreement all round.

"I can't shag him, we work together, it would be weird," pff why don't friends listen.

"Yeah but if you shag him then you would get it out of the way, then you could concentrate on actually doing work, it's a win win."

Mumbles of agreement and giggles all round.

Very offended by Matt's last statement so slammed fork down on plate to begin my protest when strange man gingerly knocks at kitchen door.

Matt and Damo have suddenly gone quiet and are concentrating on their plates in front of them.

I think I might slip out the other door and pretend I need the bathroom.

Hope he doesn't recognise us.

"Excuse me," he said, "is there a possibility I could get more coffee?" he asks, holding a tray of used dishes.

"Certainly," said Sid in his 'dealing with guests' manner of politeness as he rises from his seat, "I'll bring it up to you."

Sid takes the tray from the strange man who seems satisfied by the service and I take the opportunity to slip out of the room, I look up just as he shoots me a glance.

He looks very familiar, like I've seen him somewhere before but cannot place him. He's not bad looking, must be young, although he has one of those baby faces. Wonder if he wants babies?

Made it to the safety of the bathroom and shut the door.

Don't need to pee but do need to think. I mean it's not like I'm 'in love' with Daniel or anything but I do think I have a little crush.

Or maybe I'm just horny.

Think I'll read his text message again.

Washed hands even though I didn't pee but good to keep in the habit, and reached for the door.

"Oh I'm sorry," said startled strange man as he appeared on the other side of the door reaching for the handle, "the bathroom upstairs is being cleaned, the man said I could use this one," he continued.

"Oh, err, go ahead," I said keeping my head down.

"Are you a guest here as well?" he plugged on.

Oh god, strange young man wants to have a conversation while I'm in smelly PJ's and have morning hair.

And after effects of smoking bongs in the back of youth's car.

"Um… no, I actually live here. Okay, um, bye."

"Oh really?" he said with a polite smile, "so you must be the co-owner?"

Okay, he wants a conversation and cannot see I'm not in the mood for it so I'm going to have to just start walking away.

"Yes I am the co-owner, very busy doing owner stuff, so must dash."

Walk away fast before he says anything else.

Back in the kitchen I rejoin Matt and Damo to finish my breakfast. Millie and Sid have gone so it must be mid morning now as that's when Sid does the cleaning and washing.

Thank god it's Saturday and I don't have any work on. I was meant to help Daniel today organise a family reunion event but we made a policy when we joined forces that we would give each other the day off on our birthdays.

And occasionally when I have really bad pmt.

"So whatya got planned for your born day?" Matt asked, followed by a belch.

"Nothing."

"So you just going to sit around depressed 'cause no-one will shag ya?"

"Oh my god Matt there's more to life than just sex."

Matt and Damo look at me blankly.

"… and besides," I continued, "not much to do anyway so I think I'll go back to bed and have a nice relaxing day reading."

Matt and Damo still looking at me blankly.

"You know, as in books," I sighed.

"You know what we should do?" said Matt, "we should go clubbing in the city."

"No."

"Yeah we could crash at Bob's," mumbled Damo.

"Okay, have fun," I said.

"You're coming," said Matt with a firm no-nonsense tone to his voice.

"No I'm not."

"Yes you are, and besides, why are you even arguing, I thought you wanted to get laid?"

"Matt, it's bad enough you lured me into your bong cave last night, now you want to lure me into a room filled with sweaty young bodies and doff doff music clanging at my eardrums. And besides, I didn't say I wanted to get laid, I said I wanted to get laid and have babies."

"I know what you should do," said Matt suddenly having a brain storm, "you should go and wait for the bus in town, they have shit loads of guys on there."

"What bus?"

"The bus that comes into town every week. They stop to refuel and use the public toilets; it's full of miners heading out west. They come into town same time every week. You should go get a man from there."

"Matt are you suggesting I go and storm a bus-load of men looking for a date? Please tell me that didn't just fall out of your tiny brain."

"You said you want a man, well that's where some are, and they have jobs."

"Oh my god! Matt, I can't just rock up to a bus full of men and pick one to drag home, what am I, a cavewoman?"

"All right keep ya bloomers on nana, so you're not coming clubbing then?"

"No."

"Fine, be a boring granny with no man then."

I must be starting to snap out of my birthday blues 'cause I'm not bothered by Matt's nana name calling.

But in saying that, I still want to go to bed and wake up tomorrow.

Which I think I will.

Finishing my breakfast I take my dishes to the sink followed by Matt and Damo.

"So you're definitely not coming out tonight?" said Matt, trying for the second time.

"No."

"What about coming out pig hunting wif me and the boys?"

"Definitely not."

"Awww, why not?"

"'Cause I'm a vegetarian Matt, I'm all for animal rights."

"Since when?"

"Since Daniel told me how some pigs are housed."

"You so need to shag him, but yeah whatever, your loss."

I know Matt is trying to cheer me up but to be honest I just need to get through this day and forget there is a big possibility if I don't find a man and settle down soon then there is not a hope of ever having babies.

He and Damo head off and I thank him all the same for his offer of clubbing and pig hunting to which he said he'll call in and check on me later and he may even bring some tequila and wine.

Kitchen cleaned up and still no sign of Millie as I crawl into bed; the sanctity of the bed covers has almost made me forget about turning 39. And the scary thing is, if I'm like this at 39 then what's 40 going to be like?

Millie turned 40 last year and she said it's no big deal but it's different for her, she was married and pregnant; I'm 39 and have a dog.

Okay, I really should stop feeling sorry for myself and make a list of prospective men.

Let's see, there is Daniel… and Matt.

Okay, maybe not Matt.

So that really only leaves Daniel.

Oh and Tim from the bakery…

Oh my god I'm going to die childless and alone.

There is only one thing for it, and that is sperm donors.

With that thought in mind I drift off into a semi sleep. The words 'internet dating' keep flashing up in my dreams but I have tried that and it doesn't work for me, some people find their soul mates, I always find some overweight horny loser who still lives with his mum and wears her underwear for fun.

I try and manifest what I would like in a man if I ever did meet my perfect match over the internet when a voice flashes in my head.

Read.

Pff don't think so, decided cannot face books right now.

And besides *Fifty Shades of Grey* is NOT what I need to read.

No, reading… idiot.

Of course! I shot up, untangling myself from the sheets and recovering from the head rush caused by going from semi sleep to wide awake in .005 of a second.

Reading; I need to go get a tarot reading from Angela, she will tell me if I need to go to a sperm bank or internet dating or if I'm ever going to shag Daniel.

I quickly grab my phone from the bedside table and punch in the number. Hope she can see me today, oh well if she can't then it's obvious I'm not meant to see her.

In Angela the Tarot Reader's room.

Okay, had a little meltdown when she said she couldn't see me today so after much begging on my part, and the fact I told her it was my birthday and am on the brink of losing all hope in life, Angela has agreed to squeeze me in for a mini reading.

Didn't have time to get dressed for the occasion so have thrown on an old pair of cotton sloppy shorts with singlet top, haven't dared to look at my hair, but after all it's my birthday so if I want to go with the 'sloppy Joe I don't give a shit' look today, then I will.

Good thing about turning 39 is you really don't give a damn about the little things.

Especially the morning after you have been in the back seat of a car smoking bongs with local youths.

"Okay, shuffle the deck and focus on what urgent guidance you seek today," Angela said after the usual small talk.

As I'm shuffling I'm trying to focus on one thing only.

Will I find a man and have babies before I turn 40?

I also wanted to ask if Daniel and I are going to hook up but don't want to get questions crossed. So focus on man and babies first.

I cut the deck into three piles and Angela collected them and started dealing the cards on the table in a star shape.

"Business is going well for you at the moment," she smiled, "I see you have not just the one business."

"No," I said, "I have two."

"… and the current partnership you have is one that was meant to be; you were brought together for that purpose, you work well together in business and will continue to do so."

Yes, yes, I know that.

"I see you doing more sales over the internet than from the shop front, and I also see you doing a lot more from home."

Yes, yes.

"But feel you will have another outlet elsewhere in the future, maybe closer to the city. So as far as your business life goes my dear you have nothing to worry about as it will continue to be successful; as long as you don't take it all on board yourself and hand over a lot of the responsibility to other parties."

"I do that already," I scoffed.

I mean Sid runs the B&B; I have nothing to do with that side of things.

Grrr, why does this woman always tell me stuff that's not very important.

"Hmmm no you haven't quite done that yet," she said, "you still like to maintain a lot of the control."

Pff, do not, I think she has mistaken me for Millie.

Angela focuses on a card that looks like a young man in tights.

"Who is the young man that has recently crossed your path?"

I rack my brains but the only one I can think of besides Matt is Damo.

"He is bringing with him a great opportunity for you, I feel it's business related."

Well I can't imagine what great opportunity stoner Damo is bringing to me, in fact the thought of Damo giving me any opportunity is very, very scary.

"He will help you find what you are looking for," she said looking pleased with herself, "but be careful what you reveal because it can also do great harm to you and those in business around you."

Damo is going to help me find what I'm looking for? Okay I'm confused, what is it I'm meant to be looking for?

Unless I reveal that I have had some secret crush on Damo and Daniel gets very jealous, decides he cannot live with it and leaves, I guess that would be great harm. I mean who would cover for me when I need a day off on my birthday and when I have a bad time of the month?

Not sure if 'the great ones above' understood my question.

"An older male in your family, your Dad I think, has some health issue going on, it's nothing major and I feel it can be fixed easily by medication, but tell him he needs to stop for a while as I feel half of it is caused by stress."

Okay great ones definitely haven't understood my question, I mean they really didn't need to tell me how stressed Dad is; being on the road in a Winnebago with Mum 24/7 is bound to cause some issues.

"You seem to put too much emphasis on what you don't have and don't direct energy towards what you do have," said Angela. "Once you start looking at aspects of your life that are going well and focus on that, then the rest will come."

Okay this whole reading seems to be about business, well what about the business of babies? If I don't get some answers soon I am going to demand a reschedule of my whole life; I mean they say your spirit chooses the life you have before you are born, well if I don't have a baby before I'm 40 I am seriously going to sue for misuse of contract because I certainly didn't sign up for this.

Did Angela just say she sees a lot of men around me?

"… and you will have to choose but I feel you have been down this road before and you know to follow your heart on this one," she said, unaware I had just drifted off to my own thoughts. "But it will bring huge opportunities for your business," she continued.

"Um… I'm sorry, did you just say a lot of men around me?" I interrupt her so she will repeat what I had missed.

"Yes, and you will have to choose."

Oh how exciting, maybe Matt's right about the bus-load of men that arrives in town every week to use the public toilets, I mean not sure how that would come about as I'm a bit shy and jumping a bus looking for a date seems a bit forward, but am sure the universe is working out the finer details and is rounding up potential husbands as we speak. I mean after all I did put it on my ten moon wish list. So not going to be surprised if a bus carrying potential husbands turns up at front gate.

"Will any of these men give me babies?" I said.

"There is a child for you dear but not how you would expect; the circumstances will be a little unusual."

Well there is only one way to have a baby so not sure what she means by that but I'm sure it's all good, Angela has just confirmed what I needed to know and that is, there is a child for me, which means I was panicking over nothing. I mean pff, what was I worried about. I kinda knew it deep down anyway but good to hear it from someone else.

"You are looking much happier," said Angela, "I hope I have assisted you in answering your questions today."

"Oh yes you have," I said as I rose from my seat, "thank you, thank you."

"You know you don't always need me, follow your own instincts as they never put you wrong."

"Yes I know," I nodded in a knowing way, desperate to leave so I can go prepare for my bus-load of men arriving.

You know shave legs, dye hair, that sort of thing.

"Just one more thing my dear," Angela said as I got ready for my departure.

"Yes?"

"Be careful what you wish for."

Facebook status update.

Lisa Collins.

Would like to thank everyone for the birthday wishes, I was getting a bit worried that my life was about to run down but not to worry as I have confirmation that all is good ☺

3

Back home.

Feel much better about things now, I mean there is going to be a baby after all and I cannot wait to be a mother. And if I do have it before I am 40 it means there is not going to be a huge age difference between her and Amy so they can grow up together and Millie and I can take our prams to cafés for coffee and talk mother talk.

Okay we do that now but I don't have a pram or a baby and it's only Millie who talks mother talk, another reason why I need to have a baby, so Millie and I can be balanced again.

Thinking seriously of ringing Matt and telling him I'll go clubbing with him after all.

But then again I cannot imagine I would get home at a decent hour so maybe not.

Maybe a quiet BBQ would be better.

I unload supplies in the kitchen which consists of grooming essentials for preparation for bus-load of men arriving and a box of chocolates that was on special at the supermarket, I can hear Millie in the next room giggling like a school girl. Might go say hello as I think it's safe to do that now.

I'll take my chocolates just in case.

I enter the room, then quickly make a hasty retreat. Millie is in there talking and giggling with the strange guest like they are old mates.

"Lisa," she calls out in a voice I don't recognise, it's a happy voice with a hint of politeness and a little bit of airs-and-graces.

But it means she has seen me.

Slap smile on my face and re-enter room.

Millie is chortling about something he said and there is an amateur film camera sitting on the coffee table in front of us.

"Lisa, have you met Brendon Edsgard, he is staying with us at the moment?"

"Um, briefly," I mumbled.

Okay, Millie is scaring me, for a start she remembered his last name and even pronounced it correctly.

"He's here to do a documentary on young people and country life, he's staying with us for a while" she beamed.

Why is Millie pleased about that? She doesn't like guests staying for even one night.

Explains the film camera though.

"Hello Lisa," he greeted. "I think I met you at the bathroom door, you're the co-owner?" he asked, looking at Millie for confirmation.

"Yes, Lisa is also an event planner," said Millie like I'm not here.

"Oh," he said, his eyebrows raise in interest, "what sort of events happen around here?"

"Mainly weddings," Millie cut in like I'm still not here. "We use the grounds here for photos. Lisa is in partnership with the local photographer Daniel Cannon, so we often combine services with the accommodation, planning and venue. It's coming into its second year so we can expect it to grow further, especially now we have added the petting zoo."

What is wrong with Millie?

"Uh ha," he nods, "and this house?" he continues to ask, "what is the history behind the house?"

I open my month to answer but Millie starts talking again. "It used to be the homestead for the old abattoir back in the early 1900s," she continues, leaning back further into her chair, "it was occupied for many years but when Lisa brought it, it had been sitting empty and needed a lot done. So that's when Sid and I came on board; it took some work," she laughed.

"I bet," he beamed.

Okay so Millie is taking over, well that's fine, I'll just sit on this chair and open my box of chocolates, after all it's my birthday.

Better offer them around too I s'pose.

"So anyway," Millie continued, waving my offer of chocolate away, "after we discovered the old attic we decided it had so much potential for a country guest retreat and events venue we took the chance and built a business," Millie concluded, looking at me for confirmation.

Couldn't answer as I had a mouthful of chocolate so just nodded.

Millie left out the parts about discovering the attic because we found a secret door, after which we discovered a squatter living up there along with 150 marijuana plants. And she neglected to mention her disgust at me for buying the property in the first place after the previous owners committed suicide and 'cause I wanted to show my urban hippie boyfriend of the time that I am indeed all about organics and the countryside. Hmmm what is she playing at?

"And those two young gentlemen that were here, do they work here?" he asked, taking a strawberry heart flavoured chocolate from the box.

Grrr, I wanted that one.

"Matthew and Damon? Oh no," Millie scoffed, "they were just here to visit Lisa."

Oh my god, now I'm choking on my chocolate. What the hell Millie? Now strange man's looking at me as if I'm the local drug dealer supplying youths.

Okay I *was* selling eye pillows stuffed with marijuana at one stage, but I didn't know they were stuffed with drugs at the time; I just thought youths had a fetish for eye pillows.

Why is she trying so hard to impress this guy? I mean she can't be flirting with him as she is married to Sid and has baby spew on her shoulder.

He's only doing a boring old documentary about country life, not Steven Spielberg on location filming *The Lord of the Rings.*

Oh no, wait, that was Peter Jackson.

My god, the humidity is high today; this chocolate is melting faster than it's going in my mouth.

Lucky I have my sloppy joe shorts on, good for wiping chocolate fingers on.

"Well you have certainly done a very good job," he beams at the both of us. "You girls are obviously entrepreneurs and that's one of the things I would like to touch on in my story, the opportunities that young people, mainly in the 20 to 35 year age bracket, can create for themselves. And if they see the likes of you lovely ladies in the 35 to 45 year age bracket, that can throw caution to the wind, take the risk and be successful, I'm sure more would follow your lead."

"Absolutely," Millie beamed as they both rise from their seats.

"Mind if I take some footage of the place?" he asks.

"Not at all," said Millie.

"And I'm so embarrassed to ask this," he continues, "but I may need you to sign a bit of paper to say you have given me permission to film."

Film??

"That's fine," Millie scoffed, "yes I know what you mean, everything is all about paperwork these days."

"Oh, you're not wrong," he agreed.

What does he mean by film?

"I'll just switch this off," he said reaching forward and flicking a switch on the camera that was pointing straight at Millie and me, "and go and fetch the paperwork."

"No probs," said Millie, "I'll just go check on my baby girl, coffee is hot in the kitchen, please help yourself."

They both depart hastily.

Film? Did I hear correctly, he is doing a film, here; was he just filming me? Oh my god I'm covered in chocolate and have sloppy joe clothes on.

Nah, he was probably just testing the camera, and besides he has to have permission first. But it brings up a very good point, why has Millie agreed to this without consulting Sid and I?

All major decisions about this place are not made unless everyone is consulted and a meeting and vote takes place, otherwise it would end up in Millie running everything like she's doing now.

Well I am going to vote no, I mean it probably won't air anyway, unless it's in a classroom, and cannot think of anything worse than to have someone shoving a camera in your face and getting in your way while you're trying to work. Bit of an invasion of privacy.

I can hear Sid at the back door taking his boots off so I think it's a good idea we have a meeting now before Millie signs anything.

"Hey," Sid greets, wiping the sweat from his brow and grabbing a bottle of water from the fridge, "got the mini golf course pegged, think I may need to get online and find out the price of instant turf, don't think people would appreciate teeing off on an ants nest… what?"

I'm still so in awe of the transformation of Sid since coming out here, Sid used to be really quiet and believed in aliens and was obsessed with it all the time. He even started a group called the 'Lost Souls Movement', where a group of people would meet every chance they got and talk about their alien encounters; they had a website and 24 hour hotline to report any sightings.

But since moving to the country Sid hasn't obsessed once and has given up his position as president of the group. I even heard him talk back to Millie the other day, yep goes to show you how much the countryside can make you more balanced and normal.

"We need to have an urgent house meeting," I said, "before Millie signs us up for a reality TV show."

Sid's looking confused.

"You know? The film guy who is staying here."

"The film guy is part of a reality TV show?"

"No, no… look never mind, stay there, I'll get Millie."

"She's not here, her and that guy have taken Amy for a walk, she's showing him the remains of the old stone processing hut."

Oh bloody hell.

"Okay, well if you see her tell her not to sign anything until we have a house meeting."

"You could catch up with them, they've only just left," said Sid.

"Um… nah."

Anyway back to me and my birthday, where was I…? Oh yes, prepare for bus-load of men arriving, where is my waxing kit? Actually I'm thinking of changing my hair colour.

Currently I am a strawberry blond but I got this copper brown hair dye. I have never dyed my hair before so think I should wait for Millie as she is always dying hers.

But then again Millie will probably say it's not the right one for me and blah blah blah, so I think I might just do this on my own. Also brought a do-it-yourself waxing kit. I have always shaved my legs but figured I wouldn't have time to maintain things like that if I am dealing with a bus-load of men so think waxing is the way to go.

And besides it's like a forest at the moment and they reckon you should get to ape stage before waxing, so perfect timing.

Think the ones upstairs have my life all mapped out for me after all.

In bathroom.

Okay, have applied hair dye and now have plastic cap on my head. So while I'm waiting for magic transformation from being a fair haired Goldie Hawn beauty to a dark haired Angeline Jolie beauty, I'll start applying this wax.

The wax is a microwave one which I think I overdid as the wax was a bit too hot, so now it's cooled down to lukewarm I start to smother my legs in it.

Okay, wax applied to leg.

Better get another and do two at once,

I mean they say it hurts but I'm sure it's just like ripping off a band aid, no biggie, and if I do two at once then it will get the job done quicker and I won't have to endure so much pain.

Shit, wax strip stuck to finger tips.

Okay, ready to pull off now, one… two…

Oh Daniel's calling.

Quickly wiped hands and my heart is thumping in my chest which happens every time Daniel calls.

Which is weird.

"Oh hi Daniel," I said as casually as possible when I finally forced slippery fingers to unlock stupid phone so I could answer it.

Also still have wax strip stuck to my finger.

"Hi Lis, happy birthday."

"Oh yeah, got your birthday text, thanks."

"You're welcome, what you up to now?"

"Oh nothing much just… err… reading."

"I had a great day at the family reunion event and they gave me a little bonus."

I thought the family reunion event was an all day thing; surely it can't be that late in the day.

Oh it is late in the day.

Shit birthday nearly over.

Daniel continues, "yeah so if you're not doing anything I thought I'd take you out to dinner for your birthday… that's if you're not busy."

Oh my god did Daniel just ask me out… on a *date?* I mean pff, even if I did have plans I would friken cancel them!

Not that I think it's a good idea I start dating Daniel as we are business partners and it might be a bit weird, but then again just a tiny dabble to see if it does get weird cannot hurt, after all it's only dinner, pff.

"Yeah well since I'm not up to much, dinner should be fine," I said, trying not to sound like I'm peeing my pants in excitement.

"Cool, pick you up in half-an-hour."

Shit.

"Half-an-hour," I confirmed, trying not to sound panicked that I still have to wax and my hair is twenty minutes away from being transformed. "Sounds great, um… don't rush."

Hung up and now I'm in a real panic, how the hell am I going to get ready in 30 minutes?

Okay first things first, ditch the wax and shave.

Okay, on second thought, I'm halfway there with the waxing thing, so if I just quickly reheat the wax in the microwave and do my lower legs only.

Not going to worry about bikini line, I mean it's not like I'm going to go so far as to shag Daniel, that would be weird.

Need to rip this one off my fingers first.

Okay, now it's stuck to the cap on my head.

Oh well it can stay there, coming off soon anyway.

Unlock bathroom door, run to kitchen with pot of wax for heating. Plan is to throw wax in microwave, rip off existing strip stuck to leg and repeat while wax is heating. Then quickly do other leg, jump in shower, rinse off hair, get out of shower, apply makeup and blow dry hair; get dressed and throw self into armchair with book before Daniel arrives so he thinks that I think it's no big deal.

And all this has to be done in 23 minutes.

Think I may have to ask Sid to distract Daniel to buy me some more time.

In the kitchen, threw wax pot into microwave and pressed buttons. Think Sid is in the pantry but haven't got time for chit chat.

Right need to pull wax strip off, okay, one... two...

Arghh, feck, feck, son of a mother... that hurt...

Shit that's not Sid in the pantry!

"Abby'toir is a period homestead located in the beautiful area of Taromeo, 175 kilometers west of the city. The homestead is owned by 3 ex-urbanites who brought the property... oh!"

Okay, awkward moment in middle of waxing fest with film guy talking into oversized dictaphone.

Well thank god he doesn't have a camera.

But he looks horrified.

"Um... hi Lisa, everything okay?" he asked, averting his eyes from my wax covered legs.

"Um yes, just um... waiting on microwave to finish."

"Okay, I'll just um, get out of your hair," he said.

"That's okay, you don't have to, I'm just waiting on the... you know, to finish my... and, you know."

God microwave's still got one minute to go.

"Oh okay, no probs," he said, fiddling with his dictaphone.

Great, now we've got awkward silence.

You see this is why I don't want a snotty film guy sniffing around, I mean I can't even dye my hair or wax my legs in peace, hope Millie didn't sign that permission document.

"Um, so got any special plans tonight?" he asks, not knowing where to look now.

"Um, just a casual dinner date," I said, trying to look normal.

"Really?" he says, untangling the microphone cord from the device and switching it on, "so Lisa is the rural dating scene alive and kicking in this neck of the woods?"

"Oh errrr…"

"Let me ask you another way," he pondered, looking to the ceiling for an answer, "would you say there are limited opportunities for singles looking for love out here in the bush?"

Oh god is he interviewing me? Okay don't tell him anything, then he'll get bored and move on.

"Yes, limited yes."

"Is this because there is a shortage of bachelors or bachelorettes?"

"Both."

Oh thank god microwave just beeped.

"So on a social scale, is there much encouragement for young people and singles in this area to attend social events in the hope of finding love?"

"Um not sure, I don't get out much," I mumble, pulling my wax out.

Perfect, it's warmed up and ready to go.

"Oh really?" he looks at me surprised, "I thought it would be your area of expertise, with the field of work you're in."

Bugger, he's got a point.

"Yeah well I'm busy in other… err areas of social stuff and hadn't got round to researching that side of ummm things, sorry must dash, got to get ready."
Quick keep walking before he says anything else.

Back in the safety of the bathroom, I have to hurry this along as I only have 19 minutes left. Trying to apply wax evenly and smoothly as directed by packet but impossible when the clock is ticking so I now just apply wax strips and peel off two at a time.
Okay bad idea as very painful and think I'm going to pass out.
I remembered back to when Millie was giving birth to Amy and the breathing techniques I picked up to deal with pain, so I think I'll use those and finish off the other leg.
Or maybe just stick to Millie's coping techniques of swearing and abuse.
Panting and swearing session coming to an end, I quickly check the time on my phone resulting in more swearing when I realise I have wasted a full 12 minutes on my legs.
Quickly ditch the wax, no time for clean up, pull my shower cap off and dive under the running water of the shower.

There seems to be a lot of brown hair dye running down the plug hole, hmmm hope I have left it in long enough, I mean it's been about an hour now.

Washed self in record time of two minutes and with towel wrapped around head I'm now in bedroom deciding what to wear.

God why is going out so bloody complicated?

Problem solved as luckily I have my safe dress, you know the one you know looks good on you and you-can-wear-it-anywhere dress, yes well I have eight of them in different colours.

God now which colour to wear?

Faint knock on door followed by Sid's voice.

Oh god please don't tell me Daniel's here already, I have two minutes to go and I've still got to put my makeup on and check hair colour.

Oh god, forgot about my hair colour, which means I'll have to pick out a dress that goes with my hair.

Hope Daniel is running late.

"Lisa, Daniel's here," said Sid's faint voice behind the door.

Oh fuck.

Grabbed towel from my head and wrapped it around my body as I flung open the door to catch Sid before he walks off.

Sid's eyes widen like saucers.

"Can you stall him?" I hissed at Sid, "I need a few more minutes please."

Sid nodded in acknowledgment while backing away slowly; his eyes still the size of dinner plates.

Strange man.

Anyway, underwear carefully picked out (not that Daniel would get to see it but nice to feel good) and now it's time to see how fabulous hair colour is before choosing dress.

Ran back to bathroom in underwear and towel, can hear Sid and Daniel chatting outside which means Sid has taken him to look at the up-and-coming mini golf course.

That should buy me another half-an-hour.

Finished drying hair in more record time and looked in mirror and braced myself for transformation from Goldie Hawn to Angeline Jolie.

Shocked and stunned.

Don't look like Angeline Jolie but more like Amy's strawberry shortcake doll. You know, the one with orange hair!

Oh my god, oh my god!! What the fuck have I done?

I must have done something wrong as it's not a fabulous brown like the picture on the bloody box.

Located box from the pile of discarded wax strips and rubbish on the floor, looked in box to see if I have missed a tube of magical 'return to normal' product in there but no, nothing, just me with bright orange hair.

… and I don't think I have a dress to match it.

Shit and now I think I can hear Sid and Daniel coming inside.

Okay maybe it's the light in here and I'm overreacting, I mean I was going to text Millie and tell her to get in here and sort my hair out but I can just hear her saying to me that it's just the light too, so I'm going to save myself the bother.

Besides I don't think she is here.

Ran back to the bedroom and may have to revert to Plan B.

But as I do not have a time machine that can take me back to an hour and a half ago, I'm going to have to lessen the effect of the hair with dress colour.

Which means black is out.

So is orange, red, blue and white.

So unfair and unless I can get Sid to stall Daniel even longer so I can run to shop, get another dye, race back here, fill in another half hour waiting for dye to take effect and then pick colour of dress all over again, I think I may have to pretend I'm sick.

"Lisa!" Sid impatient voice appears at the door again, "Daniel's waiting, are you coming out?"

"Oh… yep."

Shit.

Okay well I am just going to have to suck it up, I mean it's just *Daniel,* I see him all the time. Not with orange hair but it's not like I was planning on shagging him or anything.

In living room.

After much pondering I have decided on brown dress to lessen effect of hair.

"Nice bandana," Daniel complimented as I entered the living room, "matches your dress."

New plan, decided to cover disastrous hair colour until I can get to pharmacy and get another hair dye to return to normal. It's only for tonight and it's just a birthday dinner.

"Thanks, I err, am trying a new look."

Sid knows better than to comment these days so he doesn't... love Sid, he's so cool.

Daniel is looking really nice and I think it's going to take willpower tonight, think I may have to write a wee affirmation on the inside of my hand to remind me Daniel is a 'no go' zone due to being 'just friends' and 'work colleagues'.

I am horny though.

"So you ready birthday girl?" said Daniel as he flashes a smile.

"Lisa," Millie yelled from the bathroom, "why the fuck does it look like you waxed a fucken beaver in here?!"

"Yep, ready as ever," I said as I grabbed Daniel's hand and bolted for the door.

At restaurant.

Tiny bit disappointed we ended up at the local lavender garden restaurant, called *'The Purple Patch'* and located on the highway out of town. Not that it's not a lovely place, but it's local which means local people are here and most of the staff know us. Oh well never mind, it's the thought and blah blah.

Hope it doesn't start any rumours around town about Daniel and I.

Well after all, we are business partners... so what of it? We're just having dinner.

After clinking glasses to toast my birthday, Daniel launches into conversation about his day and of course asks me about mine, didn't want to say my birthday started by waking up in a car with Matt and Damo, followed by meeting nosy film guy and ended with orange hair. And oh I did get a tarot card reading done, which told me I am going to meet a bus-load of men.

So I told Daniel my day was quiet and got a reading done with Angela and launched into telling him what she said about the business (left the part out about the men).

Actually feels like we're a married couple at the dinner table.

"So you believe that then?" says Daniel with a half amused grin on his face.

"Believe what?"

"What this Angela said?"

"Um yes."

"Okay," he shrugged.

Did Daniel just diss my reading with Angel? Is he being an asshole about it? I cannot tell.

He's obviously a non believer.

Food arrives and Daniel fills me in on his weekend, carefully trying to leave Rick's name out of the conversation, which is sweet, but I know Daniel is Rick's best mate so I do occasionally still see Rick now and then and it's not awkward between us.

Unless his new girlfriend is with him, then the daggers fly.

With her toward me I mean; not me, I'm over it.

Daniel smells so nice and he looks extra nice in this light, god I cannot stop thinking about sex.

And what's worse, cannot stop thinking about sex with Daniel.

Really need to remind myself he is a 'no go' zone. I think it's just because I'm horny and haven't had anyone for... well since Rick almost a year ago. I mean you cannot blame me for feeling this way.

Millie and Co have been trying to convince me to just sleep with Daniel and get it over with but again, it's okay for them because they don't work with the ones they shag.

Except for Millie and Sid but that's different.

And besides, can't shag Daniel as I have orange hair and am hiding it under a bandana.

Oh my god it's just dawned on me why I have orange hair! It's to stop me from jumping Daniel! Universe had plans all along to make sure I didn't go there so they made sure I stuffed up the hair colour so I would have to hide it for dinner date with Daniel to make sure it was just dinner and nothing else.

Ones upstairs are definitely looking out for me.

"So what's with this new look?" Daniel asks, pouring more wine into my glass.

Took a sip of wine to bide my time while I come up with a lie as to why I'm hiding orange hair behind bandana when Matt rocks up behind me.

"S'up peeps?" he says, grabbing a chair from the vacant table behind us and sitting down.

Followed by Damo.

Daniel looks pleased to see them as he greets them back in a manly fashion.

Makes one of us.

"What are you doing here?" I asked.

"I saw Dazza's car outside and Millie said you two were out somewhere. We're heading to the Ute Muster Ball, you wanna come?"

"Thought you were going clubbing or pig hunting?"

"Yeah was, but forgot the Ute Ball was on."

"If it's a Ball wouldn't we need tickets and nice clothes?" I said, looking at Matt's board shorts and thongs.

"Nah, it's in a cocky's shed and it's BYO. What's with the cloth on your head?"

I really don't want to go but Daniel looks like he is keen.

Now he is looking at me waiting for me to decide.

"Big Bob's got his karaoke machine set up," said Matt as if he thought that would persuade me to go.

Well I suppose dinner is almost finished and I don't really know what Daniel had planned; I mean the way he is looking at me now convinces me he hasn't got any after dinner plans.

"Yeah I'm easy," I said through gritted teeth.

"Sounds like a plan then," said Daniel, "we'll grab some drinks and head out in my car."

"Cool," said Matt rising from his chair, "but seriously Lisa, what's with the tablecloth on your head?"

4

Next morning (in bed I think).

Not sure because I'm having this awesome dream that after a night of dancing and fun Daniel took me back to his place and feed me hazelnut gourmet ice cream and rich, hot, exotic coffee before taking me to the bedroom and making love to me all night.

And it wasn't even awkward between us the next morning.

Don't want the dream to end because I'm feeling very content this morning. And no hangover if I'm feeling this good. If fact it's like I have died and gone to heaven.

Also this bed smells very nice, like a summer breeze. Millie must have changed my sheets and brought a new brand of fabric softener, she's good like that.

Thank god it's Sunday, a day of rest, as I could lie here all day.

Rolled over to adjust pillow and a wave of nausea hits me.

Uh oh!

Sudden movement not helping but must get to bathroom before contents of stomach make an appearance. My head is pounding and I appear to have no clothes on but can't worry about that, need to get to big white bowl.

Ran out of bedroom with my hand clasped to my mouth but it appears someone has moved the big white bowl.

Actually, whose house is this?

Located a big ceramic pot which is holding a lovely big plant in the corner of a passageway and made a beeline for it; so gross but when you have to hurl, you have to hurl.

"Oh my god Lisa, are you okay?" came a voice, sounding very much like Daniel's, from behind me as I continue to empty the contents of my stomach into the pot plant in my birthday suit. God I hate being sick, rather pull fingernails out. I felt Daniel cover me up with a bathrobe as I continue to violate his houseplant trying to apologise for doing so in-between heaves. Daniel is sweet and holding my hair back.

Oh shit that's right I also have orange hair.

I'm hoping this is part of a dream and I'm going to wake up soon with settled stomach and normal hair.

10 minutes later.

Feeling very low as it's not a dream; I'm tucked up in Daniel's bed with orange hair and a hangover.

After disposing of the poor pot plant into the compost heap, Daniel brings me instant coffee. He looks equally hungover and is trying to fill in the blanks but we both had a few too many drinks last night and cannot remember anything.

Well not exactly everything, I remember getting there and Matt encouraging me to do tequila shots, everything else is a big blur.

"You okay?" Daniel asks me again.

"No, I feel like shit," I said, "and sorry about your plant."

"Argh, that's okay," he said, not knowing whether to sit or lie next to me, whereas I'm too hungover to even care that he saw me naked, again.

Which brings me to the next question, why am I naked in Daniel's bed?

Oh my god did Daniel and I have *sex*?

I mean it's obvious I came home with him last night. But we couldn't have done it; for a start it would have been awkward. And who drove us here if Daniel was too pissed to drive?

"Um… so…?" I said, trying to ask the obvious question but not sure how to start. Could look for discarded condom packets I suppose.

Unless we didn't use them, uh oh.

"I'm not entirely sure what happened last night," said Daniel very quickly like he can read my mind. "I was okay until Matt started me on tequila shots after discovering they were running a makeshift taxi service for anyone who needed it. Haven't been that drunk for some time.

Which means my car must be still at McDermott's woolshed," he said like he is trying to work out how to go and get it.

I mean who cares about car, I want to know if we *did it* or not.

"Nice hair by the way," he grins.

"Oh god," I groaned, trying to hide it with my hands.

"No it really suits you, not many can carry that off like you do," he said matter-of-factly while reaching for his phone to dial.

I'm not game enough to look in a mirror in case am horrified by what *morning* orange hair looks like. What I really want to know is if Daniel woke up naked or it's just me.

I could ask him, but if we didn't do it then he might think I wanted to and that would be more awkward.

He is dressed in shorts and a tee-shirt now but they're not the type of shorts you would sleep in.

Daniel punches in a number and puts the phone to his ear. I spot my clothes neatly folded on a chair on the other side of the room.

Hmmm if you were to rip ones clothes off, you wouldn't fold them neatly and put them on a chair.

In fact, am noticing Daniel's bedroom for the first time. It's like 'Better Homes and Gardens' in here. The décor is… well a bit girly-ish.

I mean Daniel is always freakishly tidy at work but that's to be expected as it's a place of business, but so is this room. Even his thongs are evenly placed beside his bed.

At my place mine are evenly placed in different rooms.

I have been in Daniel's house a few times before but only as far as the kitchen and it's always clean but that's because he has a cleaner come in a couple of hours a week.

Didn't expect it to be anal clean though.

Oh my god I think Daniel is talking to Rick and is asking for him to come and pick him up so he can get his car.

And he just mentioned I'm here!

And he said it like it's not awkward.

Rick is my *ex* and Daniel's best mate, why would you mention to your best friend that you have his ex girlfriend in your bed, naked?

Well he didn't say naked but don't have to be a genius to work it out.

Daniel winds up the conversation and puts down his phone.

"You can go back to sleep if you like," he says, "you look terrible."

Bit offended, but fair call I suppose considering I threw up in his ceramic plant holder and killed the plant.

"I'll just go and get my car," he said slipping into his thongs.

"I'm a bit worried about it and it's been raining overnight

so I don't want to get it bogged in the paddock. When I get back I can run you home."

Perfect and while you are gone I will look for evidence in the form of discarded condom packets.

"Okay," I said in a sleepy voice.

Daniel made me another coffee, a real one this time while he waited on Rick and brought it into bed on a saucer and coaster. Think Daniel may be hinting to me he doesn't want spillage, he is so sweet though and I am really hoping we did do it last night 'cause it doesn't feel weird between us at all, if fact Daniel looks totally relaxed about everything.

I semi drifted off until I heard Rick's car pull up and Daniel leave. Not wanting to waste time I spring out of bed to look for evidence of perfect night of passion.

Knelt down and looked under the bed as that's the first place you would be if you were a discarded condom packet.

Hmm there's nothing under here, not even dust; in fact under Daniel's bed is so spotless that even if there were discarded condom packets, I'm sure he would have tidied them up as he went along. I'm shocked as I have known Daniel for a year now and I never knew he was this fussy about cleanliness. Man, it's amazing what you find out about a person when you're naked in their bedroom.

But if Daniel did clean up, that means I need to locate a rubbish bin.

And have a little snoop at the rest of the house while I'm at it.

Tour of Daniel's house.

I have never ventured passed the kitchen but I must say the house is very well laid out and a bit of a strange design for this neck-of-the-woods as it's quite modern, a bit like a loft style apartment with a lot of glass; and of course the framed photography on the wall matches the décor well. It looks very much like an interior designer has been through here.

But still trying to locate garbage bin. I mean I am in the kitchen, how hard is it to find the bin?

Okay, found it.

And of course it had to be hidden in a cupboard and disguised as a retro tin can.

Quickly slammed door in shock because I cannot believe what was lying on top.

Better have another look.

Yep there it is, not one, but two discarded condom packets; man I must have been on fire last night.

Certainly don't feel that way.

But that's confirmed it, Daniel and I must have done it 'cause I know for a fact he has been celibate for months now, so there cannot be anyone else; in fact I think he is a bit unlucky with the girls, so it must have been from us last night.

Shut cupboard door and pondered about last night, maybe Daniel doesn't remember it either, he seems very relaxed about things this morning, unless he doesn't see it as a big deal. I mean Millie is always reminding me it's just sex, why get hung up about it.

I think I may hide condom packets under discarded paper anyway, if Daniel doesn't remember and he discovers condom packets he may start to feel awkward, which may ruin things between us. I mean I'll do enough awkwardness for the both of us anyway.

The rain is starting to settle in again and it's making me feel cold, not that it's cold but when you're still naked, walking around a house with a lot of glass and it's raining outside then it's certainly going to make you feel cold. I s'pose I should go and put some clothes on.

Making my way back to Daniel's bedroom I located another bedroom and pushed open the door. This one has such a funky colour design to it, very bright shade of green with purple drapes, sounds bad but it seems to work really well.

Argh! Room also has Matt dozing on the decorative bed with decorative pillows.

"S'up," he mumbled, hearing my presence.

Shit, naked, must get clothes.

Oh and there's Damo.

"Howzit," he grinned.

Matt, Damo and me (now in clothes) in Daniel's kitchen.

"More coffee?" Damo grinned as he held up the plunger filled with freshly brewed coffee. I shake my head.

The third plunger of coffee made so far.

Mind you it's a very small plunger, very chic, goes with the miniature tea pot.

"Last night was sic," said Matt.

"Fuck yeah," Damo agreed.

Not sure what 'sic' means but I'll run with it.

I'm trying not to give away to Matt and Damo that I can't remember anything as they reminisce. If they realise, they might start telling me stuff I did. And the reason that's bad is because I think they may make stuff up. So I'm just agreeing with everything they say.

But still being discreet in extracting information.

"So what time did we get back here again?" I said putting my casual face on, "I forgot."

"Oh Lis you were so wasted," said Matt chuckling and skimming over my question, "especially when you stood up on the shearing platform and took the karaoke mic off that other drunk chick in the middle of her song, man I thought she was going to smack you in the teeth."

"Well she must have sounded… err, terrible."

"Oh yeah, then you started head banging to Guns'n'Roses and the scarf fell off your head and everyone went silent 'cause you had orange hair, ha ha, that was da bomb."

Oh shit I forgot about my hair colour. Okay, thinking I may not want to know what happened.

"Oh and you got jealous 'cause Daniel was talking to that Gina chick from the produce store."

Now we are getting somewhere, did I get jealous and Daniel saw how much I was into him and finally got the courage up to take me home I wonder?

"Oh fuck, that's right," said Damo, cracking up at the memory, "Gina was asking Daniel if he would consider doing glamour shots. And you got sooo dirty on her when Daniel told Gina she had beautiful features to work with, you butted in and said Daniel can't work miracles unless she provides the bag."

"Oh yeah, the look on her face," Matt cracked up.

"Yeah, Dan was like 'oh fuck'," Damo chuckled.

Okay not liking what I'm hearing so far and remind myself never to purposely cross paths with Gina from the produce store, I think they need to shut up after all.

"Oh yeah and remember that film guy was there with the camera and you told him to fuck off. Man you're a funny chick when you're off your tits."

What?

"The film guy was there?"

"Yeah he's doing a doco or something, duno, but me and Damo are going to be in it, we're going to be famous."

"Did he say what this 'doco' is all about?" I asked, disinterested. I mean a bunch of people getting slaughtered on alcohol and bad singing; combined with an old homestead converted into a B&B. What could possibly be interesting enough about that to make a film of it? No I really think this 'doco' is just a front, what he really wants to do is get videos of people doing stupid stuff to post on YouTube in the hope it goes viral.

"I duno, didn't ask him," shrugged Matt, pulling me back to my original question, "but after he asked Damo and I if he could interview us, he made us sign this contract."

"Contract? I hope you mean a permission form."

"I duno," Matt shrugged, suddenly scrolling through his phone.

Well he can't have filmed much about me because I know that even in my intoxicated brain-dead state, there is no way I would sign anything to say it was okay to film me, I know that for sure.

But think I need to give up drinking and actually maybe I *should* find Gina from the produce store and apologise before I run out of chook food and have to go and buy some more.

I mean she may drown me in fertiliser or something.

But that still doesn't answer the question of whether or not Daniel and I had sex. Don't want to press Matt and Damo for further information just in case they start telling me I was pole dancing in the sheep yards or something, so I am going to presume everyone was as drunk as me (after all it is a Ute Muster Ball in a shed with kegs) and not worry if Daniel and I did it or not, I'll carry on as if nothing happened.

Back home.

Starting to feel semi-normal again. Daniel arrived back home after collecting his car and insisted we stay for a cooked breakfast. Matt and Damo looked slightly uncomfortable when Daniel served it to us garnished with fresh herbs and laid the table with starched cloth napkins and shiny knifes. Means they had to eat with the cutlery instead of their hands.

But I have to say I was a little disappointed that Daniel dropped me home before Matt and Damo. I couldn't exactly test the level of awkwardness with those two around, not that Daniel seems even slightly fazed at the fact I woke up naked in his bed.

Millie was sitting waiting for me like my mother when I entered the house, the only difference being is my actual mother would have a look of utter disapproval on her face when I crawled through the door the morning after being dropped off by a boy, and Millie has a big grin on her face and is almost drooling with anticipation of hearing all the details.

I'm just going to tell her I got drunk and spent the night on Daniel's couch fully clothed.
Who am I kidding; I'm going to tell her everything.
Millie's expression fades as I enter the room.
"What's with the hair?" she gasps.
Oh yeah, keep forgetting about that.

"Never mind that," I said, taking a seat opposite her while her eyes scan my head, "guess what happened last night?!"
"You got drunk and dyed your hair orange?"
"Tch, no! Guess whose bed I woke up in?"

"Oh no Lisa, don't tell me you slept with Matt again?" she chuckled.

Millie still thinks it's funny that I got drunk once and slept with 19 year old Matt.

God it wasn't *that* funny.

"Noooo," I said in my frustrated voice, "I slept with Daniel."

I was waiting for Millie's jaw to drop in disbelief but all she said was, "yeah I know."

What the?

"How do you know?"

God Millie annoys me, she thinks she knows everything.

"Because Sid gave you, Damo, Matt and Daniel a ride home. Problem was you refused to come home with Sid and told everyone there was a party at Daniel's."

Oh, well that explains how we got back to Daniel's.

"He also gave Brendon the film guy a lift home as well; he is such a nice guy."

"Yeah Sid's pretty cool," I said.

"I was talking about Brendon."

"Really Millie?" I said with dry tones.

Millie ignores my remark and finishes, "yeah so Sid dropped you, Damo and Matt off at Daniel's, he didn't mention your hair though."

"So did Sid indicate that Daniel and I looked a little…? I don't know… closer?"

"Oh my god, not again Lisa," Millie starts giggling, "you don't know what happened last night do you?"

"I do!" I said.

"What happened then?" asked Millie.

"I woke up in Daniel's bed."

"And…"

"He made us breakfast," I said.

"And…"

"And that's all."

"So you really don't know what happened last night?" Millie chuckled, "oh Lisa how priceless you are."

"I know," I wailed, "I'm not even sure if we did it. I mean I woke up naked and messed up his pot plant. And there were discarded condom packets in the bin but I'm not sure if that means anything!"

"So when did the orange hair happen?" Millie asked, and quickly backtracked when she saw my glare.

"Okay, look," she said sighing, "worse case is you bonked each other's brains out and both of you want to avoid the subject… so carry on as normal. Best case is you didn't bonk each other's brains out and you woke up naked 'cause you didn't have appropriate clothes to sleep in and you were both too drunk to care about a little flesh, so carry on as normal.

But in my opinion it sounds like you did indeed bonk him... so carry on as normal."

"Great Millie, sooo helpful. Oh god," I moaned, "why can't I just have a normal date?"

"Excuse me," came a meek voice from behind me, "sorry to eavesdrop, but I was hoping to do an interview about singles in rural areas. Did you mention you went on a date Lisa?"

Oh great, now nosy film guy wants to know about my love life.

Actually, how much did he hear?

"No you misheard," I said sticking my nose in the air a little, "I said it would be nice to have a normal date."

Shit why did I just say that? Now I've made out I date nothing but weirdoes with fetishes.

Okay has been known to happen from time to time but what the hell.

"Oh okay, my mistake," he said in polite, apologetic tones, "didn't mean to interrupt. I was hoping there would be someone around these parts I could interview for my film on dating in the bush."

"Well there is not," I said in my hoity tone.

"I thought you were doing a film based on rural life and the opportunities it brings?" Millie said fluttering her eyelashes at him.

Very, very disturbing.

"Yes it's going to be based on the whole social structure of the area," he said enthused and pulling up a chair to join us, "I think the biggest social issue in the area is the dating scene. There seems to be a big gap."

"How so?" said Millie pretending she is interested.

Okay so Millie *is* genuinely interested; it's me who is bored.

"Well there seems to be a lot of young singles, like from 20 to 35, but very limited from 35 to 45."

"Yes I think Lisa is the only one," Millie joked.

"I am not," I said with dignified tones, "there is Daniel of course and Tim from the bakery."

"Sorry, make that three," Millie said turning to Brendon.

"Exactly!" Brendon said, "there seems to be a gap. You have the youth dating scene which is alive and active, the middle dating scene, which consists of your age group Lisa, and of course the older generation who have lost spouses to age and require companionship. In metropolitan areas there are a lot more social activities so the dating ratio across all ages is higher. What I am trying to touch on is bridging the gap in non-metropolitan areas and how active is social dating and does internet dating have a place in the bush?"

Oh my god, 'in the bush', we only live two hours from the outskirts of Sydney we're hardly in the outback. Man these city folk seem to think we live in the pioneer ages.

76

"Sounds fascinating," said Millie.

Think I'm going to be sick again.

Brendon dived into conversation with Millie about his project and how he plans to put it together and blah, blah, with Millie occasionally shooting me glances and expressions as if to say 'are you hearing this?' but to be honest, I switched off ages ago.

I'm actually thinking of Daniel.

Bits of last night are vaguely coming back to me. I do remember a conversation we had about relationships and I'm positive at one stage I was holding his hand. In fact I think I was crying. Actually I *was* crying and we were sitting outside on one of the hay bales and I was telling him about my whole fear of turning 40 and being alone and he was comforting me. Oh god I hope he didn't sleep with me out of sympathy.

Millie's looking at me as if I need to respond to something they are talking about.

"I'm sorry?" I said, snapping myself out of my thoughts.

"Daniel's here," Millie said in a huff like she has been trying to tell me for the last two minutes.

What the… I was just thinking of him.

Wonder if this is a sign, I mean this morning felt so natural and Daniel didn't seem fazed at all, so it's obvious he feels comfortable with the whole situation... and well he did take me on a date last night and he's here now, and it's not a work day.

Daniel made his way to the door as I sprinted to greet him.

"Oh hello," I purred, "just thinking of you."

"Hey Lisa, I just come back to see if you're okay."

"Never been better," I beamed.

"Oh that's good, you look better, um also I need to talk to you about last night."

Oh my god, a small leap of warm fuzzies appear in my stomach.

"I want to apologise for last night," he continued, "I hope I didn't come on too strong."

"Not at all," I scoffed.

"It's just that our friendship and working relationship means a lot to me and I hope my actions last night didn't damage that relationship."

Oh my god that means we *must have* done it and Daniel remembers.

"Pfff no!" I said a little too enthusiastically, "I mean I for one would have had a part to play so it's not all your fault," I scoffed.

"Well I don't see how you could have," he said, a little puzzled, "but I'm glad we can accept this, put it behind us and still be friends."

What?

"Um… sure," I said trying to slap a grin on my face.

"Thanks Lis," he said reaching out for a hug, "your support means a lot, it's not easy to let go after so much anticipation, I'm so happy you understand."

"Yeah, um… no problem," I said, feeling him squeeze me a bit harder.

Which is a bit weird, I mean I'm so disappointed Daniel just wants to be friends and his comment about the letting go after much anticipation means he too had been feeling the sexual tension between us, but come on; he's getting a bit emotional over a shag.

Facebook status update.
Lisa Collins.
Never ever drinking again!

5

Monday at work.

Still disappointed with the whole Daniel thing.

I can't help flicking him glances across my desk as he rearranges a photography display. He seems so happy; in fact I haven't seen him this cherry for a while. Maybe he hadn't had sex for a long time. Explains why he got so emotional over it.

After Daniel left yesterday Brendon, the nosy annoying film guy, was still trying to talk me into an interview. I have managed to avoid him so far, claiming I was tired from the big night and had to deal with orange hair, so he wants to meet up some time today at work.

But I have to say, thank god for Millie, as she managed to lessen the effect of the hair colour using some awesome product. Hair's still orange but an acceptable, trendy orange. Although it's probably a bit too late anyway, as Matt had tagged a picture of me on Facebook with a shot of tequila in my hand, eyes half closed, bright orange hair, with the caption *'epic nite with Lisa Collins'*.

God I wish I had a normal man.

Not that Daniel isn't normal but if he didn't take me to that stupid party then maybe the whole drunken sex bit would have turned into a night of sober lovemaking, well maybe, but at least I would have fricken remembered it.

Typical. The only time in ages I have any physical contact with a man and I miss the whole thing.

It's Matt's fault for showing up at the restaurant and dragging us off to the Ball, in fact I'm going to text him and tell him what I think of him.

"You okay?" Daniel asked puzzled as I press send.

"Fine," I said trying for a smile.

There, take that Matt you little shit.

"Hi ya," Millie greeted as she entered the shop, negotiating the door with the pram.

It's normally Sid that negotiates the shop door with the pram when Millie is working but she has the week off.

"How's it going?" she asks, looking slightly breathless as she falls into the chair beside the desk and applies the pram brake.

"Okay I s'pose," I said leaning over the top of the pram to poke tongues at Amy, something I have been teaching her to do every time she sees Matt.

"Busy?" Millie asks again, her eyes scanning Daniel's new display.

"No not really," I answered as Matt's reply text message arrived on my phone.

Hmm, is that the best comeback he has?

"Coffee Millie?" Daniel asks as he proceeds to the back of the shop.

Hmpf, did he think to ask me?

"Yes please," she smiled back pulling off her scarf, not that it's cold out but ever since Millie become a mother she has traded her trendy battered jeans and skinny tops for a more stylish and sophisticated look with lovely accessories; mainly to make her feel she is not constantly covered in baby goo.

"So how are things between you two?" mumbled Millie when Daniel was out of earshot, "is it a bit weird?"

I did fill Millie in on what Daniel said to me about coming on too strong and he doesn't want to ruin our friendship or working relationship and blah blah, but she seems to think Daniel may have been testing the water to see what my reaction was.

"Apart from him being in the best mood all year it's fine," I said, a little deflated as I replied to Matt's text message.

"Well just take it for what it was," said Millie, "it hasn't damaged your working relationship with him so I guess you have to be thankful for that."

Why is it that non-single people don't consider it may actually be the end of the world for single people when things don't work out with someone when you're nearly 40 and childless?

Ohh another text just arrived from Matt trying to worm his way out of the truth.

Pff, what Matt doesn't realise is I can do this all day.

"Brendon is on his way for that interview," said Millie, "he is just taking some footage of the town first."

"What!? Oh no Millie, I'm not really in the mood to talk to anyone about what a failure I am, why are you so keen for me to get involved with his stupid zitty assignment?" I snapped, sending another text reply to Matt.

"What's this?" Daniel said making an appearance, balancing three coffee mugs.

"Brendon the film guy who is staying with us," Millie elaborated, "he wants to do an interview with Lisa on the social dating scene in rural areas."

"Oh yes," Daniel said handing me a mug of coffee.

You see this is the type of man I want, one who doesn't need to ask if I want a coffee he just knows I do.

"He spoke to me about it at the Ute Ball the other night," Daniel continued, "I told him the dating scene for the likes of me in these parts is dead on arrival."

Dead on arrival? What am I, chopped liver!?

"He has got some great ideas on how to promote the area," said Millie taking a sip of her coffee. "It's the type of thing we need to put this place on the map."

Daniel agreed but excused himself when his phone rang, interrupting what he was about to say.

I'm a little bit offended with Daniel's comment about the dating scene being dead out here, I mean I have to agree, but it's not the sort of thing you say to a perfectly good single woman sitting opposite you, with whom you may or may not have had a sexual encounter with in the past 48 hours.

"What's wrong with you?" Millie asked reading my gloomy expression.

"What do you think?" I snapped.

Millie rolled her eyes at me as the doorbell tingled and Brendon made an appearance.

"Hi," Millie greeted in an enthusiastic voice, leaping from her chair and grabbing the heavy door for him as he came in with his hands full of equipment.

So not in the mood for him, or watching Millie bow to him as if he is Russell Crowe, but I have a feeling he is persistent so I'll just have to suck it up and get it over with so he will leave me alone forever.

Another text message from Matt.

"Hi Lisa," Brendon greeted as I typed in yet another reply to Matt, "ready for your 15 minutes of fame?" he chuckled as he set up his camera.

What a twat.

"S'pose," I mumbled, stuffing my phone back into my bag after sending off my text.

"Excellent," he said pulling up a chair while Millie positioned herself just off to his side so as not to get in the camera shot.

Should check my hair and makeup.

Nah.

"Okay so Lisa just act natural, like you and I are having a conversation," he said switching on the camera, "what normally happens when making a film or documentary such as this one is I ask a series of questions to which you respond, then later on I add voice over and edit your responses into it. So you ready?" he asked.

"Yeah," I shrugged.

"Okay," he said glancing over his shoulder to see if Daniel had finished his phone conversation.

"Sorry," Daniel mouthed to him while he wound up his conversation and grabbed a seat to listen.

Hmm if Daniel is listening in maybe I need to get a subtle message across to him that both him and I are almost 40 and childless, therefore we need to consider the possibility that we should at least discuss having babies together.

"Lisa, you're 39 and single?" he started.

"Yeah," I muttered.

"And you come from Sydney?"

"Yep."

"And did you have an active social life when you lived in Sydney?"

"Yep."

"Did you date a lot in your younger years?"

"A bit."

"And two years ago you moved out of the hustle of the big city to start a business in small town Australia?"

"Yeah."

"So as a single woman in her prime, what attracted you to these parts?"

Oh god he wants the whole story. I'll just give him the short answer I think.

"Real estate."

"Real estate?"

"Yes."

"Anything else?" Brendon probed.

"Not really."

Well I wasn't going to tell him the long answer; that I bought a rundown shack in the middle of nowhere because I had a romantic vision of shacking up with hippie boyfriend in wonderful bliss of rural paradise who instead decided to end things at my time of purchase, leaving me with rundown rural property, no man and Millie sending me here to live with hillbillies and take responsibility.

Except there were no hillbillies, only hot Jake who ran off with an older married woman.

But let's not go there.

"Okay," Brendon sighed flicking his notepad, "so coming from a highly populated city to a town of 2,000 how did you adjust to the lack of social interaction?"

Don't really want to tell him that it only took hours after moving here to be introduced to the young hot farmer by his aunty, who happened to be my nosy neighbour who brought me casseroles, while her other nephew who was just as good looking, if not more, happened to be squatting in the ceiling of my home unknown to me until strange things started happening; so I didn't really have to go looking as they all came out of the woodwork... literally.

"Yeah it was a bit of a challenge," I muttered picking something out from underneath my fingernails, my thoughts drifting off to memories of the past two years.

I can feel Millie's eyes boring into me; I bet you anything if I glance in her direction she would be glaring at me for my lack of 'enthusiasm'.

"So what do you think needs to happen for that to change?" Brendon asked sounding slightly frustrated.

I paused to ponder his question as this is the opening I need.

"Well," I said sitting upright in my chair and looking straight at Daniel who was sitting directly behind Brendon, "I feel the lack of matches for singles in the area is a major issue, especially for people in our age group who want to settle down and have families. I mean on the one hand they love it out here and have made a successful and comfortable living and working environment, but on the other hand, the lack of eligible single men and woman makes it impossible to have any sort of dating life within the town."

"Okay," said Brendon also straightening up in his chair and running with my sudden burst of enthusiasm, "so would you…"

"Let me finish," I interrupt him. "There is internet dating and social media of course, that makes the whole dating process a bit more widespread but out here there isn't the potential people to choose from that don't require long distance relationships, therefore you learn to appreciate the people around you," I turned my attention to Daniel as Brendon opened his mouth to try and slip in another question. "So," I continued, holding Daniel's gaze, "I feel that if two people of a similar age and status get on really well and enjoy this type of quiet lifestyle, then why go seeking love from outside when it's all right in front of them," I beamed.

There. Message delivered. I hope Daniel receives that loud and clear.

The shop door flies open and in storms Matt.

Oh god he's got a sour face.

"What the fuck do you mean when you said my manhood and brain are both the size of a bean and about as useful?"

Oh god.

"It's just name-calling Matt, stop being a princess," I said, trying to get him to shut up so I can gauge Daniel's reaction to my comments.

Why does Matt have no discreetness about him?

"Well game on Lisa! If you've got something to say, say it to my face, don't text it," Matt ranted holding up his phone.

Brendon's eyes are darting between Matt and myself.

"Matt your manhood is the size of a bean," I said snarkily, "now can I talk to you later, I'm just in the middle of something," I added turning back to Brendon.

"Yeah well didn't hear you complaining the night you took advantage of me," whinged Matt.

Oh god. My face is burning and Daniel looks like he spat his mouthful of coffee back in his mug. Bloody Matt.

Well that secret is out.

"What's this fight all about anyway?" Millie asks puzzled.

"Lisa's having a go at me 'cause she reckons I hoe'd in on her and Daniel," Matt answered before I could open my mouth, "she reckons if I hadn't shown up at the restaurant the other night she would have had a chance with him, I mean as if you would Lisa."

Arrgh.

"I didn't say you *'hoe'd in'* on Daniel," I said trying to rectify my embarrassment, "I simply suggested that next time I'm on a date could you be more respectable of my space, you know, in case I have a real date."

Brendon has this look of smugness on his face like he has stumbled onto something.

"Not the way the text read," Matt said scrolling on his phone to retrieve it, "I'll read it out."

"No you won't!" I said leaping across the desk to snatch his phone from him, "that's a personal text Matt, have you no respect?"

"Well you hurt me with your cruel words."

"So let me catch up," said Brendon, a little bewildered as well as smug, "you had a relationship with this man and he crashed a date you had with your colleague here?"

"No not exactly!" I said a little frustrated, "look, never mind."

"So is it a jealousy thing?" said Brendon, like he is still conducting my interview.

"Nah, it's Lisa bitching 'cause she tried to score with Dan here but he went wif us on the piss instead, but truth is she's been trying to get into his pants for ages," said Matt holding his phone in the air so I can't reach it.

"Oh my god Matt that is so untrue and by the way that's not what I said!"

Well I said something along those lines but not telling them that.

Okay so I texted Matt and told him next time he wanted to rain on my parade and get my date so drunk that it ruins any chance of having a pleasant evening, he should make damn sure he has insurance on his private parts. Matt replied with the argument that I wasn't on a date as it was only with Daniel. I said, yes indeed I was on a date with Daniel. Then Matt came back with the argument that I wasn't, then I said I was and he wouldn't know a date if I smacked him in the head with one, then Matt said he can tell the difference between a date and a non-date and I wasn't on a date 'cause Dan wasn't into me as he could tell when a guy is into a chick and Daniel isn't. I then said how the hell does he know if he is into me since his brain as well as his manhood are the size of a bean and then well… then the fight really started.

"So there must be a lack of singles around these parts," Brendon joked to Millie, "especially if these two are fighting over the same man."

Millie chuckled at his joke.

"Um Lisa can I talk with you for a moment?" said a stern and slightly embarrassed Daniel as he abruptly got off his chair bringing the room to a silent standstill.

Okay, awkward moment and all eyes boring into me as I follow Daniel to the back of the shop.

"The other night," Daniel started when we were out of earshot, "I know you were expecting more and I thought I told you why I can't be with you on a romantic level Lisa."

"You did and I wasn't," I said enthusiastically, trying to hide my embarrassment because I don't really know why he cannot be with me on a romantic level, but I'm guessing it's because of the whole 'working together' thing.

"Pff don't listen to Matt," I continued, "he's just seeking attention; it was well… um s'posed to be a joke."

"Yeah I guess he can be a bit sensitive," Daniel agreed.

"Pff, just a bit," I scoffed, "soft as a marshmallow that one."

"Yeah," Daniel chuckled, "anyone would think he was the gay one instead of me. Okay glad we cleared that up, I was getting a bit worried you got the wrong impression. Now you better get back to your interview, your fans are waiting," he grinned.

Chuckling I made me way back over to my desk. Matt was still there but now sitting in the corner with his head in his phone pressing buttons.

He's obviously over his rant.

"Everything okay?" Brendon asked still looking slightly smug.

"Fine," I said sitting next to Millie who was feeding Amy, "um sorry about that," I said.

"Oh, no problem," said Brendon, enthused, "that's the type of emotion that makes documentaries real, don't hold back just because I'm around," he grinned, settling in for another round of questions.

Hmm surprised he's not into drama films.

"Well actually, I think that's all I really have to say, not much happens around these parts."

"Oh, okay then," Brendon said, slightly taken aback.

"Like I said," I continued, "my take on dating is that if two similar people get on really well then why go seeking love from outside when it's all right in front of you?"

Hang on. Something's not right and it's just hit me.

Shocked and a bit confused, I turned to Daniel.

"Did you say you *can't* be with me?" I asked him suddenly catching up with the earlier conversation.

Daniel's eyes flick between Millie, Matt and Brendon.

"Um yes."

"Is that because we work together?" I asked trying to get the words out around the lump that has suddenly formed in my throat.

Please tell me it's because we work together.

"No Lisa," Daniel said gently like he was trying not to create a scene, "it's because I'm gay. Remember?"

Facebook status update.

Lisa Collins.

It's official, I'm dying alone with a psycho dog.

6

Back home.

"I knew that," said Millie in a matter-of-fact voice.

"You did not Millie," I snapped.

God why does she have to make out she knows everything?

Millie, Matt and I are sitting around the table discussing the fact that Daniel came out of the closet while Brendon the film guy is upstairs editing my earlier interview.

The awkward moment when the guy you have been attracted to for almost a year and thought you had sex with, turns out to be gay.

And if that wasn't enough it was even more awkward that Daniel had to remind me he had told me the other night at the Ball he was gay after I proposed marriage and babies to him in my tearful drunken state. And that resulted in us having a heart-to-heart chat about things and we agreed to be friends who support each other.

Which of course then led to me feeling even more sorry for myself and getting more intoxicated and requesting to Daniel that I stay at his because I was feeling poorly and lonely.

Not sure what me waking up in his bed with no clothes on was all about but we can definitely rule out that any sex happened.

I think I want to crawl in a hole and die.

"Yeah I knew he was too," Matt agreed as he frantically pressed buttons on his phone. "He's never had a serious girlfriend and he's always reading those gay men's health magazines."

Oh for god's sake, suddenly everyone's an expert on gaydom.

"You did bloody not Matt, you were as surprised as Millie here," I snapped.

"Well you didn't know," Matt said. "Even Damo knew," he added, holding up his phone so I could see Damo's text message across the screen, *'yea new dat'*.

"Doesn't matter who knew and who didn't," said Millie adjusting Amy's baby-grow top, "as long as Daniel is now comfortable around his friends I think it's great."

Millie would think it's great; she can now set him up with one of her gay friends.

"Yeah I don't care," said Matt still frantically pressing buttons on his phone "as long as he leaves my ass alone."

"What's happening?" said Sid, catching the last of the conversation as he made his entrance.

"Daniel's gay," said Millie.

"Oh yeah…? I knew that."

Excused myself as didn't want to join in mini celebrations of Daniel's gayness, instead I'm lying on my bed thinking of the potential singles in the area now Daniel is off the list.

Well it only leaves Tim the baker.

Can feel a wave of depression coming on.

Think Angela the tarot reader got it wrong as she said I'm meant to have choices, well Tim is not a choice so where are all these potential single men she was talking about?

Maybe I should get back into the internet dating scene in the hope I find someone who is willing to move out here.

Deflated, I opened my laptop to reactivate my account. Not really that excited about having to weed out the Brad Pitt wannabes and players. Maybe I should edit my preferences a bit.

Okay here I go again:

Lisa Collins.

Age 38 and 368 days old.

Better change *'Looking for a man to father my children'* to *'Looking for friendship and possible relationship'*.

Interested in men.

Also better change my character profile after all I'm not a *'retired underwear model that has retreated to my ranch in the picturesque setting of the Blue Mountains to ride horses and write poetry'*.

Well at the time it sounded better than the truth of *'retired highschool dropout who buys underwear from K-Mart and resides in country B&B located in the feral town of nowhere land with wayward friends and psycho dog'*.

Don't judge me.

Okay so changed character profile to *'I run a small event hire business in a small town west of Sydney. Also owner/operator of a country B&B. Have normalish friends'*, actually better change that to *'have friends'*.

What else? *'I like walks on the beach'*; better delete that as I don't live anywhere near a beach. I like... *'socialising'*, yep that sounds good, *'and bushwalking'*.

No better delete that.

'Skydiving'.

Not likely.

'Golf'.

Hmmm, no!

'Dog breeding'.

No.

'Juggling'.

Oh my god I seriously don't have any hobbies!

Okay, so *'socialising'* and… *'being me'.*

Which is a lie 'cause sometimes I would like to be a retired underwear model, but can't think of anything else.

And lastly add current location.

Which is going to drop the statistics of potential matches from thousands to possibly three.

Okay so character profile of Lisa Collins is basically that I'm a small town business owner who likes socialising and being herself.

In other words, boring as batshit.

Internet dating site account is now live but I don't know why I bother, I would be lucky to get matched with Mr Potato Head.

So I won't hold out much hope.

Closing lid I slumped back on bed in depressed manner.

Cannot believe I have no hobbies, I mean my mother was always enrolling me in different things like ballet and karate but I never really stuck at anything. I did do meditation recently which I really liked and would have worked out if I didn't go chasing my ghost friend Larry down the street and wrestle him to the ground in front of my fellow meditates.

I don't think I'm a failure, just disinterested in stuff.

Unless in involves men and babies.

Maybe I need a project to take my mind off things.

Think I'll just lie here until the universe gives me a sign, because I got nothing.

I can hear Brendon chatting with Millie so they must be close. Actually I think they may be wandering around the grounds outside my bedroom window.

I love it here and the old place is looking really nice but this is more Sid's project than mine. And Millie used to do kickboxing and had her work until she had Amy, now she has Amy but I don't have anything.

Matt's project in life is to get wasted and laid.

And Daniel's passion is his photography.

Okay yes, the event planning I love, but that's all I seem to have and that's more like work.

Well I s'pose I should be thankful I'm not making a documentary on social interaction among singles in a small town like *some* people around here. I mean how boring is that.

Poor guy, I wonder if he was labeled the nerd in his class at school.

If I was into filmmaking and had to come up with a project on social sciences I would do something far more exciting like 'My Kitchen Rules' CWA style or 'The Bachelor' country style.

Sat up and logged back onto my internet dating site to see if the universe has matched me up with perfect man yet. I should just delete it; I mean I have been down this road before; it's always easy to hide behind a dating profile. It would be so much easier if you invited potential single men to a lineup, picked out say five matches and then spent time with each before even making a date.

God how perfect would that be?

Yeah I think I will delete my dating profile for good as I think the bald headed man who claims he is Brad Pitt is back.

Unless.

Wait a minute…

Oh my god why didn't I think of this before?!

Outside running across lawn like Forrest Gump but with bare feet.

Typical, when you don't want a boring film guy they're always in your face but when you actually want one… nowhere to be seen.

Bloody Millie's obviously taking him for another 'tour', god what does she want to show him now? The remains of an old decaying log.

Spied Sid who was still engrossed in marking out the mini golf course.

"Sid have you seen Brendon?" I panted when I finally got to him.

"Yeah he's just gone up to Mrs Crankshaw's to ask her about previous generations of families living here; I think Millie and Amy went with him."

Oh bloody hell.

"Okay well if they come back before I catch him tell him to not go anywhere or do anything, I have a brilliant idea!"

Ran to car, jumped in, jumped out, ran to house to retrieve car keys, ran back out to car, jumped back in and now driving frantically to Mrs Crankshaw's in bare feet.

If I had time right now to slap myself I would because I cannot believe I hadn't thought about this before. Okay yes I thank the universe for the sign but bloody universe must've been on holiday because it took its time giving it too me.

Driving up Mrs Crankshaw's smelly drive, dodging the dairy cow herd that is occupying the grassy edges, I can see Brendon's car parked out front of the house and I cannot get there fast enough; contemplated jumping out of car while still moving and running to house while car parks itself but have a Toyota called Lizzy and not Kit from Knight Rider.

Noticed a strange brand new twin-cab ute parked in front of Brendon's car, don't recognise the vehicle so wonder if the Crankshaws have finally retired the old farm ute.

Just as I suspected, can hear chatter and biscuits being consumed as I run into the house.

"Lisa dear," Mrs Crankshaw greeted as I hastily entered the kitchen, "just in time, the kettle's boiled but I wish you had phoned me first dear, you see…"

"Brendon!" I said abruptly, interrupting Mrs Crankshaw, "I have a great idea for your film project."

Millie's giving me a wide-eyed stare as if she is trying to tell me something.

"Oh really, what's that?" said Brendon, slightly interested, looking up from the pile of photo albums displaying pictures of the old farming area and bullock wagons in front of him.

"Instead of doing a documentary about country life… why don't we do a reality series?"

"Um well that's what a documentary is," said Brendon.

"No, no, not like boring stuff, no-one wants to watch *that*. Why don't we do something fun like 'The Farmer Wants a Wife'?"

Millie just choked on her coffee.

"It'll be perfect," I continued, running with my enthusiasm, aware that the room feels a bit tense but not really caring.

"I'm the single one, so obviously it won't be 'The Farmer Wants a Wife' *per se* but I am looking for love, so we advertise on the 'net or in the Sydney Morning Herald and get some single men here who want to take part and are interested in moving to the country. We could offer free accommodation and in turn that should give us a bit of advertising for the B&B. We can call it '*The Country Girl Wants a Husband*'."

My god I'm such a genius.

I stopped to catch my breath and let Brendon catch up and process my idea.

Millie is really giving me a wide-eyed and flick stare, not sure what she is trying to tell me.

Mrs Crankshaw looks a bit embarrassed for some strange reason and Brendon looks like my idea has just sunk in because his expression has changed.

And it's looking positive.

Oh I think I just got goose bumps.

"So… what do you all think?" I said getting a bit impatient with the silence.

"I think it could work," said Brendon still considering the possibilities, "I'd have to look into the legal side of things and maybe get a solicitor to draw up a liability contract, but after all, my film is a film based on social interaction in the bush so I guess this would fall into that category."

Millie hasn't said anything but is continuing to try and grab my attention. For god's sake why doesn't she just spit it out?

"Well I think it would be a splendid idea," said Mrs Crankshaw, "but Lisa dear, um… can I talk to you for a moment?"

"Think what this could do for the CWA," I continued, interrupting Mrs Crankshaw once again, yes rude of me but it's not every day I discover I'm a fricken genius.

"I mean if I mention I'm in the CWA as a semi-young thing it could get more woman interested in CWA stuff."

My god what is up with Millie's eyes?

"So is that a yes?" I look at Brendon hopefully.

"Sounds good to me," said an amused male voice behind me, "where do I sign up?"

Oh my god I feel like someone has just punched me in the stomach, all of a sudden my insides are in knots.

Millie just buried her head in her hands and Mrs Crankshaw looks both tense and embarrassed.

I turned around to confirm.

Jake!

7

Oh my god he is back!

Lower then lowlife, bastard Jake!

Well I didn't say that out loud to him I just… well not sure what I did, think I just stared at him in disbelief.

Cannot believe the nerve of him showing up at his auntie's house after deceiving his family by selling the farm to mindless developers, blackmailing his twin brother, having an affair with Matt's married mother Pamela using her to siphon funds from the CWA, while making me go all gaga over him and suggesting we move in together, then taking off in the middle of the night without so much as a howdy do!

Not to mention just now ruining my moment of geniusness.

And here he is, back and looking all gorgeous and sexy with an obnoxious expression plastered all over his face.

Bastard!

I abruptly excused myself and casually strutted out Mrs Crankshaw's door like I am poised and in control and I don't give a flying toss he is here but really I had to leave before I lost control and threw saucepans at him.

I also found myself being oddly attracted to him again.

No, no, no! Must remind myself he is a cold deceptive bastard that has no feelings for others. Apart from for older married woman.

Back in the safety of my home.

"I tried to tell you he was there," said Millie when I shot her my 'what the fuck' look when she came in behind me minutes later. "Not my fault you can't read facial expressions."

"Yes well, very hard when your facial expressions just looked like you had something in your eye, now did he say why he was back?"

God I hope he is just passing through.

"Nope," said Millie, carefully putting Amy into her highchair, "didn't really say much, just that he's visiting for a few days."

Oh thank god.

Obviously Mrs Crankshaw has forgiven him if she has allowed him back into her house. Cannot believe the nerve of him.

Wonder if Rick knows he's back?

He must do, after all they are twins even if they do want to rip each other's heads off, aren't twins supposed to have some sort of telepathic connection.

"I wouldn't sweat on it," said Millie twisting the top off a jar of apple puree, "he's not worth the air around him.

Now what the fuck were you going on about some reality TV show you wanted to present?"

Oh my god nearly forgot about that.

"I won't be presenting it Millie, I'll be starring in it, I'll be called *'The Country Girl Wants a Husband'*."

"Tell me you're not serious."

"Totally and why not, it's a win win, Brendon will avoid getting a bad review for making a boring old fart documentary, it'll be good publicity for the B&B, I'll finally get a man, and Amy will have a playmate."

Millie looks flabbergasted.

"Lisa I can see two things wrong with that plan: one, how are you going to convince any man to come out here and give up his time for no money and not even a guarantee he is going to get laid? And two, Brendon is an amateur film maker so where is this 'publicity' going to get recognised? It's not like it's going on national prime time TV."

God here it is, Millie the fun police, at it again. I'm starting to think she doesn't want me to settle down and have babies.

"Look Lisa," Millie continued as she tried to force the spoon into a stubborn Amy's mouth, "I want nothing more than to see you settled down with children if that's what you want but I don't want you to end up with the wrong guy out of desperation."

"I'm not desperate!" I shot back.

Millie raised her eyebrows.

"Okay maybe I am, but Millie I didn't marry Rick 'cause it didn't feel right. Think about it, if I was desperate I would have gone ahead anyway."

"Yes true but I also don't want you to flaunt yourself and get forced into choosing a guy just because he has shown up for a television show which may not even make it to the screen."

Okay Millie's not only the fun police, she just got promoted.

"It's not going to be like that," I scoffed, "it's going to be a bit of fun, and *anyway* who said I was doing it to find a husband huh? Did you ever consider Millie I'm doing this because I think it's going to be good for the business and B&B?"

Which is totally not true but that's what I'm going to tell Sid, as it's him that will be making up the extra beds and accommodating for more guests.

"Just trust me Millie," I added after she gives me a look of total and utter disbelief.

"Lisa! Oh you're here," said Brendon making an appearance. "I've just spoken with a director, and he has put me in touch with a solicitor and it looks like it's not going to be too complicated.

But here is the best news of all, free-to-air tv is launching a new television channel soon dedicated to amateur films and documentaries and if this goes well we could get a spot for the series," Brendon beams.

Millie is now banging her head on the tray of Amy's highchair. Oh my god it's going to happen and I'm so excited and obviously Brendon is as well because we are now in an excited embrace and dancing around the kitchen. And the best part of all, it will be on tv, me… a celebrity, ohh who am I going to tell first? Mum… no wait I'll tell Daniel, hmm maybe not yet, he's just revealed to me he is gay, don't really need the competition.

Ohh phone's ringing.

I peeled myself from Brendon's excited embrace which had gone on longer than it should have and answered my phone.

"Hello, Lisa Collins Celebrity speaking."

Where the hell did that come from?

"Err, I mean Event Planning."

Brendon excused himself and indicated to me he was going to make a start on the advertising draft.

"We didn't get a chance to catch up," said the male voice on the other end which made my body run cold but oddly, my ego inflate.

Jake.

"Yes well I have far more busy and important things to do," I said coldly.

"Like your television show?" he enquired.

"Err yes, among other things."

"Like what?" he asked me in a genuinely interested voice.

Millie is giving me a puzzled look wanting to know who it is, I mouth to her it is Jake.

"Like err stuff, work stuff… well must go now…"

"Aunty tells me you turned the old place into a Bed & Breakfast, wow you have done really well," he continued, trying to keep up the conversation.

Millie is frowning at me and indicating for me to hang up.

"Umm yes, extremely, well must go."

"Lisa wait," he said sounding all soppy and genuine.

"Yes?" I soften.

"Hang up!" Millie growled under her breath at me.

"I was hoping we could catch up in person it's just that…"

"Hang up!" Millie growled again.

'I can't!' I mouthed to her.

"I think I owe you an explanation," he said.

My god I don't know what to say.

"For god's sake," Millie said, ripping the phone from my hand and pushing the end call button, "don't give him any more of your time."

"But Millie he was just about to offer an explanation," I wailed.

"Don't you dare get sucked in," she warned rather sternly, "he's back in town for a while and probably wants a booty call. What possible explanation could he offer to justify what he has done? Let it go Lisa."

Jeez Millie has taken her controlling grumpy pills today.

But she has a point, Jake is a bastard and I'm not interested in his 'explanation' as to why he sucked me into his world, convinced me he is a god and then took off.

No, from now on I'll just ignore him; hopefully he will be gone soon.

Anyway I have bigger things to worry about, like becoming a celebrity.

Ohh I just got goose bumps again.

My phone is ringing again and a quick check on the display screen confirms it's Jake, so I ignore it. Anyway if he wants a booty call why doesn't he just ring Pamela?

Ohh just felt a stab in the heart there.

Wonder if she knows he's back. After all he did the dirty on her as well.

Oh well she did deserve it.

Brendon is back and shows me the draft of the advert we are going to place nationwide.

It reads:

The Country Girl Wants a Husband!

If you are a single male aged between 29 and 50 and looking for love in the peaceful setting of country life NSW, then we want you.

Applications for an amateur dating reality television show are invited. Successful applicants will then be invited to audition.

Please forward a current photograph along with a one page profile describing yourself and your interests and hobbies to application@thecountrygirlwantsahusband.com.

"So what do you think?" Brendon asks.

"Hmmm 29 to 50; isn't 50 a bit old?"

"We have to put a wide age group out there Lisa otherwise it may be slim pickings. Besides what does age matter when you're in love?"

"Yeah I s'pose," I sighed.

"Anyway I can weed out the older ones if it comes to that."

"It's perfect," I beamed, "so when is it going to run?"

"Um excuse me," said Millie playing bad cop again, "Lisa we have house meetings on things like this, don't you think we need to sit down with Sid first, after all we need to accommodate for this tribe of potential victims."

God Millie is so negative.

Official house meeting with Millie, Sid and Brendon (even though he's not part of the house, I thought I should have him there on my team).

Sid's looking flabbergasted but I think I have finally convinced him.

"So you're telling me you want to do a reality television show to promote the Bed & Breakfast and the area, and you have decided the best way to attract tourists is to offer your hand in marriage to anyone willing to take it?"

"Uh ha," I beamed encouragingly.

"How many are we talking?" said Sid, "we only have accommodation for two doubles and one is being occupied at the moment."

"Well I was thinking we have my room and then we can also move the junk out of the rumpus room. We have a spare bed."

"And I can move to the motel in town if you need the room," said Brendon.

"And where will you sleep?" Sid asks me.

"With Amy."

"No, not a good idea, Amy is unsettled at night as it is and it still leaves the problem of bathrooms," said Millie putting her discouraging two cents worth in.

"Yes that's true," Sid agreed, "I'm sorry Lis it doesn't seem practical."

Still amazed and extremely proud at Sid's newly found confidence for speaking his mind but on days like today why oh why does he not revert back to his old ways of being scared of swearing at a fly.

"Well that settles it then," said Millie, "either you find another venue to accommodate these psychos or cancel."

God Millie and Sid are sooo unfair.

"Well can I suggest…" said Brendon trying to calm me down before I throw myself on the floor in a toddler tantrum fit, "… we can still do the filming of it here which would work out better, and we can see if the motel in town can give us a discount for a bulk booking," he said as the sudden realisation at lack of available funds becomes apparent on his face.

Oh yeah I forgot about funds.

"My budget is limited," he said, "so I'm not sure it can stretch that far."

Silence fell around the table and I can see Brendon's mind working overtime as he is trying to figure out if this is going to work or not.

Why is the universe doing this to me? I mean I did ask for a bus-load of potential men to be delivered to my door so I can choose a suitable mate. Why are they making it so hard?

Think I'm going to cry.

"Well if it's meant to be, it's meant to be," said Millie, gathering her empty coffee cup and heading for the sink. "If you come up with a solution for accommodation then Sid and I agree the B&B will be fine for the filming location."

Gee Millie, should I grovel at your feet now?

Didn't say that out loud though.

So Brendon is happy; and away to make a call to the motels which I said will probably make him unhappy. And I've gone for a walk to sulk to the universe and ask for money to fund potential television hit series.

I wander down to Bonnie and Clyde's pen, my two pet goats I got when I first arrived here before the menagerie of animals we have here now, and proceeded to complain to them as they nibble at my fingers.

The one opportunity comes along where I can be both famous *and* find a husband, which is so rare, and one simple thing like a lack of beds hinders the whole thing. If I had less people living here and having their say then I wouldn't have a problem.

Oh, speaking of, Millie is hollering at me.

"Lisa, Daniel called!" she yelled out to me, "he wants you to call him back."

Oh god I haven't really seen Daniel since the whole gay thing came to light. But I know I have to face him some time, after all we have a wedding at the church to cater for this weekend. Better put sulking over lack of potential men behind me and get into work headspace.

Crying down the phone to Daniel about lack of potential men.

"Okay calm down Lis," he soothed, "so you're saying the only thing stopping you from finding a man to have children with is lack of funding for accommodation?"

"No," I sniffed impatiently and proceeded to fill him in about the whole operation *'The Country Girl Wants a Husband'*.

"… and Millie and Sid said they won't have them staying here and Brendon doesn't have enough money to put them in a motel," I wailed.

"Ohhh now I see," said Daniel, sounding like he has finally caught up with the whole idea.

"And these potential bachelors, how many are we talking here?"

"Oh I don't know, 10 maybe 20."

"Think 20 may be a bit much Lis."

God why are people so negative?!

"Okay fine, 10."

"Is this the total number you have had applied?"

"No we haven't been through that process yet."

"And is Brendon directing the whole thing or has he got a team involved?"

God so many questions.

"Um no just him… and me."

Daniel fell silent on the end of the line but not a bad silent, a silence like he may offer a small glimmer of hope any moment now.

… any moment now.

"I'll call you back," he said quite abruptly before hanging up.

Oh bloody hell.

"Okay so the motel said they have 8 double units," said Brendon making an entrance and looking deflated, "they can do a discount if booked for 14 days, but it's stretching the budget so we still may have to find an alternative, and we'd have to give them a definite date for booking soon because the annual flower festival is coming up, and the chook races."

"So is that a positive on the accommodation or a negative?" I pushed.

Brendon's looking at me as if to say 'what do you think?'.

"Well it's possible," I shot back.

"Lisa," he sighed, "I like your enthusiasm but it's not just the accommodation, it's also the catering and transport here, finding people willing to spend their own money on air fares or bus fares to get here. There's a lot more to it. So what do you think?"

Don't want to tell him what I think because I think Brendon's not trying hard enough.

I can feel the lump in my throat again and I think I'm going to cry. I mean they are grown men; can't they cook their own food and find their own way here?

Oh Daniel's calling back.

"Okay Lisa, I've done some digging and I think we can make this work to our advantage business-wise," he said, sounding happy with himself, "we will sponsor the accommodation, my place has five rooms including mine. I can get hold of Roy at the furniture rental place and get a discount off another 5 single beds, that way if we get 10 applications then they can double up two to a room and I'll stay at yours."

Oh my god Daniel is brilliant!

"Oh my god, oh my god," I chanted down the phone.

"But in return," he continued, "I want free advertising for the business so we are going to have to sit down with Brendon and propose that we..."

"On our way," I interrupted him.

8

20 minutes later.

Oh my god, it is happening.

I mean it is really happening.

And I owe it all to Daniel; he's so brilliant with all his convincing.

Millie and Sid agreed to the B&B being the location for filming, on condition there is to be no disruption to Amy's routine and Millie can sit through the auditions and help choose the successful applicants.

Debbie from the nursing home said we can borrow the resident's van for transportation to and from the accommodation and B&B on the condition that it's back on Tuesday mornings for aqua aerobics and she can sit through the auditions and help choose the successful applicants.

Mrs Crankshaw agreed to Brendon's offer of a large donation made to the CWA for catering the meals on the condition that their efforts are acknowledged in the credits and the members can sit through the auditions and help choose the successful applicants.

And of course Daniel has offered to give up his home and stay at the B&B as well as donate money for the food for the CWA on condition that *'Cannon and Collins. Photography, Event Planning and Supplies'* is the main sponsor for the show and he can sit through the auditions and help choose the successful applicants.

Matt and Damo said if we don't get enough applications they'll see if some of their mates want to do it on the condition that we supply them with a couple of dozen cans of Johnny Walker and a slab of Four X Gold.

So the advert runs tomorrow.

So, so excited.

Brendon also slapped together a website and Facebook page and uploaded pictures of the B&B and Daniel's house. And tomorrow Daniel is going to take some glamour shots of me to put on the website.

But now I'm sitting up in bed, pen and paper in hand because Brendon has requested I compile a profile of myself and what I am looking for in a perfect partner.

And you know I thought that would be the easy part but it's not.

I even asked Millie to help me but she only came up with boring stuff like 'honest and romantic'.

I mean don't get me wrong that's all very good but what about other things like 'good with a hammer' or 'leaves the toilet seat down' or 'does not go out in public wearing board shorts with runners'.

You know, the little things.

Anyway Millie eventually gave up, saying there is no such thing as a perfect man, unless I mould him out of clay and call him Michelangelo and I shouldn't be so picky. But this may be my one chance of getting what I want, so I have decided to make a list of all the men I have gone out with and pick out their good points only.

So this is what I have come up with:

My first real boyfriend was Samuel the personal trainer; I liked him for his athletic body and realistic nutrition intake, so that can go on the list.

Joe my hippie boyfriend for his spiritual and sensitive side.

Jason the jockey for his love of animals and ability to ride a horse.

Andrew because he was good around the house and a good dancer.

Darryn because he kept himself well groomed and had great dress sense.

Rick for his honesty.

122

And Jake for his sexy looks, nice tanned body, charisma, skills in bed, and ability to swing a hammer and build almost anything.

So in summary:

Lisa Collins' ideal man:

- *Tall with dark complexion, must have rock hard abs, nice athletic limbs and maintain good nutrition.*
- *Have good cooking skills as well as maintain good housekeeping skills.*
- *Does not go out in public in ugg boots, brown shoes, anything that has orange in it, caps worn backwards, track pants, overalls, or pants worn any higher than the navel.*
- *An appealing allure to his personality and must have a spiritual side and believe in angels. Must not be afraid to cry at sad movies and happy endings. Definitely must be an honest man who doesn't keep secrets. Animal lover is essential.*
- *Must hold the following skills – farming, fencing, building, car maintenance, fixing leaks, able to hang curtains, clean animal pens, ride horses and dance.*

There, think I have covered it all.

Couldn't be bothered getting out of bed to give it to Brendon so I'll just email it to him then send a text telling him I have emailed it to him.

Pressed send on both devices, pushed my laptop away and snuggled into my pillows. I'm so excited about this, it's like I have finally found something that I can have a chance to truly shine at, don't get me wrong, running my own business has its rewards but it's not like I'm doing that all on my own as I have Millie, Sid, and Daniel to compromise with. But this is going to be about me and me only; my talents, my personality and what I want for me.

And about time, as it seems to be about everyone else around here.

Feeling chilly so wrapped the dooner around me and snuggled further down in bed, really must get some beauty sleep for tomorrow's photo shoot but I'm so hyped up. Still haven't figured out what to wear, I was going to go with my black figure-hugging knee length dress and black high boots but as Brendon reminded me, this is *'The Country Girl Wants a Husband'* not *'Nightclub Goer Looking for a Hook Up'*.

So Daniel suggested leaving it with him and he will take care of the wardrobe side of things, he is coming at 9am tomorrow.

Drifting off to sleep feeling content with potential stardom when my phone ringing pulls me from my sleepy daze.

Bet ya it's Brendon so I should just ignore it; he can come down and talk to me if it's important as don't want to put my arm out because it's cold. But then again he may have spotted a flaw in my perfect man profile so better answer it.

"I'm sorry, were you sleeping?" came the male voice that sent cold chills through my insides.

Bugger, should have looked at the caller display first.

"Yes Jake I was," I said, trying to muster a frosty tone but really kinda feeling a bit tickled pink he's called.

"Okay I'm sorry to wake you, I'll let you get back to sleep," he said in a quiet voice.

"No it's okay," I said a little too quickly. Shit that sounds like I'm pleased he rung, better change tone. "Um I mean, well, what do you want?"

"Just to see how you're doing," he said as I can hear the flick of a cigarette lighter.

"So you're still smoking?" I shot back.

"Yeah bad habit, need to quit," he said like he was trying to justify it to himself, "so how's things with you?" he asked, changing the tone as if he is settling in for a full blown phone conversation.

I can hear Millie's earlier words in my ears *'hang up, hang up'*.

Really want to launch into telling him about the show and the photo shoot; actually a tiny bit of me misses him.

Yes I know I didn't go out with him for long and he did use me and spit me out. I mean I had a longer relationship with Jake's twin brother Rick than I did with him, but for some reason Jake got under my skin.

Or should I say, is still under my skin.

Shit, shit, shit. Why did I let him do this to me? Need to say a disappearing chant.

Um… *evil demon be gone.*

"Lisa, you still there?" he said when I hadn't answered him.

"Um yes, I'm fine, a little tired. Okay good to talk to you, take care, bye."

Quickly pushed end call button and breathed sigh of relief.

Really need a Jake repellent 'cause that was a close one, for a brief moment there he had me sucked into his web of charm and sexiness. Millie will be proud of me when I tell her I didn't speak to him.

Actually better off Millie not knowing.

So from now on better start focusing on a new man who will be a hundred, no, a thousand times better than Jake.

Also better drown phone in bucket of water 'cause Jake is calling back.

3pm following day.

Okay didn't drown phone in bucket of water, ended up having marathon conversation with Jake.

Once we got talking it's like we couldn't stop.

He apologised for what happened between us and said he got a bit gaga over Pamela and he thought she loved him and it was her idea to embezzle funds from the CWA and sell off the farm for development so they could elope. But he got scared and took off and that's when he realised Pamela just used him and he felt terrible about the whole thing; so he has come back asking for forgiveness.

I mean what a bitch Pamela is, I always knew it was her pulling the strings.

But he said I deserve better than him and he just wanted to say sorry and how he felt he'd ruined his chances with me.

I mean he has really changed.

But I'm not going to get sucked in so I told him we could be friends and he said that would be great so we talked some more and I told him about the filming and that the advert was running today and how excited I was about it all. He said he couldn't wait to get the paper to see, good luck with it all and any man is lucky to have me blah, blah.

Rather sweet and I don't care what Millie says, talking to Jake has closed a lot of doors for me and I'm feeling pretty good about myself.

But I've decided I'm not going to tell Millie anyway, she will just put a negative spin on it all.

"Righto that's enough," said Daniel after the last click of the camera went.

I must say Daniel is brilliant with his wardrobe choices as I'm looking pretty good in my wrangler jeans, nice cowboy boots, a shirt that shows off my curves but gives a slim fit, and long blond hair with a hint of orange protruding nicely from my cowboy hat.

It's been an awesome day, Daniel got here at 9am as planned and started going through my wardrobe while I attempted to get out of bed (after late night conversation with Jake) but after finding nothing suitable and a quick breakfast of jam on toast, he took me shopping for some country gear from the local emporium. It's so much fun shopping with Daniel and I now know why so many chicks prefer to shop with gay friends, it's like having a best girlfriend but without the bitchiness or in Millie's case, the boredom, Millie hates shopping. In fact from now on I'm only going shopping with Daniel and the best part is, I didn't even have to pay for it.

How cool is that.

I have had a text message from Brendon telling me that we have had no applicants so far but have had one enquiry which is brilliant considering it's only been a couple of hours. Brendon also said he was going to advertise locally to get some local lads to apply and because the age group criteria is over 29, I can safety say none of Matt's spotty mates will apply. But downside is, Tim from the bakery can.

But no matter, as it's up to me to decided. I did ask Brendon if I can take a sneak peak at the applicants to which he said no, it's up to the selection committee to decide who gets in at the start or not. A bit worried as I know Millie is on the selection committee but it has been decided they can only act on the credentials I have set.

So all photos of self are done and loaded to website, advertisements are underway, legal liability documents have come back from lawyers and bus-load of potential single men is on its way.

All I have to do is wait until closing date for applicants in a couple of weeks time then it's all go.

I'm soooo excited!

Facebook Status Update.

Lisa Collins.

Would like to thank fellow facebookers for their concerns about my last update in which I stated I am dying alone with my psycho dog, it's all good as truck-load or should I say bus-load of potential singles on its way now and I shall keep you all updated.

Also remember to like our facebook page, *The Country Girl Wants a Husband'* and share with your friends for your chance to vote.

9

Audition day.

And I'm feeling slightly anxious. Not because bus-load of men is arriving today, but because bus-load of men arriving are to face the wrath of the selection committee, which consists of the following people:

Millie (of course, she likes to be in control).

Mrs Crankshaw (apparently she will be able to tell a lot about their character by her body parts, for example if her gout starts playing up when he presents himself he's no good).

Fran, Betty and Mary from the CWA (they state since they've been around for a lot of years, they can smell a scoundrel a mile away; also Fran hasn't seen that many men in one room for a very long time and doesn't want to miss the opportunity).

Matt and Damo (I don't know why but according to Matt, their stanch presence alone will send a silent message to the applicants 'not to fuck wif you').

Debbie from the nursing home (because she is lending us the resident's van).

And of course Brendon and Daniel will be observing from the side, I can understand why Brendon will be present but I think Daniel just wants to perve.

And I'm not allowed anywhere near it.

Which is so unfair I mean this is my future husband at stake here…

It's been a long couple of weeks since we ran the advert and I've been trying to keep myself busy with work but it's so hard when you know you're about to become a celebrity. Jake has texted me a few times asking how things are going with the applicants. Nothing full on, just a friendly text now and then. He has decided to stay a bit longer with his aunty and apparently he and Rick have spoken, still a bit raw but they can tolerate each other again.

Not that I'm going back down that road. In fact I should stop thinking about him.

Brendon's not being very forthcoming with information regarding the responses for the adverts but assures me it's all fine and I'm to leave it up to him. Millie and Sid are also being very secretive and Matt and Damo have assured me they have got the situation covered but wouldn't elaborate on what they meant by that, so it's understandable I'm a bit nervous.

But auditions are happening today which means they must have got enough guys.

Ohh I think I need to pee again.

"Okay time for you to go," said Millie knocking on the bathroom door, "they are here and you shouldn't be."

Apparently they have appointed Max Crankshaw to come and collect me to spend time with him down on their farm while potential men are being grilled by roomful of mostly old and controlling woman. Millie said not only would it be a good idea to have someone there to supervise me so I'm not tempted to spy, it would also be good to spend time gaining real knowledge about the country and farming as the title of this project suggests.

Finished in bathroom and made excuse to Millie that I needed to collect something from my bedroom so I can at least get a glimpse of them from my window. Max is waiting by the back door to escort me and I can hear the bus pulling in at the front of the house. We have opened up the verandah and living area to accommodate the guests for today's auditions. Sid has put a lot of time and effort into the lawns and gardens and the place looks fantastic, in fact I hardly recognise it, it looks like something out of a house-and-garden magazine. Love Sid, he is the best and weirdest amateur landscape gardener ever.

I move to the window and can just see the front of the bus, the angle makes it a bit difficult, so I press my right cheek to the glass to get a better look. Oh my god the bus is a big one and it looks like it's full. No wonder Brendon is being a little reserved about the applicants; he's probably trying to spare my nerves and excitement, and he may be a little overwhelmed as it's obvious he's had a huge response. The bus door opens which obscures my view further. I can see movement inside as they are gathering their things and heading to the door.

Oh my god this is it.

My heart cannot stop pounding as the first one steps from the bus, hard to see from this distance but oh my god he is hot, wonder if I should text Millie and tell her to put him in the final six.

Oh my god, so is the next one.

"Lisa!" Millie yells, appearing in my line of vision down below, scaring the bejeezes out of me. "Go!" she orders as Sid bangs on the bedroom door behind me.

Bloody hell. So unfair.

3 hours later, still down at the Crankshaw's farm.

"… and that Lisa my dear is how you artificially inseminate a cow," said Max proudly as he puffs his chest out while the vet disposes of her long glove.

I cannot concentrate and I've been texting Millie all morning but she is not responding to my messages. I'm so anxious and really want to know what is going on.

I'm also bored.

And I really thought Jake would be here but there has been no sign of him all morning.

I did hear from Daniel, who assured me it's all going well but wouldn't say any more. He did say two of the women from the CWA had to be removed from the room after they asked the men to strip.

So now I'm back in the house making the tea for the visiting vet and Max who are just cleaning up from a morning of sticking things in cows. I have to say this is the longest morning ever. And if I was truthful I have to admit I'm a bit nervous about the whole thing. I mean I always seem to end up stuffing up relationships. Is it because I attract the wrong men or because I haven't found the right person?

What if the right person isn't in that bus-load of men and I go through another relationship only for it to crumble and me to once again end up back on my own with my psycho dog?

Oh my god what was I thinking doing this? I'm setting myself up for a fall; why do I do this to myself? Maybe I should just ring Brendon and call the whole thing off, I mean what if none of them are suitable and I have to force myself to choose one only to end up sending him packing.

I think I'm about to hyperventilate.

"Dollar for your thoughts," said Jake behind me, startling me and causing me to let out an involuntary yelp.

"Are you okay?" he said as his expression changed from one of amusement to concern.

"Yes fine," I said gripping the counter and trying to gain my composure, "just making tea."

Jake looks really nice with his clean shirt and jeans, wonder where he has been.

"I'll help you," he said noticing my hand shaking slightly as I negotiated the tea cups to the tray.

God I need to get out of here, think I'm having an anxiety attack and am suddenly freezing.

About to tell Jake all is good and excuse myself to hide in the bathroom when my phone starts to beep.

It's Daniel telling me auditions are over and Sid is on his way to pick me up.

Okay, anxious moment over. Bring it on.

Back home.

"What the…?"

"Calm down Juliet, they have just gone back to Daniel's to settle in," said Millie clearing the plates.

Oh thank god, I thought Millie had scared them off already.

"So where are Mrs Crankshaw and the others?"

"We've all got tasks to do Lisa," Millie said sounding frazzled.

"So what are they like?" I asked, "are they hot?"

"Hot enough that Fran and Betty had to leave the room before they threw their bloomers at them," Millie teased, "but other than that you are just going to have to wait and see."

Millie is such a bitch.

"Oh and we got one local," she called from the kitchen, "but Lisa I want you to know it wasn't me who decided on him I got out-voted okay?"

"Oh god it's Tim isn't it?"

Millie came back from the kitchen and went to answer but stopped herself.

"You'll see," she said as she proceeded to gather up more disposable plates.

"Lisa!" Brendon greeted with an enormous grin, "great success so far, I'm so pleased you suggested this, I can see it's going to be a great social experiment as we have some great characters amongst them, everyone seems happy and they are all at Daniel's settling in at the moment. So I have asked Matt and Damo to bring them back round at 3pm and we will start filming the introductions."

"Matt and Damo are chauffeuring them?" I asked a little alarmed.

"Well we couldn't find anyone else to drive the van," Brendon said puzzled.

"What about Sid?"

"Busy," called Sid hurrying passed me with an arm full of bedding.

"But Matt hasn't got his full drivers license."

"No but Damo has, they've each taken a week off work," said Brendon, "thought that was rather good of them, they're only doing it for a slab of beer and a couple dozen cans of bourbon."

Having visions of van-load of potential men parked on the side of the road sucking down bongs provided by Matt and Damo.

"Right no time to lose," Millie said grabbing me by the arm as I shake the image from my head.

"Change of clothes and makeup needed. I'll be up to help you right after I tend to Amy."

Ohhh, goose bumps.

But shit what am I going to wear?

"Put on the clothes you wore in the photo shoot," Millie called as she went to attend to a crying Amy who just woke up from her nap. My god that woman is a mind reader.

But now the nerves are setting in and I think I'm about to be sick. But rest assured I will be poised, calm and elegant.

I just need a wee wine.

2.58pm.

Okay Millie is a total nervous wreck.

So is Brendon.

Don't know what the fuss is all about, I'm feeling fine.

"Bloody hell, drink this," said Millie handing me a cup of coffee, "can't believe you drunk the whole bloody bottle."

Okay I overdid it a little with the wine but the closer the time came for meeting the men, the more nervous I became, and I'm only slightly tidly. It's like you're about to give a speech in front of your peers at school and haven't got your cue cards.

But should have eaten somefing 'cause I fink the wine is going to my head.

Millie is fussing with my makeup and insisting I change my top to an even tighter one. I know she is trying to help but to be honest I already look like a bit of a tart with the shirt unbuttoned too far but Millie and Brendon insist I look fine so I'll run with it.

I can hear the van pull up at the back of the house, any moment now they will be led in one by one. Earlier in the day Brendon filmed an introduction which he will edit in later. But right now I finally get to be introduced to future potential husbands. Plan was, I'll be standing in the courtyard and Daniel (who volunteered to be the host so he can have front row eye-candy seats) will introduce them as they come in one at a time, you know like the real television show.

"Okay change of plan," said Brendon as I poured the last of the contents of my coffee down my throat. "We can't do this show the traditional way you know because of err, copyright issues," he said shooting a glance at Millie, "so instead of being introduced one by one Lisa you are just going to make an appearance on the lawn where they are mingling and having cocktails and finger food."

"And?" I said waiting for my instructions for my grand entrance being the bachelorette starring in the *'The Country Girl Wants a Husband'*.

"And we'll be in the background filming things and we will edit all the introduction voice over later."

Seems a bit odd, I mean wouldn't you just film everything at once?

"So all you have to do Lisa, is pretend you are attending a garden party."

I looked at Millie who gave me a cheesy thumbs up.

Hmmm, Millie's acting weird.

"So Daniel will take you out and introduce you to the lads," said Brendon.

Oh now I get it, phew. There is going to be an introduction after all, just in a social environment, nothing formal. Thank god, for a moment there I thought they were going to just throw me out onto the front lawn with a group of drunken men.

"Your guests are waiting," said Daniel making an appearance, "are you ready?"

Oh my god I need to pee.

"No time," hissed Daniel as I head for the bathroom door.

Um hello, do I need to point out we are not on a tight schedule and after all I am the star and it's fashionable for the star to be fashionably late.

Oh never mind, urge to pee gone now.

10

2 hours later.

Is it illegal for a woman to have multiple husbands?

Might look into that.

It's been an awesome night so far.

And I have to say it is going well as I'm having no awkward moments with them whatsoever, if fact we are into the hugging stage.

Really need to pee again as haven't had a chance to do so with all the natter and chit chat. Drinks went on a bit longer than expected and I'm feeling slightly wobblier than before. We're all now sitting down to dinner prepared by Mrs Crankshaw and Betty. The CWA have decided to do the meals in rostered shifts, which was organised by Sid so there were no arguments as to who got more shifts than the other, seems bus-load of young men have caused a bit of a cat fight amongst the CWA. It was also decided they were to prepare the evening meal only as they have free access to the kitchen at Daniel's place for the rest.

I was a little surprised when Daniel first took me out there and introduced me because from the amount of men arrived on the big bus this morning only seven remained, but as Daniel reminded me we didn't have a lot of accommodation, so I suppose. It seemed a bit weird to begin with as I stepped outside, one of them hooted and whistled and told me to get my gear off. Bit disrespectable, but Daniel quickly went over to him and after a mumbled exchange of words, the guy apologised and said it had been a long time since he saw a woman as good looking as me, so sweet, yes he is forgiven.

I'm trying to look out for Tim the baker since Millie said a local had been voted in. I'm presuming it's Tim as there doesn't seem to be a lot of other potential guys in the area that fit my criteria, but can't see him anywhere so hoping he got cold feet.

Before dinner I was allowed to have some one-on-one time with them down in the garden. When I say 'allowed' it's because Millie thought it may be better if I stayed with her at all times and we mingled as a group.
In fact I don't want to think about what she thought I was going to do on my own, gee thee have little faith.

So let me introduce them all.

Slade and Steel are twins born 2 minutes apart, Slade has blond hair whereas Steel has dark hair, they are even in the same profession as they both work in the mines. I informed them there is nothing funny about their names sounding like an '80s cop show, to which they replied they didn't think there was any humour to their names and they sound nothing like an '80s cop show, but they seem really nice and have good jobs so I think they should definitely be on my final list.

Darcy is soooo cute and works in the mines. Like me, he too had a little accident with hair dye so his hair is slightly orange as well. I couldn't help myself; I had to spike his hair and pinch his cheeks, now he looks like a wee troll doll, but cuter. He's a bit shy but likes a cuddle and I don't think he minded that I thought he looked like a fictional character so I think he should definitely be on my final list too.

Jamie feels we were connected in a past life and have been reunited to finish our path of purpose together and I couldn't agree more because after all, he is here. I told him all about my ghost friend Larry and how I came to meet him. Jamie thinks it was Larry who came to see him in the night and told him to find a group of miners and get on a bus.

I said it doesn't surprise me as Larry is always doing stuff like that but what really blew me out of the water is Jamie said just as he was looking out for a sign in the form of a passenger bus while he was hitchhiking to see his cousin, as he thought that's what Larry was referring to, he got picked up by a bus-load of people who work in the mines.

So funny and spooky.

Jamie is so spiritual and so nice I think he should definitely be on my marriage list.

Derrick, who I have named Captain Sweatpants on account of his oversized stomach and baggy track pants, works in the mines as a technical engineer and was not at all offended when I told him he's not so hot in the looks department but has a lovely personality and because of that I think I'm going to put him on the final list. You know because everyone deserves a chance.

Paul works in the mines, is a bit shy and not much of a conversation man. He said he's not much into meeting woman as has had bad experiences so not sure what he is doing here, to be honest I don't think he even knows. But he looks okay, wears glasses and full length cargo pants, doesn't seem to drink much so I think definitely will be on my final list.

Bevan, who is affectionately known as 'Bear', works in the mines, can crush a full sized beer can with his forehead, and is missing his two front teeth. Not sure how he fitted my criteria as he is very loud and seems to like swearing a lot. In fact he was the one who told me to get my gear off so I think Millie and the CWA woman must be blind because he seems like a bit of a thug. I'm surprised Mrs Crankshaw's gout didn't play up when she met him. But he can tell the funniest jokes and you know, once you get passed the other stuff, he seems kinda nice and he does think I'm a good looking gal. I have never dated a man with as many tattoos as him before so I think he should definitely be on my final list.

But the awesome thing is all of them are paying me attention and I feel like I'm the goddess of this party and they are all biding for my hand in marriage.
Oh wait…

I am *so* drunk but not that drunk I'm making a fool of myself or being very loud. In fact I feel elegant, poised, and in control. And still need to pee.
But dinner is almost over and Brendon has stopped filming. Millie, Sid, Daniel, and Brendon are now joining us at the table and there are murmurs of conversation everywhere.

Matt and Damo are also here and I know their 'stanch presence' was meant to be intimidating but honestly wearing dark glasses at night is just ridiculous. Sid is talking with Captain Sweatpants and Paul which doesn't surprise me as Sid is a bit of a nerd himself, Millie is in conversation with the twin gods Slade and Steel about fitness and how to lose her baby weight since they are gym junkies, and Brendon is having a yarn with Darcy. Bevan, aka Bear, is chugging back drinks and Jamie is talking to me about animal totems.

Not that I'm paying attention to him as not only trying to focus on not peeing, but I'm also doing a quick head count. Millie said there were eight all together as the van can only transport ten minus Matt and Damo but a quick head count only reveals seven.

Quietly excuse myself in poised and calm manner and leaned over to Millie who was still wedged between Slade and Steel.

Oh my god those twins are even hotter close up.

"I thought there were meant to be eight," I whispered to Millie, "what happened to Tim?"

"Tim? What makes you think it's Tim?" she whispered back.

"Well he's a local; you said there was one local guy."

"Um… yes, he's running a bit late, should be here any second but Lis…"

"Could I have everyone's attention," said Brendon standing from his chair diverting my attention from Millie, "first of all I would like to thank each and every one of you for staying and being a part of this social experiment, and we hope you have an enjoyable stay in the country," he said in a speechy manner.

'Stay'? And what does he mean by 'thank you for staying'?

"Just a friendly reminder you all signed the agreement that we can film you in this social environment and even though we will take the utmost precautions to ensure your privacy and any personal information is not disclosed, your full cooperation is most appreciated," Brendon continued.

Murmurs of 'no worries' came from around the table.

"So enjoy your stay, hope you have a great time and get ready for a week of fun."

Brendon sits back on his seat and conversation starts up again.

Hold the bus. Why was there no mention of me, or anything about why we are here? Hmmm think I need to say a few words.

"Excuse me," I said clinking my glass while getting to my feet as Millie's eyes widen in horror at the fact I am about to open my mouth.

My god, why does she do that!

"I would like to say a few words," I said when everyone finally looked my way.

Shit I better make this quick as still really need to pee.

"Well I would personally like to thank each of you for coming. And I hope you haven't been disappointed so far," let out a small chuckle but no one else seems to smile. Except Bear as he has just hollered at me to 'get ya gear off' again, seriously, no wonder that man is single.

"Back when I first got this idea for this show I wasn't expecting such a bus-load of fine young men to turn up at my door. I am looking forward to the week but it's also going to be a tough week faced with hard decisions and disappointment, not only for some of you, but for me also."

Jamie the spiritual guy seems to be the only one nodding in agreement with what I'm saying, the others are looking blank. Except Millie who is looking awkward and embarrassed.

God I sooo need to pee, better wrap this up.

"I am looking forward to spending time with you all but I just want you to remember in your own individual way you are special and have lots to offer any girl, but sometimes you just may not make it over the…"

"Um Lisa," Brendon interrupted leaping to his feet, "we have another visitor and also I errr, need to speak with you, now!" he said looking at me as if to say 'shut the fuck up'.

God what is their problem, I mean I am the star here, and the visitor is just Tim.

Okay just ignore Brendon and end on a positive note.

"So what I am trying to say," I continued, glaring at Millie who is trying to tell me with her eyes to sit down and shut up, "that no matter whom I choose you are all special and have lots to offer a girl, but sometimes you just have to leave it to fate to decide. And it's important to know that there is someone waiting out there for each and every one of you."

Okay soooo better wrap this up, think a tiny bit of pee is coming out.

"So hope you enjoy your time with me and remember don't take it personally. I shall now retire to my quarters and I look forward to seeing you all tomorrow, bye."

Turned to run towards toilet and walk smack into Jake who is standing behind me holding the biggest bunch of flowers.

What the hell is he doing here?

But don't have time for accepting flowers and small chit chat as really need to pee.

In bathroom.

My god, cannot believe I made it to the toilet.

The relief is overwhelming; it has to be right up there as one of the best feelings in the world.

I could hear cheering and whopping coming from the table as I quickly ran passed Jake almost knocking him over and crushing his flowers.

Didn't mean to knock flowers out of ex boyfriend's hands, but when you gotta go, you gotta go and now I have Millie, Brendon, and Daniel standing outside the bathroom door asking if everything is okay.

God can't a girl just have a moment?

Called back to them informing I'd be out shortly to satisfy their need to know why I am on toilet. And gave myself a moment to reflect as to why Jake would want to participate in an amateur dating show.

Well it's obvious from the phone calls and texts he wants to make a new beginning and give things another go between us. Ha! I always felt he would come crawling back. And to be honest I wasn't completely shocked when I turned around and saw him there. It's like a tiny bit of me knew he would show up somewhere and to be honest I'm a bit pleased he did.

Not that I would go back there but nice to know a girl is wanted again after rejection.

A tiny knock on the door followed by Millie's quiet voice pulls me from my thoughts. Also pee is finally over.

I can hear whispers through the door and can only guess Millie, Brendon and Daniel are still standing out there and no doubt talking about me.

Think I'll just sit here till they leave.

Finally their whispered conversation falls silent and only a faint tap on the door alerts me to the fact they are actually still there.

"Lisa are you upset with me?" said Millie through the door.

Does Millie think I ran from the scene because of Jake? Millie is feeling remorseful? Oh my god I think I'll just run with this.

"I just want you to know," she continued when I didn't answer, "it wasn't my decision about putting Jake in, I was a bit outvoted and because he was the only applicant, um, like *local* applicant and Brendon felt it was a good idea to put a local in, well he kinda got in by default."

I'm loving this and should tell Millie I'm not upset at all Jake is in but it's not every day the opportunity comes along that Millie is sorry for anything so I'll just pretend I'm upset.

I unlock the door wearing my annoyed face.

"Sorry Lis," Millie said again, attempting to hug my rigid body, "I know it was a bit shocking but think of it this way, at least you get to reject him in public this time, think of the humiliation."

"Yeah I s'pose," I mumbled.

"Lisa is everything okay?" asked Brendon sounding a little annoyed I ruined his party but obligated to ask about my wellbeing.

"Fine," I said as bright as I could but down enough for Millie to think I'm still annoyed at her, "I just errr needed to pee."

"Jake Crankshaw and Lisa have some unpleasant history," said Millie spilling the beans.

"Oh… sorry I didn't know," said Brendon suddenly sounding shocked and genuinely remorseful, as Daniel lifted his brow in surprise, "I got told you two were old friends, I can ask him to leave if it's too much," said Brendon turning towards the verandah.

"No!" I said grabbing at his arm, "I mean no, it's all good, this way I get to um, reject him in public, aye Millie."

"That a girl," said Millie.

"Okay that's good, well just let me know if it's too awkward," said Brendon, "oh and by the way Lisa, um, we were just talking and we decided if you could be so kind as to leave the speeches to us, in fact it would be so cool if you could um, not say anything at all and just have fun," he said in a coy and guilty way.

Millie nodded in agreement with Brendon as Daniel shuffled his feet.

What the? I cannot believe he just said that. I mean I am the star here so why can't I say a few words?

"It's just that, well it's kinda not really what you think it is." Brendon said elaborating when he saw the look of confusion and annoyance on my face.

"What do you mean 'not what I think it is'?" I asked.

"He means," Millie interrupted shooting a glare at Brendon, "that, err, it's better you say nothing, after all this sort of subject is, um, a delicate issue so maybe we should leave the finer details up to Brendon," she said as Daniel's eyes dart between the two of them.

Hmmm not sure I'm liking what I'm hearing. Either they're not telling me something or it's because Brendon is afraid I will outshine him on the film front so he is trying to keep control. I mean I know Millie always wants to be in control but it seems a little odd that they don't want me to say anything at all. I mean looks are all very fine but they need to know I have some personality and all Brendon wants is for me to stand there like I'm some sort of painted doll.

"We're not saying don't say anything," said Daniel like he can read my mind, "we are simply saying we're not sure how emotionally stable these men are so we should just treat them like, um, mutual visitors and not put pressure on them."

Millie and Brendon seem satisfied with Daniel's answer and are nodding enthusiastically.

Okay, now I'm suspicious.

But fine, if they don't want me to mess with the men's 'emotional stability' by talking, then I will just stand there like a doll, poised and in control. I mean why stop there?

Why don't they make a cardboard cutout of me and save a heap of hassles.

"Oh Lisa stop dramatising everything," Millie snapped before walking off.

Shit did I say that out loud?

Facebook status update.

Lisa Collins.

Well just like to report bus-load of men have arrived; please stand-by for updates.

11

Day One: 5.20am.

Yes 5.20am and I'm walking down country road like crazy healthy people do in cool morning air.

Only because I decided not to join in on barbarian beer fest and instead resign to my quarters like a princess last night. Millie came up several times throughout the evening and tried to get me to come down and join the party and every time she did, she seemed drunker than the last time.

I told Millie I'm locking myself in my room so I'm out of the picture as I wouldn't want to tip the guys over the edge with my talking. But also bus-load of men can then see they don't have to live up to any expectation of mine and their true colours can surface so Millie has a chance to be my eyes and ears on the ground. She can report back to me on who is worth keeping and who should get the boot.

Didn't really mean for her to do that but it was the only way I could get her to shut up, stop coming into my room and accept I would not be joining her in drinking marathon.

Millie loves doing stuff like that so she accepted her new role as spy chick with passion and bounced away happy.

Also left me in peace to text Jake.

Yes I texted Jake, so what of it? He left soon after I knocked the bunch of flowers from his hand in desperate flight to bathroom to relieve myself. And for the record he texted me first and asked me if I was okay after I left the party to hole myself up in my bedroom for the evening. I didn't want to tell him I was trying to act poised and in control, not drunk and out of control; so I just said I was okay and it had been an exhausting day and I needed my beauty sleep. Then he texted back and said *'ok then well sleep tight'*, so I had to quickly text him back and tell him I cannot sleep due to noise outside as didn't expect he would end texting conversation so quickly.

So he suggested I sneak out and he would come and pick me up and I was welcome to use the caravan that resides at the back of Mrs Crankshaw's place if I needed to sleep in peace, even his nosy aunty wouldn't know I was there.

Which was a great idea until Millie started showing up every five minutes with reports on which potential single was doing what, so then I had to go to Plan B, which was locking the bedroom door, putting pillows under covers to make a person shape because that's what you do, and telling Millie I had a headache and want to sleep; to which she said she will secretly film potential singles in their booze habitat; and then escaping out the window, crossing over neighbours cow paddock to a waiting Jake and his ute down the road.

And no nothing happened, in fact he was rather sweet. We ended up talking all night about the potential men and my thoughts on them all. Jake thinks they are all losers including him and I deserve better. Then he also suggested I go and hop into the spare bed as I needed sleep, after he had made me a hot chocolate.

Didn't want to sleep, wanted to savour the evening, so I suggested we play a game of monopoly as it would help me get to sleep. After one game of monopoly and five games of scrabble, Jake suggested a little impatiently that maybe we both should get some sleep as it was 3.30am.

Jake dropped me off down the road and I am going to sneak back into the house before Millie or anyone else notices I'm gone and asks me where I was.

I mean why can't they just let me do what I want without questioning me? I'm nearly forty.

Okay shouldn't use the 'f' word, fills me with dread.

Approaching the house I can see a faint light beaming dull in the glow of dawn which means either Amy has woken early and got her hungover parents out of bed or someone's left the light on from last night.

Which means either way I'm going to have to go back in the same way I went out and that's through the cow paddock followed by my bedroom window.

Entering cow paddock I carefully negotiated my body through the barbed wire fence trying not to snag my clothing, when excited hippy man came running up to the fence line.

On god. Can't go bloody anywhere.

"Lisa!" exclaimed Jamie as he held the wire down for me so I could climb through, "I had a feeling I'd be graced with your presence in the beauty of this new day."

Well I suppose this reaction was better than 'what the fuck are you doing climbing through a fence at 5.30 in the morning?'.

"So pleased you decided to make it," he beamed. "I did get a message from your spirit friend Larry telling me to join you in this morning ritual."

"Larry? Ritual?"

"In giving thanks to the earth and Mother Nature," he said a bit puzzled, "we talked about it last night you said you do this every morning."

"I did?" bloody Larry.

"And what a beautiful place to give thanks amongst these beautiful animals."

Shit just spied Millie with Amy looking in this direction, she must be on her morning cleaning rampage she does after every party, in fact she looks like she is squinting hard to see what we are doing judging by the hand over her brow to shield her eyes from the glare of the rising sun.

The one time I decide to sneak back into my own house and suddenly everyone is a morning person!

"All right," I said quickly turning back to Jamie, "we better make a start, err, you lead the way."

"Are you sure?" he said, "after all I don't want to impose."

"It's okay, um, visitors first."

"That's very kind Lisa," he said taking both of my hands and facing me.

Even the cows have stopped grazing and are staring as if to say 'what the hell?'.

Jamie has his eyes closed and is inhaling the air as if it's the last bit of oxygen on earth.

Better do the same, I can still feel Millie's eyes boring into me.

The cool air is hurting my nostrils; also think one of the cows has just planted a fresh cow pat as the smell of dung is getting stronger.

"Mother, Mother feel our love, feel our gratitude for your precious earth," Jamie suddenly stated loudly.

Jeez almost jumped out of my skin at Jamie's sudden outburst, I didn't realise we had to say a few words.

"Mother, Mother we feel your love beneath our feet, you are growing, always growing and we are growing as one with you."

Jamie squeezes my hand as if to say 'your turn'.

"Um… yes, oh great and powerful Mother Earth."

"Mother, Mother," he continues, "hear our voice, hear our gratitude, queen of the earth, queen of the sea; we give thanks for the food we eat."

Oh my turn, "err yes, oh great one, many thanks."

Oh god we're deep breathing again. And I can feel myself being lowered to the ground.

Okay now we're on the ground.

We are lying on the ground on our backs spread out like angels.

Okay now we're rolling gently from side to side.

God I really hope Millie is not still watching.

"Can you feel her energy Lisa, can you feel the growing energy from the earth, can you feel her gentleness?"

"Um yes, oh great and powerful earth."

Think I just rolled in cow pat.

Snapped open my eyes as I can feel a presence, I'm so hoping it was my ghost friend Larry but no, it's Brendon. Brendon and his intrusive camera.

Followed by a sniggering Millie.

"Just pretend I'm not here," whispered Brendon.

Okay think enough thanks has been given. Jamie gives one last inhale followed by a long exhale before opening his eyes. He doesn't seem at all fazed by the fact we are being filmed and mocked at the same time.

"Good morning," he beams, lifting himself off the ground, "are you here to join us?"

"No, no," said Brendon trying to keep the straightest face he can muster, "I'm just capturing the morning's activity."

"Isn't it great?" said Jamie enthused, spreading his arms wide to hug his surrounds. "Lisa is so lucky to have such a quiet place to meditate amongst nature."

"Oh is that what you were doing?" asked Brendon camera still rolling.

"Yes we were giving thanks to Mother Earth. Thank you Lisa for allowing me to share in your morning ritual."

"Errr…"

"Maybe we can all join in tomorrow morning," said Millie with a smirk, "since it's part of Lisa's morning ritual."

Grrr, Millie is a bitch.

"Great idea," said Jamie, "we often lose ourselves in our daily lives. I think it would be good for all our souls to have a quiet moment and give thanks for our surroundings."

"Yes and Lisa you can lead the meditation ritual since you are so practiced at it," said Millie.

I take that back; Millie is a *queen* bitch.

"Okay it's a date then," said Jamie squeezing my hands and bowing to the cows who haven't taken their eyes off us.

Back at house.

"Lisa why is your bedroom door locked? How did you get out, it only locks from the inside?" Millie asked.

"Err…"

Judging by the fact that bus-load of potential husbands are still here and passed out amongst the empty bottles of alcohol, must've been quite a party last night. In fact Daniel is still here, and Matt, so I don't think it's the bus-load of men's fault they are still here, think it's due to the fact that their sober driver and accommodation host were too drunk for words.

"Lisa?"

"Oh I don't know, maybe the door accidently locked itself as I shut it this morning when I was going, err, meditating."

"Do you have a key for it?"

God so many questions.

But interrogation aside I'm feeling rather good about last night. Am so pleased I decided to be poised and in control and spend the evening playing board games with Jake.

But what I am alarmed about is the amount of passed out bodies in the living area. I mean Millie is always going on about Amy's environment and role models being healthy and normal, I mean she barely lets Matt in unless he is wearing proper pants and has cleaned his teeth, so why is she suddenly okay with having a raging party with strange men and allowing them to pass out on any available sleeping surface?

Brendon appeared in the kitchen, also looking like he had been dragged through a thorn bush backwards actually.

"Get much sleep?" Millie beamed at him as she strapped Amy into her highchair for her morning feed.

Millie doesn't do hangovers.

"A bit," he said reaching for the coffee, "but I think the night was successful. I hope this isn't a taste of the week to come though," said Brendon looking slightly worried.

"It was a great night," said Millie mixing up Amy's weetbix, "such a lovely bunch of guys."

Okay I know what's going on here.

Millie is trying to make me feel guilty for retiring to my quarters instead of joining her and potential husbands for social evening of drunk and disorderly behaviour. Well I'm just going to ignore her.

That's why Millie must never ever know that I climbed out my bedroom window and went to Jake's last night.

"I'm just heating up the BBQ," said a tired looking Sid coming through the kitchen, "I think our guests might want a sausage sizzle breakfast when they wake up."

"Good idea," said Brendon finding his second wind, "then Lisa you can mingle with them some more and we'll get some filming of the night after. Later we'll sit down and film you with a comment on each of them and what you found about their characters and we can edit it in later."

"Did you have a good night Sid?" asked Millie, catching him before he departed with a bag full of sausages.

"Yeah was great," said Sid departing like he was on a mission.

Still ignoring her.

But I'm not ignoring Brendon.

I thought after introductions and dinner, they'd all get driven back to Daniel's, then the next day (today), I pick a rose which has a name attached (pre-organised) and have a date with that person.

Hmm think I better pin *him* down for interrogation for a change.

Thank god I still have a copy of the week's itinerary in my pocket to state my case.

"Um excuse me," I said with all the politeness I can muster, pointing to the bit of paper in my hand, "I thought I was meant to be surprised by a single rose that held the name of my first date and the location."

Millie and Brendon flick a sideways glance at each other.

"Oh do you still have a copy of the *old* itinerary?" scoffed Brendon, "silly me, I thought I gave you a copy of the new one, hang on I'll fetch you one."

"New one? Why did we change it?"

"Because that show style has been done before by the professional dating shows," said Millie, glaring at Brendon as he hastily departed, "we are trying not to infringe on any copyrights, remember *Lisa*?"

"But the whole idea of the mystery date *Millie*, is what any dating show is all about. I go on a date with each individual while they go out of their way to impress me and in the end I choose one I have an attachment to."

"Um well... yes, but we have also decided not to do that either."

"What?"

"Instead we've decided to have group activities," sighed Millie wiping regurgitated weetbix from Amy's mouth.

"Group activities?"

"Here it is," said a bubbly Brendon re-entering the room and handing over a piece of paper that held the week's program on it, not to mention with camera in hand, "the new itinerary."

I quickly scanned over the page. It only had what's happening today, it doesn't have the list of activities for the whole week. What the…?

'Welcome to day one of our mystery country tour, starting with breakfast at 9am. Bus departs at 10.30am, picking up your beautiful host for the week, Lisa Collins, for a fun day of activities which our picturesque region has to offer. Finishing off with dinner in the beautiful gardens of Abb-toir Bed and Breakfast'

Alarm bells are ringing in my ears. Nothing in there mentions anything about *'The Country Girl Wants a Husband'*, in fact it sounds more like we are running a mystery bus tour.

Okay need to find out what is going on.

I fix a stare onto Brendon.

"All right, all right!" said Brendon, like he has finally broken down from all the interrogating, "I'll tell you why," he cried, Millie is chucking her hands in the air in a frustrated manner.

Man that was easy.

Daniel staggers into the room in a sleep induced haze as Brendon continues, "I know we were going to do a dating show the same as *'the bachelor'* but we kinda had to re-think things as there seemed to be a lot of legal issues surrounding this."

"… and we only got one applicant," said Daniel reaching for the coffee.

"One applicant!" I spluttered.

"Yes," said Millie gently, "one applicant, Jake; and because we advertised and Jake replied we have to involve him."

"So where did these men come from?" I asked puzzled.

All three of them exchanged glances with one another, "Matt arranged it," said Brendon, "so we had another think about it and after consulting with the selection committee we decided it would be better to use it as a way of promoting the area combined with my documentary about social interaction in rural areas."

"What!?"

"Yes," said Millie enthused, "and by adding a slight mystery to it all, it keeps it interesting."

"Yes," agreed Daniel, following on from Millie, "and because we are trying to promote the B&B as a country retreat we thought country based activities were a good idea."

I cannot believe what I am hearing. Not to mention a little alarmed with Matt's involvement.

"So why am I mentioned in this as the host?" I continued, trying to get some answer to all this.

"Because there are seven potential single men out there Lisa," said Millie, "so if you spend time with them then maybe one of them may take your fancy. Okay so it's not a dating show but…"

"So what are the activities?" I asked with a slight hysterical edge to my voice, trying not to imagine us sitting around a fire pit plucking chickens.

"Um… well we're not going to reveal the activities till the day," said Brendon. "Only us three and Matt will know the destinations."

"Not going to reveal the activities until the day," I repeated in disbelief, "only you three and Matt know what's going on."

"Well you wanted mystery dates," said Millie.

"Just trust us," said a bleary eyed Daniel as I opened my mouth to explode, "follow our lead Lisa, we know what we're doing okay?"

Back in bedroom after climbing back through window.
Abruptly left room without saying any more to send them a silent message that I'm not happy about the change in production.

But forgot that bedroom door was locked from the inside and couldn't get in to abruptly slam door behind me, so I had to storm back passed production team, mumbling something about going for a walk so they wouldn't suspect that I'm actually going to enter my bedroom through the window. And now I'm lying on my bed feeling a little mixed up about the whole thing.

I mean what a bunch of control freaks. One minute we were planning the next big reality television show with glamour and romance, and the next minute we're going on a mystery tour to learn how to pluck chickens.

Okay well maybe not pluck chickens but my point being; how the bloody hell would I know what is going to happen? I mean we *could* be plucking chickens for all I know!

So no red roses, no real mystery dates, no romantic strolls, no elegant evening wear, just a week full of plucking chickens and binge drinking.

Think I'm going to cry.

Okay, okay, so maybe I'm exaggerating, it's only day one, there's five more days to go, but Brendon is right when he said if last night was anything to go on it's going to be a long week.

Slight knock on the door and I know it's Millie coming to justify the change of plan,

I mean when were they going to inform me, the day we rock up at the Crankshaw's to milk cows?

Okay more dreaded thoughts about the week ahead are flashing before my eyes.

Better sort this out.

"What the hell Millie?" I said as I abruptly opened the door.

Millie rolled her eyes as she entered the room.

"Lisa," she began, rubbing her brow, "I know this sudden change of plans has thrown you off but it's still an opportunity for you, just not in the way you thought. Besides, do I need to spell it out for you, your original title was '*The Country Girl Wants a Husband*' so tell me please, because I'm a little confused, what part of that doesn't fit into the current plans of country based activities?"

So Millie is pulling out the sarcasm gun, which only means one thing, her intention of ending this conversation is with her way or the highway.

"Because I was kinda hoping for a more elegant and sophisticated week with romance and dinner dates Millie, not cow pats and shearing sheds."

"Well then go on Next Top Model if you want elegance and sophistication," she shot back, "but if you're going to sulk for the week tell me now so I can cancel it."

Grrr, she always knows how to get me.

Didn't answer her, just let out a huge sigh and folded my arms, sending her a silent message that yes I will cooperate but I'm not happy about it.

After all there are a couple of the men that do have potential so I'll go along with it.

"I have some sneaky pictures of last night," she beamed pulling out her phone in an attempt to soften me up, "wanna see who is cute when they are drunk?" she teased, waving the phone at me.

Couldn't help myself, Millie is so good at cheering me up.

"Okay," I said as I sat on the bed next to her in giggly teenager fashion.

"Oh maybe take a rain check," she said disappointed as Sid made a silent appearance at the door.

"Matt has just gone home to shower and will be on his way back to pick everyone up shortly," said Sid, "everything okay?"

Oh my god of course! Matt is the chauffer for the week, which means he will have insider knowledge of what is going on, which means all I have to do is manipulate him into giving me the itinerary, stage a coup on the whole production and kidnap seven men for the week and run the show my way. Now why hadn't I thought of that half an hour ago?

Just need something to blackmail Matt with so he is on board, but what? Hmmm have to think that one through.

"All good," I beamed at Sid, "just had a wee meltdown but fine now."

"So you still want to do this?" asked Millie.

"Of course," I smiled at her.

"Good," she said giving my cheek a quick peck, "because there was too much organising for you to back out now."

There goes Millie, thinking of herself again.

She closes the door behind her and I glance at the paper in front of me, a little note at the bottom reads *'Day one activities – apron and boots required'*; a combination that can only mean one thing and that is – boredom beyond belief.

Right that is it. I definitely need a plan.

12

CWA headquarters (aka kitchen room of town hall) accompanied by bus-load of hungover men wearing boots and frilly aprons.

This is day one of the mystery tour, today's activity; a cooking demonstration with Mrs Crankshaw and the CWA.

"I thought you would be pleased," Brendon whispered as we stood around the table in the back room kitchen of the town hall, "aren't you the president of the CWA? It's good promotions."

"Lisa dear are you paying attention?" Mrs Crankshaw growled as Brendon reset the camera on his shoulder ready to film again while Sid stood behind him dangling a microphone. Didn't know Sid would be part of the filming which means it's going to make plans of a coup more difficult because as soon as I start something he will go and tell Millie.

Jake is also here and gave me a secret wink from across the room.

It's now very late in the afternoon and we have only just got here, mainly because everyone was sleeping off the night before and by the time everyone got back to Daniel's and settled in, well day one was almost over.

The talk at breakfast however was just as dull, as all they seemed to rant on about was the antics of last night and because I retired to my quarters all elegant, poised and in control, I could not join in on their reminiscing. Even Matt and Damo have made a few new 'drinking buds' by the sounds of it and I guess their 'intimidating and staunch presence' is no longer working now the guests have seen the real side of dumb and dumber.

"Okay dears now the secret to damper bread is to treat it rough," Mrs Crankshaw demonstrated while Mary, Betty and Fran stand by her side ready with extra flour and looking very flushed.

All right so I need to put this plan into action, it's been a hectic few hours but I have managed to push a few cards up my sleeve that see Matt becoming part of *'Team Lisa'* and not *'Team control freaks who have no idea about producing a decent show'*. Also have the second part of my plan organised and that is to arrange my first date, but not sure who to start with. I had a secret date with Jake last night which I must admit went very well so it will be a bit hard to compare now.

Slade and Steel seem okay but a bit into themselves, in fact I don't see any difference in personality, and they share the same interests so I think I need to organise a double date with them but not today.

Jamie is loving this damper making; he said it would be great skills to learn so when the apocalypse arrives at least we know how to turn ordinary flour into tasty treats when we all go underground, I think he is a little distracted. In fact I'm surprised he is not making yin yang shapes out of the dough, he's that into it. But I kinda feel I will be having a date with him every fricken morning at 5.30am thanks to bloody Millie, so not him today.

Bear asked me yet again to get my gear off this morning which is starting to get a bit old and so far he's not too interested in cooking but more in drinking so maybe not today, I may save that one till last.

So it's between Paul, the shy guy who once again doesn't look like he wants to be here, or anywhere for that matter. Derrick, aka Captain Sweatpants and sweet little Darcy.

Okay not Paul and Captain Sweatpants; both of them seem very disinterested and Captain Sweatpants has just pulled out his mobile, I mean how rude. In fact I don't think they are even interested in social interaction so why are they here?

I guess I choose Darcy as my first date. Now just to convince him he needs to do the same.

Mrs Crankshaw is still going on about dough and I am trying hard not to look at Jake who is flicking occasional glances at me. Now thinking about sex with him.

"Lisa dear!" snapped Mrs Crankshaw, pulling me from my thoughts.

"Um yes?"

"Tch, still with your head in the clouds, and what are you wearing! Put this apron on dear, your clothing is not appropriate for this task. Did anyone inform Lisa about the dress code? Okay, no-one, tsk, tsk," she scolded not waiting for an answer, handing me a flower patterned full length apron and tutting at my footwear. Well at least the apron will protect my elegant purple sequined dress.

Yes okay, I'm wearing an evening dress and heels all right. It's all part of my plan so what of it?

"I was just telling these lovely lads here about your talent for making blueberry jam," Mrs Crankshaw continued, "I saved a jar from the entry you put in the annual fair before they barred tasting due to tampering, such a shame," she drifted off into her own thoughts before continuing, "anyway I thought once we have made our lovely bread, they can complement it with your lovely blueberry jam."

Oh my god.

She saved the jam. The one I entered in the fair when I first moved here to impress Jake and show Pamela I'm all about the country. The one I accidently used salt instead of sugar in and then proceeded to get it back from the judging tent by suggesting there was some tampering with the homewares, causing a whole investigation of the way they have been running the whole section.

One lick is going to send their taste buds running for the hills, perhaps never ever to eat anything that slightly resembles conserves again.

The one my future love is about to try.

Okay don't panic, deep breath, remember poised and in control, we haven't made the bread yet so I have time to make the jam disappear. Which will have to fit in-between getting Matt into a corner and convincing him to hand over top secret information and arranging a surprise date with Darcy.

So much to do!

"So," Mrs Crankshaw ordered, "there is plenty of butter and flour here but because we only have one oven we will head outdoors to cook it over the open fire which my darling nephew Jake here prepared earlier."

So Jake knew what we were doing, hmmm maybe I need to bring him over to *Team Lisa* as well.

Everyone seems excited, like they have just accepted a challenge in fear factor and are now racing to get to the flour first.

I cannot believe this is happening. This is meant to be a fricken dating show! Not My Kitchen Rules.

Captain Sweatpants hasn't attempted to get involved; in fact he's leaning against the wall by the door with his head still in his phone. And Brendon's not helping, as he is actually filming Captain Sweatpants leaning against the wall.

Just so rude, he is definitely off my list.

There seems to be a lot of boyish antics over damper making, in fact I feel like we are back in home economics at school and I'm an awkward teenager. I'm actually really embarrassed and not sure what to say to any of them, it's like I haven't bonded with anyone. And none are taking this bread making demonstration seriously so I don't see the point of it, in fact Bear has brought a can of bourbon with him; actually, come to think of it, a can of bourbon hasn't left his hand since he got here. What the hell was Millie thinking?

Mrs Crankshaw must also agree with the level of disrespect while bread making because she is now threatening them with her rolling pin.

There, that has brought some order to the kitchen.

"So done it wif any of them yet?" asked Matt, sauntering up behind me wearing shorts to expose his lily white legs accompanied by his heavy mechanic work boots and an apron with boobs on it.

"No Matt," I hissed, horrified by the volume of his voice, "I am not looking to 'do it' with any of them, I'm looking for a life partner, a soul mate, future husband. Not a one night stand," I whispered.

"Yeah well, forget about doing it with those twins ova' there," he said, glancing at Slade and Steel, "bet they're both gay, probably gay wif each other."

Since Matt has learned about Daniel being gay he thinks any man who has an inkling of pride in their appearance is also gay, in fact it's like he has taken up a whole new hobby, bit like bird watching, trying to find the pretty wren in a flock of seagulls.

Brendon wanders passed with the camera and I wait till he has moved on before starting on *'Operation bring Matt to Team Lisa'*.

In fact he has come to a standstill and is filming me.

Okay, poised and in control.

Wish he would just leave.

Matt is playing up for the camera, I don't know why because he's not even part of this show. Actually what is he doing here, isn't he just the driver?

My eyes flick to Captain Sweatpants who is standing in the entrance to the open door sucking on a cigarette while talking on his phone, the cigarette smoke is drifting back inside right passed the sign on the door that says no smoking.

While in front of him Bear has made an oversized penis out of his damper dough, stuck it to his groin and is attempting to chase Mrs Crankshaw with it, while she smacks it with her rolling pin.

Hmmm think the chance of a decent potential date may be slim.

"Matt where did these men come from?" I said.

"From the bus."

"Yes I know that Matt but where did the bus come from?"

"From town, the one that stops here every week, the mining bus."

Oh my god.

"Yes," Brendon said as he stops filming and lowers his camera to explain, "thanks to Matt's quick thinking he jumped on the bus while they were having their routine stop and asked them if they wanted to be part of a social experiment. Luckily they were the bus that had their compulsory two weeks off and were heading home, we did have more, but because they had to be single, only seven remained."

A large clang of baking utensils distracts Brendon and he's off again with his camera, followed by a bored looking Sid.

"You look fucked off again," said Matt as he starts to mix his dough, "why do you always looked fucked off, is that part of being 40? Like menopause or somefing."

"Oh bloody hell Matt! I'm only 39 and no, I'm annoyed because Brendon was supposed to be producing a dating show staring me, all elegant and poised while men grovel for my hand in marriage. Instead we are making… actually Matt what are *you* making?"

"A joint outta dough," said Matt sounding like a preschooler who has painted his first picture.

"Okay Matt, whatever floats your boat. My point is exactly, well this," I said, pointing to the floury blob in front of me.

Matt opens his mouth to answer my question but I cut him off, I mean now the flood gates of frustration are open I cannot stop.

"… and also it was my bloody idea for the show and I thought we had an agreement it would be run my way. That twat Brendon would have no chance of ever producing anything half as good if it wasn't for me and now all he wants to do is sabotage it with alcohol and dough. I mean I haven't had a chance to bond with any of them Matt and they are only here for five days! Five days to get to know seven men, one of them could be my potential future, and what are we doing, making models of illegal substances out of bread dough."

"What's up?" Jake said, sliding in beside me sounding concerned.

"I duno, think it's menopause," said Matt, concentrating on his creation.

Deep breath; poised and in control.

"Listen," said Jake in his soft and calming voice, "think of this as a bonding activity," he grinned, placing his hand on the small of my back for comfort.

Jeez that sent shocks through my body, think I need to grab a piece of dough to keep my hands occupied before they reach out and grab him.

Oh, he's moved back.

"Well you are being a bit of a snob," said Matt placing his dough joint carefully on the baking tray.

"Pardon?" I spluttered, "how so?"

"Well you haven't spoken to any of them, and you didn't even come and have a drink wif dem last night."

"Excuse me, I had a drink."

"Yeah like one, then you made some dumb-arse speech and went and hid in your room. Thought it was funny when you knocked Jake's flowers out of his hand though and ran away, man the look on his face was priceless, he's such a dick."

Horrified I looked behind me to see if Jake was still standing there, thank god he had moved off and didn't hear.

Matt's not so keen on Jake since Jake has, quote, 'done it wif my Mum'.

"I did not Matt and besides I was trying to make a good impression on them."

"Yeah well they all think you're a bit of a snob and a bit of a princess who thinks she's better than them."

"Who does?"

"They do."

"They do not."

"Yeah they do, they all said it, I mean you're even wearing a dress. I told them you're a pretty cool chick when you're not fucked off about being forty but they reckon you're fucked off about everything."

"I am not fucked off about everything; I'm just fucked off about the way this doco is going to turn out. I think you're full of shit Matt, I bet you all of them would want a date with me given the chance."

"Well do you have a date wif any of them?"

"Not yet, haven't had a chance, too busy getting drunk and making bread."

"See told ya, snob."

"I'm not being a snob Matt, I am being poised, elegant, and in control."

"But you're none of those fings," said Matt puzzled.

Think I need to give up trying to explain to Matt the power of etiquette.

He is distracting me from my plan to brainwash him.

Looking around to see if anyone was listening, I went in for stage one of my coup.

"So Matt what are we doing tomorrow?"

"Can't tell ya, it's secret."

Thought he may play it this way.

"But you can tell me anything," I said putting on my tone of voice that is reserved for secret best friend conversations.

"Nah can't, they made me swear."

"Does Damo know where we're going tomorrow?" I asked, trying not to sound frustrated.

"Nah."

Bugger.

"But if you just tell me I won't be so fucked off."

"Nah still can't, Millie said if I tell ya she was going to put my nuts in a vice, and I'm a bit scared of her 'cause she'll do it, she even showed me the vice."

Bloody Millie.

"Can you give me a little hint then?"

"Nah."

"Is it plucking chickens?"

"Nah."

"Milking cows?"

"Nah."

"Making billy tea?"

"Nah."

"Matt just bloody tell me."

"Nah told ya, can't. I need my nuts."

Okay so he's not going to play ball, well I just have to pull out the big guns.

I reached down and pulled a big white envelope from my bag.

"Matt if you don't tell me what we are doing tomorrow and for the rest of the week, I'll show everyone this," I said waving my envelope at him, "and then when I finish showing everyone this, I'll put it on National TV when I become famous," I said with a hint of power and control to my voice.

"You're going to show 'dem a big envelope?" he said not sounding too concerned.

"No, I'm going to show them the embarrassing, no, mortifying, shit on you that I hold inside this envelope."

"What is it den?"

"Can't tell ya," I said, "unless you get me a copy of the week's activities, then we will do an exchange."

"You've got nuffing," he scoffed.

"Oh I have."

"Have not, you're such a liar."

"So Matt do we have a deal?"

"Nah."

"What?"

"Nah, unless you show me what's in there, which is nuffing. You don't scare me Lisa."

Bugger, bugger, bloody Matt, the little shit.

"Fine then I'll just pull this out now shall I, and show everyone?"

"Go ahead then."

"Okay everyone," Mrs Crankshaw clapped to get everyone's attention, "if you have all made your damper mixture, head outside and we'll cook it up."

"Oh sweet," said Matt, picking up his creation of a joint and heading off out the side door to the grassy knoll outside.

Panic has just set in as I glance up at Darcy who is also taking his damper bread mixture and heading for the door, followed by Betty, Mary, and Fran, who seem to have taken a wee liking to Darcy.

Shit, okay need to not worry about Matt for now; need to put part B of my plan into action and that is to set a date with Darcy.

Also need to have a quick word with Mary as she seems to be the only one capable of helping me with my plan.

Stuffing Matt's dirty laundry evidence into my big bag of tricks I head for the side door, Jake is out there tending a lovely camp fire which has now burnt down to hot embers. There are camp chairs set up around the rock circle that houses the fire, and dusk is settling in so it looks really romantic.

Which is perfect for what I have in mind.

I just have to get to Darcy and beat off his fan club of old women.

After grabbing Mary and having a quick word with her I joined the others settled around the fire with our damper bread on sticks. Jake brought out cold beers for everyone and suddenly Captain Sweatpants is interested and has put away his phone to join us.

Bear is getting the most attention with his penis made out of dough (which he has affectionately named 'damper dick'). Matt looks a bit put out as no-one has noticed his model of a marijuana joint, but have no time to sit and observe. Fran has nestled herself next to Darcy and Betty's on the other side of him. I'll need to fit myself in-between them. Betty may be a little difficult to move but Fran will not be so hard so I'll grab a seat and make my way over.

Wish I hadn't worn these ridiculous heels as I almost tripped over as the blasted things wedged into the grass.

Mrs Crankshaw is looking at me as if to say 'I told you so'. Well if I had known we were cooking a blob of flour outside I would have worn something a little more appropriate. Like flat shoes to go with dress.

"Lisa what is in there?" Fran asked as I struggled to settle my chair next to her. "That's an awfully big bag," she gasped, "mind yourself, don't want you to do an injury."

"Oh just a few creature comforts," I said as I pulled out a little fold-out table, nice tablecloth to accompany it, bottle of champagne, bottle of wine (you know, gotta have choices), red rose in a vase (fake but it's television who would know), and two glasses. I proceed to set it up between Fran and myself. There that's nice.

Now just to get rid of Fran and my date with Darcy is set.

Keep thinking I'm forgetting something though.

"Okay dears, keep rotating your sticks to evenly cook our lovely damper shall we?" Mrs Crankshaw said as Brendon positions himself and the camera for a shot of the fire.

Oh great, Fran has pulled out her knitting, looks like she's settling in.

Oh! I know how to get rid of her.

"Fran," I whispered before she settled into her row of stitches.

"I think I have torn my dress. I may need you to grab something for me out of my car."

"Sorry?" she whispered adjusting her hearing aid.

"My dress, I think I have torn the back of it you know in the bum area."

"Oh your dress," she said loudly forgetting the tone here was one of a whisper, "well stand up and give me a look then," she sighed irritably.

"No, no, it's embarrassing."

"It's just knickers dear, stand up," she said even louder, also forgetting there are men present, "I have a darning needle here somewhere."

"No, no, I'm err, wearing a thong."

"A what?"

"A thong, you know, g-string."

"You want a piece of sting?"

"No, no, look don't worry, just move over."

"Pardon?"

"Move!"

Bloody hell, I swear old people do this on purpose.

"Look just hang on," I said and proceeded to drag Fran and her chair to one side.

"Where is your dress torn?" Betty asked straining her neck passed Darcy to look at my behind as a very freaked out Fran is grasping at the sides of her fold-up chair as I proceed to drag her around my wee table so I can fit my chair next to it and Darcy.

"It's not, don't worry."

Good thing she is light as these heels aren't helping.

Okay, there, done.

"Are you sure dear? I can't tell in this light."

"No, no, it's fine," I said smacking Betty's hand away as she grabs at my dress.

Oh good Mary is here.

"So Darcy," I said, sliding myself into the chair all poised, elegant and in control, "wine?"

Darcy looks a bit stunned.

"Um… no thanks I've just opened a beer… oh okay then," he backtracks as I proceed to pour the wine in his glass anyway.

"Lovely evening isn't it?" I said as I popped the wine back in the cooler and lifted my glass, "to a pleasant evening," I toasted, raising my wine glass.

"Um… yes, a pleasant evening," he said hastily picking up his glass to toast mine.

"Excuse me dear?" Mary said leaning in on the table between us holding out a video camera, "is this thing working, I can't tell?"

"The red light is on, so yes," I said through gritted teeth.

"Oh of course, silly me, okay, as you were."

I borrowed Sid's alien encounter video camera to record my date, if Brendon wants to do his own show filled with a week of plucking chickens with a group of men and one chick well then he can do that till the cows come home, I on the other hand will be doing my own show of *'The Country Girl Wants a Husband'* filled with romance, elegance and candlelit dinners.

Oh which reminds me, forgot the candles.

Oh never mind the glow of the fire is enough.

"So Darcy," I said grabbing his attention as he continued to show a look of bewilderment on his cute face, "tell me about yourself."

Darcy glances around at his peers before turning back to me.

"Um... what do you want to know?" he said snatching a sideways glance at the camera Mary has now pressed up against his ear.

"Oh you know," I said, hand signaling to Mary to move back a little, "where do you work, what do you like to do, what would be your ideal woman?"

I'm hoping he will say me, but if not I can edit that in later.

"Oh okay, err well let's see, I work in the mines as a driller."

"Yes, yes," I said leaning closer to expose a bit of cleavage, "how interesting, and where do you come from?"

I can feel Jake's eyes boring into me from across the camp fire; I'm so loving this attention.

"Born and bred in Bendigo," Darcy continues, "no siblings, was raised by my father."

Explains the attachment old woman have for him, it's the need for a mother vibe he is putting out there.

"Aww," I said tilting my head slightly sideways in sympathy, "that must have been hard."

"Nah wasn't too bad, my old man's pretty cool," he said lighting a cigarette.

"And what kind of woman do you like?" I asked, hoping for a 'moment'.

"Lisa what are you doing?" asked Brendon, glancing at the romantic setup between Darcy and myself.

"Excuse me," I said, smiling at Darcy with all the grace I have, "I'm having an innocent drink with Darcy," I hissed at Brendon.

"Do you want me to stop filming dear?" asked Mary as Sid arrives with the sound mic.

"No you keep filming Mary," I said, turning back to Darcy, ignoring Brendon's puzzled reaction.

"Wahoo, you there Darce?" Bear bellowed from across the fire pit causing all eyes to turn toward me.

Darcy grins and raises his wine glass.

I glance at Jake again but cannot read his expression, it's a bit of a blank one so cannot tell if it's a look of jealousy.

Uh, oh.

Shit, shit, I knew I'd forgotten something.

Resting beside Jake is my jar of jam, which has been opened and a good blob of it is now residing in a pile of saltiness on top of Jake's damper bread.

And he is about to eat it.

"Nooooo," I shouted, leaping from my chair and throwing myself across the lawn towards him in an attempt to knock it from his hands before he takes a bite. Would have all gone smoothly in one swift movement if blasted heal didn't get wedged in soft grass causing foot to leave shoe and now I'm lying on top of Jake on the damp grass as my clumsy tackle resulted in him falling from his chair to the ground and knocked his damper bread clean out of his hands.

"Get ya gear off," shouted Bear from the sideline.

Not knowing what to say in this situation so I started with 'sorry' in the hope that a reasonable explanation would follow, when Matt thrusted a picture of him naked in a paddling pool at the age of three in my face.

"Where the fuck did you get this from?" he said sounding slightly upset, "you've been in my stuff."

Oh shit, Matt must have snatched the envelope from my bag.

"Doesn't matter where I got it from," I said trying to climb my way off an amused and stunned looking Jake, "you shouldn't have gone into my bag, we had a deal Matt."

"We had shit," said Matt, "and I didn't go through your stuff, it was lying on the ground."

Shit it must have dropped out of my bag.

"You've been stealing photos of me in da nude just because you want what I've got, not cool Lisa."

"I didn't steal them, I acquired them."

"From who?"

"Doesn't matter."

"Well it matters to me when you take a dude's dignity like this," he whinged.

"Oh my god Matt, you were three years old."

"Doesn't matter, wasn't my choice to be photographed in da nude."

"What is going on?" said Brendon, running over with Sid and camera in tow, "is everyone okay?"

Shit need to silence Matt's whinging arse before he spills it to Brendon that I was trying to blackmail him into handing over the mystery itinerary so I can stage a coup.

"Nothing," I quickly said, leaping to my feet as Jake does the same in one swift sexy move, picking up the chair and returning it to its rightful position.

"Matt here was just, errrr, reminiscing over an old photo of himself," I said glaring at him with all the threatening expression I can muster.

"Lisa dear what are you doing?" Mrs Crankshaw tutted also racing over and dusting me off and checking Jake is okay. "Honestly you're like a dog on heat sometimes."
"Argh!" exclaimed Bear shaking his head in agony and desperately wiping his tongue, causing everyone to abruptly turn in his direction, "what the fuck is this shit?" he exclaimed holding up my jam jar.
Oh god.
"Lisa dear," Fran came up behind me and whispered in my ear, "you've torn your dress and I can see your bum cheek."

Facebook Status update.
Lisa Collins.
Someone drown me now.

13

Day two: 5.16am.

Yes 5.16am and walking in crisp morning air for second time in my life.

Yes walking. Well not all the way, Jake dropped me off down the road again so Millie doesn't discover my absence.

And yes, Jake. I am walking home in crisp morning air for second time in two days after scrabble session for second time in my entire life.

Well who can blame me after the little fiasco last night? Not off to a good start and it's so unfair my date with Darcy getting cut short because I was trying to stop Jake and his tastebuds being assaulted by my blueberry jam; and Matt discovering I was trying to blackmail him into giving me this week's mystery itinerary by acquiring nude pictures of him in a paddling pool at the age of three. And then Bevan, aka Bear, sampling my blueberry jam and deciding he was assaulted, *then* discovering I had actually torn my evening dress while trying to save Jake.

After which everyone decided it was fun to use my jam in a truth or dare game, bit like fear factor according to Bear, while I got driven home by Jake to retrieve normal clothes wearing Mrs Crankshaw's flowery apron around my waist to cover exposed arse cheek.

Kinda didn't feel like going back out after that so I quickly checked in with Millie and Sid and said was going to bed, ran to bedroom, got changed, locked bedroom door, and climbed out window to Jake's waiting car down the road.

Jake said I looked a bit annoyed about the evening's events so he suggested I come round to his for a round or two of scrabble to try and cheer me up. Really, really just wanted to go to bed and crash but remembered Jake must have insider knowledge of up-and-coming mystery events as he took his own car to the town hall to set up the camp fire so he must have known what was going on. So thought a quick game of scrabble, to hide the fact I'd planned to casually slip into the conversation about the whole mystery itinerary in the hope that Jake will give top secret information away, would be harmless.

I can't remember who won because I woke up with scrabble letters stuck to my cheek so think I may have fallen asleep during the game with Jake.

He was so sweet about it though as he covered me with a blanket but said he can't tell me anything because he doesn't know any more.

Bugger.

But now I must get home fast as the sun is coming up and I better get back before…

Uh oh!

"Good morning Lisa," exclaimed Jamie as I arrived at the barbed wire fence, "we're all here for morning meditation of thanks and gratitude, I'm thrilled with the turnout. So we're just waiting on you to start us off."

Oh no.

Everyone is standing there looking at me; Matt, Bear, Paul, Darcy, Slade and Steel, even Millie and Captain Sweatpants. In fact the only people who aren't here are Jake and Daniel. Even Sid is here holding Amy.

God does anyone believe in sleeping in any more?

Which means Millie is going to want to know why I was attempting to climb through the neighbouring barbed wire fence at 5.20 in the morning.

Shit.

"Morning Lisa," grinned Brendon, mounting the camera on his shoulder, "everyone seems keen to give this meditation a try so when you are ready, lead the way."

"Oh… um, I thought Jamie could lead, you know, take turns."

"Oh Lisa you are such a beautiful sharing person," Jamie mused, "but I think I have imposed on your morning ritual enough, I would love for you to lead me, well us, into giving gratitude and thanks to this beautiful planet this morning."

"Yes Lisa," Millie smirked, "show us how it's done."

I shot her a glare, to which she then reminded me in front of everyone that I was indeed a spiritual advisor because it was listed on my Facebook profile and she would just love some spiritual guidance right now. Millie is such a bitch, she just loves digging up stuff like that and using it against me.

God where is Larry my ghost friend when you need him?

Okay, there's no time to dwell on absent ghost, everyone is poised in anticipation, including the herd of cows surrounding us.

And Millie is a tiny bit right, I have had experience in spiritual stuff, okay maybe I only attended a couple of meditation classes but surely this stuff is all the same.

And besides I don't want Millie to think she has landed me in it, so I will show her I'm all about spiritual stuff and lead a professional meditation.

"Ahem… okay everyone, err, gather in a circle," I said remembering I saw this in a movie. "Now hold hands, close your eyes and take a deep breath," I mused.

"Bit gay," mumbled Matt loud enough for everyone to hear.

"Now… ummm… feel the earth under your feet."

"Are we meant to take our shoes off?" asked Captain Sweatpants.

Murmurs of agreement to the question all round.

"No, you're good."

"But if you want us to feel the earth through our feet then we are going to have to take our shoes off."

More murmurs in agreement.

Bugger, fair point.

"Yes, yes, okay, take your shoes off."

Shuffles of shoes being removed.

"Okay where was I? Um… oh yes, feel the earth through your feet and ummm, feel you're naked at one with nature."

"Do you want us to get our gear off?" bellowed Bear.

Okay set myself up for that one.

Chuckles all round this time.

"No, no, clothes are good."

"Are you sure?" piped Jamie, "I think if anyone here is wearing tight fitted clothes they should loosen them up so the energy can flow more freely."

Nods of agreement.

"Okay then, if you must," I sighed.

"Better not take your jocks off," complained Matt, "Lisa would probably want to take a photo, she might need it one day."

God Matt doesn't let things go easily.

"No, no, leave your underwear on and just loosen clothing," I snapped.

God Millie is loving this.

Faint shuffles of belts and clothes being loosened and removed, followed by more giggling as Bear lets out a loud belch and claims he is 'releasing his energy'.

Okay now someone just farted.

"Go ahead Lisa," snapped Jamie, shooting a glare at the circle.

Murmurs of 'sorry' from the group.

"Umm… okay Mother Earth, hear our um… voice as we speak to you of um… gratitude and love."

Murmurs of gratitude and love all round.

Shit, mind has gone blank.

Quickly opened eyes in the hope inspiration will come to me. Quickly shut them again as I discovered Bear has actually removed his pants completely.

Oh, I know.

"Mother Earth, we give thanks to the trees we see and um… the branches of fruit you bear," now don't ask me why but it appears I'm waving my arms around like a tree.

Well I don't know what else to do.

"That's it Lisa, be the tree," said Jamie as everyone opens their eyes and follows my lead.

Shit.

"Um… wave, wave your branches around," I instructed flapping my arms around.

Everyone is flapping their arms like mad people except Matt who is reaching in his pocket for his phone.

"Now, err, be the tree, swaying from side to side."

Everyone's swaying and flapping.

"Now umm… be the seed floating in the air."

All right now we're running in circles flapping our arms.

Not sure how it came to be that we are running around flapping our arms like airplanes but can safely say all dignity is now gone.

So not how it's done on TV.

Captain Sweatpants looks like he is about to pass out with the sudden exertion.

Better wrap this up.

"Okay now bring your tree to, umm, a standstill. Close your eyes again and breathe in the cool morning air."

Sounds of deep shallow breathing all round.

"Namaste," I bowed, before hastily moving towards the safety of the house; leaving a bewildered but slightly amused half dressed bus-load of men standing in a field of cows.

Back at the safety of the house.

Sooo glad that is over.

"Nice circus," said Matt coming in behind me, "man wait till I upload this to YouTube."

"You filmed that??"

"Yep, fark it's gonna go viral," he said sounding like he had had a victory.

"Don't you dare Matt. That was a legitimate meditation giving thanks to the earth, have some respect."

"You didn't have any respect when you were gonna put a picture of me in da nude on national television."

Oh god why does Matt remember some things and not others.

"Oh that," I scoffed trying to keep him sweet as he headed over to the desktop computer to upload his video, "I was just joking about that, I mean pff, as if I would Matt. I'm better than that. I was just trying to find out where we would be going, it's frustrating not knowing," I wailed.

Truth is, I wasn't joking, not that I would let that slip to Matt at the moment. But the last thing I want is Matt uploading a video to YouTube of morning meditation with group of half naked potential husbands in a cow field playing airplanes. I mean I'm in business, Matt isn't, so I have a reputation to uphold and Matt doesn't.

God why couldn't life be simple?

"Not knowing what?" Millie asked, overhearing the last bit of the conversation as she saunters in with Amy in her arms looking like she has just had a good belly laugh.

"Oh nothing."

"Lisa tried to blackmail me last night," said Matt taking a seat at the computer.

God I could kill Sid for giving him the password to the desktop.

"I did not try to blackmail you last night," I scoffed, "I was simply, errrrr, playing a wee joke on you. I mean god Matt you can be so sensitive at times, lighten up."

"Why did she try and blackmail you Matt?" asked Millie.

Oh great, now Millie's getting involved.

"'Cause she wanted to… ouch."

Tried to silence Matt by throwing cow-pat stained running shoe at him.

But not going to work as Millie will press Matt until he tells her, then Millie will be forced to put Matt's nuts into a vice, then I'll never know what the week's secret itinerary is going to be.

"Um, no reason," I quickly said.

"Matt?" Millie pressed, ignoring me.

God I wish Larry my ghost friend was here so I could get him to divert Millie while I can quickly silence Matt or come up with a reason other than the truth.

Matt went to open his whiney mouth again when Amy let out a burp, followed by regurgitating white goop all down the front of Millie's top, but not before Millie's mobile phone started ringing and Brendon entered asking if he could speak to her.

I'm overwhelmed with emotion, it's like Larry *is* here helping me, I mean that couldn't all have been a coincidence.

See universe does want me to blackmail Matt into handing over plans.

Millie gives me a look as if to say 'it's not over yet' and proceeds to deal with the distractions.

"Matt," I hissed as he logs on to his YouTube account, nursing the back of his head where the shoe hit him,

"I'll make you a deal, you don't upload that video and I'll hand over all incriminating evidence including naked pictures of you as a toddler."

"How can I be sure you don't have any more? I mean that was not cool Lisa, a dude has his dignity you know."

"I don't, I promise, hand on my heart. Just don't upload the video, or tell Millie why I want the itinerary."

"But that's two things," Matt said looking annoyed.

"No actually it's one," I corrected, "remember? The reason I tried to convince you with the photos was to get information about up and coming week's mystery tour. So technically it's one."

"Two!" Matt said and pressed 'login' to his account.

Shit I can hear Millie winding up her conversation with Brendon while cleaning Amy up.

"Okay, two then," I caved, "I'll hand back all photos of you, if you cancel that upload."

"Okay done. But I want them back to me by 6pm or this goes viral. Oh and I want to know where you got them from."

"Matt I can't tell you that."

Matt starts to upload the video, little shit, he really means business.

"Okay, okay, it was Debbie, Debbie from the rest home remember, she used to babysit you."

"Thought so," Matt said, sounding outraged.

"Never mind that," I urged as I can hear Millie's presence getting closer, "now I need a copy of that itinerary, name your price, I promise I won't tell Millie where I got it from so your manhood will be safe."

"How can you guarantee my nuts will be safe?" asked Matt.

"I'll errr… tell her it was Brendon okay? I promise I won't let on."

Matt pondered this for a while; I mean jeez, time *is* a factor here, what is there to ponder?

"Okay," he agreed, "but on one condition."

"Sure, what's that?"

"Don't go near Jake Crankshaw."

"Pff, what? I've hardly seen him."

"Really?"

"Yeah really but hey if that's what you want, it's a deal," I said sticking my hand out for him to shake.

Matt ignores my hand and folds his arms across his chest.

"So you're telling me you haven't seen tosser Jake at all since he came back?"

"Well only, you know, around here… which is hardly ever."

"Is that your final answer?"

"God Matt we're not on a game show here."

"Well have ya?"

"Pff, of course not."

"Well explain this then," he said in a smug voice, handing over his phone.

Oh my god! Bloody Matt has been stalking me to get some evidence and has even taken pictures of me getting out of Jake's car this morning after our night of playing scrabble. It looks like he was hiding behind a bush when he took them. Bloody, bloody hell.

"Okay, okay, I can explain," I said.

"He's bad news Lisa, he did it wif my mum ya know."

"Yes I know but…"

"Can you imagine me doing it wif your mum?" he went on.

One mental image I can do without. But I can see his point.

"He's nuffing but a tool," Matt went on winding up to a rant.

"Yes, yes, he's a tool," I said trying to keep the conversation moving before Millie gets back. "But there was an innocent explanation for it, now do we have a deal?"

"What was the explanation den?"

"I'll explain later," I hissed, "now do we have a deal?"

"Not yet, there's one more thing."

"But that's two conditions," I spat, "you only said one."

"Nah technically it's two things, if you want the itinerary then stay away from Jake. But if you don't want me to tell Millie you blackmailed me then that's two things."

Grrr bloody Matt, when did he get all sneaky and grow a brain?

"Okay fine," I sighed, "what is it?"

"Go out on a date wif Damo."

"Pardon?" I spluttered.

"Go on a date wif Damo, he fancies ya and he doesn't care that you're 40."

"39! And Matt I can't go out on a date with stoner Damo."

"Why not?"

"'Cause he's um… stoner Damo. And besides I'm a sophisticated, respected business owner Matt I can't be dating Damo. He's half my age."

"But you shagged me."

"God Matt would you let that go, you and I both know what happened there.

"So what's wrong wif Damo? You know he would have applied to get a chance to get into your pants if you hadn't put the age limit on it. That's so age-est."

"Because *Matt*, Damo is like 20 years old, smokes pot, still lives with his mum and as far as I know, doesn't have a job. I can't be dating the likes of Damo."

"Well that's where you're wrong.

He's 23 actually, has a job and lives with his grandma, not his mum which goes to show what a caring person he is, moving in to look after his Nan. See I told you, you're a snob, you don't even know him."

"He's still a pot smoker."

"Yeah he only does that 'cause his job is so stressful he needs somefing to unwind. If you had his job you'd be off your face too."

"What does he do for a job?" I asked puzzled, unaware that Damo even had a job.

"Not telling ya, you can ask him when you go on a date wif him."

"Matt I'm not going on a date with Damo."

"Okay then I'm telling Millie you tried to blackmail me into giving you the itinerary."

"Matt you are not being fair," I hissed aware that I can hear Millie's footsteps getting nearer, "you can't make me go out with someone I'm not interested in."

"How do you know you're not interested in him? You don't even know him, you don't know these guys either but you want to shag them."

"Date them Matt, date them. Not shag them."

"Same thing."

"It is not and besides, I'm not looking for a one nighter, I'm looking for long term. Therefore Damo won't have a shot."

"How do you know he's not wanting a long term thing? Go out on one date or I'll tell."

Oh god I can see Millie's reflection in the computer screen as she is marching back towards us like she is on a mission to extract information from Matt.

Who am I kidding that's exactly what she is about to do.

"Okay, okay," I hissed under my breath at Matt, "I'll do it but just one date and that's it. Now quickly make something up."

"Oh hi Millie," I beamed as she stood over a very smug looking Matt with her hands on her hips.

"So why did Lisa try to blackmail you Matt?" she asked in her intimidating voice.

"'Cause she wanted me to set her up a date wif Damo and said she was going to show a picture of me in da nude if I didn't."

Oh my god!

Driving in van to mystery destination.

I'm so tired and have a headache.

Not because it's late in the day or because of the early morning start, it's simply because I have had Millie on my bloody back all morning about 'why didn't I just date the local youth to begin with if that's what I wanted' and spare her the trouble of getting bus-load of men out here and blah blah.

Didn't have much of a defense thanks to bloody Matt landing me in it, so I had no choice but to sit there and take her lecture like a naughty child.

But no time to dwell on up-and-coming date with stoner Damo because I actually have a copy of the day's events thanks to Matt.

Not sure about the entire week yet as Matt has only given me the information for the one day when he picked me up and must say, after looking at the program, I'm pretty impressed. I mean a morning visit to an olive garden for tastings and a pressing demonstration, followed by lunch at the Old Stone Mill House, it sounds very romantic. Not riveting stuff but better then damper bread and chicken plucking. I can just see me walking through the rows of olive trees with my date.

The program said 'dress for a garden party' so it gave me the opportunity to wear my big floppy country style hat I had bought for the Melbourne Cup function at the local race track last year but never got to wear due to poor weather that saw me replace sophisticated racing hat with yellow waterproof rain hat to save expensive salon hairdo.

And I have to say, complemented with my causal summer dress I look rather graceful and ravishing.

I quickly phoned Mary and told her the destination to meet me with the camera. Mary's not exactly discreet but because she also runs the information centre in town once a week, if Brendon asks why she has a camera, then I have an excuse all ready to give him that it is for tourism and promotions, as long as he doesn't ask Mary of course.

Now who to arrange an actual date with? Which is going to be harder now as I have a feeling Brendon suspects I may be staging a coup on his whole production.
Think Matt may have told stoner Damo that I agreed to go out on a date with him too because he's been making eyes at me all morning.
Okay just try not to look at him.

So far I have had drinks beside an open air fire with Darcy. Okay yes just half a drink before having to rescue Jake from the horrors of salty jam but there didn't seem to be any spark between Darcy and I, so moving on.
And I think Darcy may feel the same way because he hasn't approached me for another date. If fact he's acting like he hasn't even been on a date with me. Why does it seem to be me doing all the bloody chasing around here? I mean anyone would think these men are here for the free bed and food.

Well okay technically they are, but they're all bloody single. You would think they would jump at the chance of courting a perfectly good semi-normal, successfully, and single, good looking girl like myself.

Jake is on the bus this morning and I can feel him trying to catch my attention but I'm trying so hard not to look at him as Matt is watching me like a hawk.

The mood on the bus this morning seems to be relaxed and happy as everyone appears mellow, even Bear has downgraded his compulsory can of bourbon to a can of light beer and has only asked me to show off my breasts once since meditation. I would like to say it was my morning ritual of giving thanks to the earth that has turned them all into relaxed and happy men, except for Captain Sweatpants who looks like he almost died of exhaustion, but as Millie pointed out laughter is good for the soul as it releases endorphins so morning meditation may have done them the world of good, but not in the manner I was thinking.

I pointed out to Millie that given the short window of time I had to prepare such a morning ritual, i.e. none, I thought it went well and I would like to see her do better.

To which she then asked if I didn't know I was going to host morning meditation then why was I climbing through a barbed wire fence at 5.20am; after which I decided not to press the argument any further.

Slade and Steel seem to be inseparable since they got here and I'm not sure which one I like more since they are very similar. I think I need to spend time with both of them today then decide who the better one is.

Not sure where this olive garden is as I have never heard of 'Oliva Place' and was surprised to hear it was local but it sounds very romantic and have to say things are looking up.
Now to arrange a date.
I sidle up to Slade and Steel who both have ear buds in listening to music.
Not sure where to begin so think a casual conversation to warm things up may be the go.
"So how are you guys finding the area so far?" I said as I smoothly leaned myself against the head rest on the seat trying not to glance at Jake who is within eyeshot in the seat behind.
"Pardon?" Slade said, removing his ear buds, while Steel continues to look out the window.
"How are you finding it?"
"Finding what?"

"The area," I beamed followed with a hand gesture like I was demonstrating the safety features on an airplane.

"Oh the area… um well… yeah it's nice from what I have seen so far."

"Oh good, good, so… um you having a good time?"

"Yeah not bad."

"Excellent," I said glancing out the window not knowing what to say next. Steel hasn't acknowledged that I'm here but I can hear his music through his ear buds.

"So," I said, glancing back at Slade as he went to put his ear buds back in and paused midair.

"Um… looking forward to today?"

"Yeah I think so," he said lowering his hands.

"So umm… yeah good, okay catch up later."

"Okay yep, catch ya."

Connection established.

Well with one of them anyway.

Ohh, text message.

Oh it's from Matt, wait, isn't he driving the van.

'ask damo on a date'.

Oh for goodness sake.

I text back.

'when I'm effing ready'.

Jake's eyes are boring into me and I'm trying so hard not to look back at him.

Another text message.

'now or I'm telling'.

Oh for…

'Matt just watch the road'.

'I am, do it now or I'll ph Millie'.

'you can't rush these things matt u have to find the right moment'.

'I'm calling Millie'.

Looked back at Matt and the little shit has his phone to his ear. Bloody hell.

'okay I'll bloody ask him'.

Why am I texting back when he can see me and talk to me?

Oh god Matt's texted back. How is he doing that *and* watching the road.

'k but don't let on I told u he fancies ya'.

What! Oh god that's going to make it even more unbearable, well here goes.

"Hi Damo," I said grabbing the seat next to him as Matt throws his phone back on the dashboard with a victory smirk.

"Oh hey Lisa," Damo says as his cheeks turn a slight shade of pink.

Man Jake is really playing with my instincts today as I can feel his stare with every move I make.

"So I was wondering, um, if you would like to, um, you know…"

Oh god I'm not sure I can bring myself to do this and Damo is not helping with his awkward silence, you think the least he could do is fill in the blanks.

"So what was I saying? Oh yeah I was just thinking…"

Ohh text message.

'so wot he say'.

Okay really need to find my inner calm blue ocean with Matt before I completely lose it and shove his phone up his nose… wait a minute.

Instead of glancing at Matt to send him a silent glare that he is a total and utter twat, my eyes dart towards the windscreen, I can't help but think this road looks familiar.

Oh no it better not be…

Abruptly standing to move to the window opposite, I can feel the panic rise in my throat as I glance out to see the row of olive trees approaching.

Oh no.

Oh god, please don't turn into the driveway Matt, please, please, please.

No, no, no, no, no.

Oh noooooo!!!!!

14

So it turns out 'Oliva Place' is proudly owned and operated by skinny arm waving Italian man that once lured me into thinking he had white animals for my petting zoo only for me to arrive and find he only had a white dog, now my Monty. But not before tricking me into tasting his olive oil which then led me to offer him marriage advice causing his wife to come after me with spiteful words of how I propositioned her husband before she threatened me with certain nastiness if I ever came near him again.

And here they both are; standing in the beautiful ambiance of the olive grove, waving their greeting as Matt pulls the van in… I cannot be here, I simply cannot.

"You going to get off the floor and come outside?" asked Jake amused but puzzled as everyone cautiously stepped over me while I took refuge on the van floor so I can't be seen.

"Um yep, just give me a moment."

Okay I have two options here; one I stay on the van floor, or two, get out and face it.

Think I'll go with option one.

"Lisa?"

Damn.

"Oh yep, coming," I mumble.

Okay I'm just going to have to stay out of sight, lucky I have my floppy hat and dark glasses.

Mary has just pulled up followed by Brendon and Sid in Brendon's car. Better get out there before they start asking where I am, then my cover *would* be blown.

Stepped out of van as discreetly as I could given that Mary hastily made her appearance by waving frantically at me. Thank god Italian man and psycho wife have turned their backs and are leading the group down a laneway before they realised she was waving at me.

"Yes I see you Mary," I said with all the firm politeness I can muster as she finally caught up.

"Oh I was worried I'd be late," she panted, "Bill caught his finger in the bathroom door and you know with his limited mobility and the fact I have to help him with his clothing I had a dreaded thought that he actually slammed his…"

"Yes, yes, now did you bring the camera?"

"Camera, oh yes dear, it's right here."

This may not turn out to be easy now I'm dodging crazy Italian people, but if I can lure Slade and Steel away from the group and into the olive groves then I have half a chance of shooting a dating scene within the olive groves followed by a romantic lunch at the Old Stone Mill House which I am just praying is in a different location to this.

Also need to do in such a way Brendon won't come after me to find out what I'm doing. God whatever happened to people minding their own business?

Daniel has texted to say the local paper has contacted him as they heard a production crew is in town and would like to do a story as to why they are here. Texted him back and said yes to a story.

My god if this publicity keeps up I'll be a celebrity in no time.

Crazy Italian lady and skinny arm waving husband have now stopped in front of a barn style shed. Which was a completely different shed to the one I was originally lured into to taste olive oil before he convinced me to take Monty home with me. In fact the whole place has transformed. To the left is a pathway leading to a beautiful garden which overlooks acres of olive trees, if only I had more time to appreciate the scenery and not spend my time staging coup on production, as it's really nice here, really looks like a little piece of Italy.

Italian man and his wife turn to address the group and I duck out of sight behind Jake. Matt has noticed and is glaring at me. Skinny arm waving Italian man has started to talk about their journey and how they came to buy the land and turn it into an olive enterprise which not only produces fine olives but olive oil pressed right here in the shed behind him.

Jake keeps looking behind at me with a puzzled expression as to why I am hunched over behind his back and gave me an even more puzzled look when I placed my finger to my lips to shush him.

Mary is standing behind me waiting for my instructions, I did tell her to start videoing some of the beautiful setting so I can edit in the dating scene with Slade and Steel later but Mary seems distracted by Jamie who is shuffling from foot to foot looking like he is going to burst out into dance any minute now.

I didn't really have a plan on how the date was going to turn out as I didn't bring any food or tablecloths or wine, in fact I don't even think I have a bottle of water but I have to say since I decided to plan my secret production by turning boring tourism documentary into exciting dating show, it has brought out my creative side as I had a brilliant idea on how to set my dating scene with Slade and Steel.

Now just to find Slade and Steel.

Skinny Italian man has stopped talking and the group is now parting in different directions.

Shit, shit, what is happening?

Feeling exposed as Jake has moved off towards crazy Italian lady who is leading a group towards the olive groves and I'm not sure which way to go first.

Brendon and Sid have a quick meeting before moving off with crazy lady's group. It's like a flock of sheep scattering in different directions.

Darcy, Bear and Jamie follow Jake towards crazy lady while Matt, Damo, Paul and Captain Sweatpants move off towards the shed.

"It seems I'm in a bit of a pickle," said Mary looking confused, "I'm not sure which group I'm supposed to be in."

"Just follow me," I hissed as I frantically searched to see where Slade and Steel have gone. Italian man has turned to see if anyone is lagging behind and I quickly duck behind a passing Damo so as not to be seen.

"We can't be in the same group dear," Mary continued, "that means it would make very uneven numbers."

Damo is looking uneasy as I grab the back of his shirt to hold him still to use him for camouflage. I spy Steel near the front of the queue near Italian man.

Cannot see Slade which means he must have followed the other group who are moving off in the other direction.

Have to say universe is not helping with my plan to stage coup on production, you'd think universe would abide my wishes and help a girl out. I turned back to Mary who is almost frantic with where she is meant to be.

"Go with that group and stick close to Slade," I whispered to her, "when you catch up with him give him this," I whispered passing her a scroll wrapped in beautiful red ribbon. "Once he opens it, get a shot of the scroll and him reading it then keep the camera rolling and don't let him out of your sight. I'll catch up. In the meantime get some footage of the olive groves."
Mary looks frazzled by my instructions but quickly moves off to join the other group.

I release Damo and move closer to the front of the queue to where Steel is. Italian man has his back to the crowd as he leads us towards the main entrance of the pressing shed. My phone beeps as I move in closer towards Steel.
we're on our way the message read from Daniel. Who is we? Never mind that now, I quickly turn my phone down and stuff it back into my bag.

I pull my hat over my eyes a bit more and adjust my sunglasses so Italian man doesn't recognise me now I'm closer. We get to the entrance of the shed and he turns to address the group. I quickly duck behind Steel.

"So if you a likey to come come," said Italian man almost knocking Matt over with his hand gestures, "we press some olives huh."

I quickly go to grab Steel's attention when Matt intercepts me.

"So, you asked Damo on a date yet?"

"Matt now is not the time."

"You didn't answer my question."

"No, not yet okay," I said, craning my head around to keep my eyes on Steel, "and besides it's hard to ask someone out if you don't fancy them to begin with Matt!"

Bugger lost sight of him.

"Well, when?" said Matt pressing the issue, "I mean you grabbed his arse before. So now you got him all worked up."

"Grabbed whose arse?"

"Damo. Just then, I saw ya."

"I grabbed the back of his tee-shirt Matt."

"Why did ya do that if you don't fancy him?"

Oh god Matt is giving me the biggest headache.

The queue is slowly moving into the shed and I have completely lost sight of Steel, who has already entered.

Chances of luring him away now are slim which means I have to stand through the whole demonstration.

God I hope Mary hasn't given Slade the scroll yet.

"Okay," I sigh at Matt, "if I ask Damo will you leave me alone for the rest of the day?"

Ohh just spotted a side door to the shed. Wonder if it's unlocked.

"Okay, deal," Matt said.

Haven't got time for this but I can see Matt is not going to leave until I do, so I quickly slide up beside Damo who was about to join the others inside.

"Damo do you want to go out for a drink some time?"

Damo suddenly looks like a possum caught in headlights… that has also lost his tongue.

Oh for god's sake, it's a simple yes or no question.

Italian olive man is now gesturing from inside the shed for everyone to gather around and Damo is just standing there looking at me.

Haven't got time for this.

"Yes or no Damo!" I snapped, "I've got things to do."

"Um, yes, that's yes," he stammered as Matt stood behind him with giant smile on his face.

"Good, I'll be in touch," I said before quickly moving off around the side of the shed to the small door. Phew and it's not locked, things are looking up.

Carefully opened it and I can see directly to the main entrance as Damo makes his appearance along with the rest of the group. Italian man is standing with his back to me beside a big shiny metal press. Steel is standing on the opposite side of the press to him.

Well not the best place to stand but because he is facing toward me and Italian man isn't, I may be able to catch his attention.

Actually on second thought, bad, bad idea, it will only take one strange look from Steel to alert Italian man to the fact I'm here then he may start feeding me olive oil again which may cause his wife to come after me accusing me of husband stealing.

I only made one scroll but can see now I should have done two. So I quickly scribbled a note down on a mini scribble pad that faintly read in light embossing '*Matt and Neroli. 20th May 2012*'. The notepads were meant for Matt and Neroil's wedding but of course that never happened so we were stuck with their wedding merchandise. Mind you the members of the CWA are grateful as Betty said she now has plenty of pens and a constant supply of message notebooks beside her telephone.

Now to discreetly hand it to him without being noticed by anyone.

Leaving the side door ajar slightly so I can use it as an escape route I quietly make my way inside the shed.

Everyone is standing in a circle around the press and it's such a wide circle I'm having trouble maneuvering around the bodies discreetly. The light in here is just shocking. Skinny arm waving Italian man must have made a bit of a joke as the group fall into murmured giggles at his presentation, I quietly steal up beside Captain Sweatpants who turns to look at me in surprise as I pause to plan my next move.

Italian olive pressing man is talking about cold pressing to make extra virgin olive oil by pouring a bucket full of olives into a vibrating tray that runs through a shoot to another vibrating tray only to get run over by what looks like training wheels off a girl's bicycle that have been molded in cement going around in circles, which then goes through this other tube and comes out looking very much like runny honey as it is tipped into a dark wine bottle.

But then again I do have dark glasses on and it's also kinda dull inside the shed so it could be a whole different process for all I know.

Everyone takes a step closer towards the press to see the oil being extracted and I continue making my way around the circle trying not to be noticed.

Man these dark glasses aren't helping but I don't dare remove them.

With that thought in mind I pull my floppy hat further over my eyes and make my way to where I thought Steel was standing. But it turns out to be Paul the boring guy. I seem to have lost my sense of direction; I thought we were standing over towards Darcy.

Oh wait that's not Darcy that's Damo.

Man anyone would think I'm in a labyrinth.

Italian olive man is now showing Paul the boring guy, who always looks like he is waiting for Scotty to beam him up, the workings of the press. Paul looks like he has finally found something that slightly interests him. Although he is an engineer so I s'pose…

"Ouch!" Matt exclaimed as I accidently kicked the back of his heal as I edged passed him. Man why does Matt have to over dramatise everything!

Everyone turns to look briefly at Matt's outburst including Italian man and I hold my breath but they quickly divert their attention to the marvels of the liquid goo coming from the stainless steel machine.

Phew that was a close one.

Finally made it to where Steel is standing and I maneuver in slightly behind him but not too close that he can sense I am there or the brim of my big hat touches him. My plan was to slip the note into his hand and take a step back out of sight so when he turns around to see who put it there, no-one is there, which will add a slight curiosity to it. Then he will read the note hopefully the same time as his twin brother reads the same note given to him by Mary, which says:

Down by the olive tree,

In row number 5,

You will be greeted by a pleasant surprise.

It may not be riches, it may not be love,

it may only be a pleasant stroll.

But if you ignore this request then you may never know,

what awaits you down in the olive grove.

Brilliant aye!

And it's me; me who is the pleasant surprise.

Although not quite sure what I'm going to do when I get them there but all the same a very romantic gesture.

If I can just get him to see the damn note.

Captain Sweatpants has appeared beside Steel to get a closer look at what is happening with the press and I cannot thank the universe enough for providing me with his robust frame large enough to slip beside and not be seen.

Finding my mojo I quietly slip the note into Steel's palm which he has resting slightly on top of his front jeans pocket and quickly turned to make my hasty getaway behind the safety of Captain Sweatpants' bulk when a whoosh of air appears out of nowhere taking my hat off my head.

"… And you see we a use the blower for clean the olives," shouted Italian man over the noise of what appears to be a giant vacuum cleaner hose in reverse.

My hat has blown in the direction of the press and I try to duck for cover behind Captain Sweatpants but it's too late, bloody Matt is standing in the way.

Not sure whose head made the sound of a crack when mine connected with Matt's but can say with confidence that bloody Matt would most likely make the biggest fuss.

And there goes my sunglasses.

Glanced over at Steel who is looking at the note with a puzzled expression.

Okay got no time to lose, better get out of here and make my way down to the olive grove before he gets there. I hope Mary has followed my instructions.

"A'cusea me, you're a hat," said Italian man coming up behind me.

Oh no, shit… okay, don't look at him.

"No not mine," I said keeping my back to him as I slowly made my way towards the door.

"It a yours, was on you head yes?"

"No."

"No?"

"No it's um… his," I said pointing to Matt who is holding his head and still looks like he is trying to work out what just happened. Luckily no-one saw it so he can't blame me.

Well I hope no-one saw it, no-one is saying anything or coming to Matt's aid.

"But it a girl hat," Italian man says.

"Yes he can be a girl."

"Ohhh you a maka joke."

"No."

"You a funny, now here take hat."

Uh oh.

He dives in front of me and like any slow motion disaster his face lights up like Christmas tree lights as he recognises me.

"Oh it'a you," he exclaims in delight, diving in and planting a kiss on my left cheek, "you take dog oh it a good you come a visit. Come, come got new oil for you to try, where is dog?"

He has his arm around my waist and is trying to lure me back toward the olive vat.

"Oh it's okay, I was just leaving, err, prior commitment…"

"Ohhh you bleeding."

"Pardon?"

"You bleeding from you head," he said pulling out a manky looking handkerchief and placing it on my head.

Oh shit, so I am.

"Come, come, we fix you up."

"No I'm fine."

"No come, I take you to house, get you fixed."

"No it's just a scratch."

"Agh," he spat at my protest as he gripped my waist tighter and steered me in the direction of the side door. I look back in alarm in time to see Steel disappear out of the main shed door. Oh no.

"Waita here," Italian man instructs the group, "justa fix the girl head."

We make our way towards his house and I fumble in my bag with one hand for my phone to try and alert Mary that Steel is coming her way and to stall them until I get there, but the glare of the sun is hurting my eyes and it's not easy when you have an Italian man holding his germ infested handkerchief to your head and directing you into enemy territory. Damn Matt and his bloody hard head.

God I only pray Italian man's wife is still outside with the other group.

We arrive at the house after what seems to be an eternity and he takes me into a little scullery off the kitchen. With all his talking and arm flapping it was hard to get a text message off to Mary to say I am on my way but I managed to pull it off before he takes my bag and shoes off me and places them behind an old wooden chair which he then instructs me to sit on.

He fumbles in what appears to be a first aid tin and starts dabbing antiseptic lotion on my head, pulling my hair back from my scalp, messing it up while the lotion runs down my head into my eye causing him to then wipe all the carefully applied mascara from my eye as he quickly catches the drip. Grrrr.

"So how is a dog?" he asked as he continued with his sabotage.

"Oh… fine," I said, trying not to indulge in too much conversation so we can quickly get this ordeal over with.

"He a make a trouble no?"

"No."

"He a good?"

"Yes."

"You have husband yes?"

"No."

"But you got married yes?" he looked puzzled as he continued to dab my forehead.

"Oh *that*, well no I was meant to you see but when it come down to getting married, it just didn't feel right you know."

Shit got sucked into his web of conversation. Be strong say nothing.

"… so I just had to tell him I couldn't marry him. Which was really difficult because it's hard to find someone around here with Rick's qualities you know."

Okay rein it in, he's not your best friend.

"… but I couldn't just marry for the sake of marrying someone. Millie is always telling me it's better to have the right person by your side then spend your life molding the wrong one to fit right but it's just so unfair."

For god's sake woman, zip it!

"… so yep I just let him go… like a discarded piece of old furniture. Giving noooo thought to the fact that I'm almost 40 and drying up like an old prune, crazy huh?"

For god's sake Lisa, shut the fuck up.

Italian man is listening intently and nodding in sympathy while applying a band aid to my forehead.

Think he needs to apply one to my mouth.

"There all a fixed," he said looking satisfied with his work, "ohhh you sad."

Yes I have to admit, tiny trip down memory lane has made me a little depressed.

"No I'm fine," I sniffed remembering that Steel and Slade are waiting and I really need to get out of here fast. Also need to fix makeup and hair.

"Ohh come a here," he said wrapping his arm around my shoulder in a reassuring hug. Oh god, me and my big sooky mouth.

"You are nice lookn girl huh, and funny, you mustn't be sad."

"No I'm not any more; I'm all good, in fact happy, happy as."

"There, there," he said trying to pull me closer. Mucking my hair up even more.

Bloody hell, is the universe hell bent on making me jump through hoops for one bloody date.

Oh shit is that a door I hear?

"Maurice where is gun..." shouted a female voice that could only be one person.

Oh shit.

"I a fetch it for you," he yelled back pulling back from his unwelcome embrace and excusing himself from the room.

I can see the shadow of her frame passing by the slightly ajar door which gives me a chance to slip out. I quickly grab my shoes and bag and make a bolt for the door, snagging the strap of my dress on the old rickety timber frame as I hastily rose from the chair. Got no time to worry about that, need to get out of here before she sees me and gets all Italian mafia on my arse for being near her husband.

Shoes and bag in hand I tiptoe towards the door, but not before catching a glimpse of myself in a small mirror above the sink.

Oh my god, need to fix makeup and hair.

Grrr, seem to be torn between bolting for freedom and looking good for my date. My phone is beeping from my bag alerting me to messages and the strap on my dress keeps falling down exposing the top of my bra.

Bloody hell, don't have time for this.

Throwing my bag onto the sink I quickly fumble through the contents for my mascara and hair brush. Argh, when you don't want a safety pin they're everywhere but the minute you need one to hold the strap up on your dress…!

I can hear crazy Italian woman's muffled voice which seems to be in another room far from this one so I get to work applying my mascara as quickly as possible.

My phone beeps a message reminder again and I know it'd be Mary trying to get hold of me, wondering where I am.
Man does that woman have no patience?

Ditched my mascara as I spot a small safety pin hovering at the bottom of my bag and I retrieve it before it disappears back into the black hole; and quickly go to work securing my dress but it's not easy when you're not a gymnast or trained in the art of bending your arm over your head to retrieve strap.
Uh oh!
The door abruptly opens and I am now eyeballing crazy Italian lady.
Man that happened so fast I didn't even see it coming.
We are both looking at one another with a gobsmacked expression on our faces as I am trying to put my dress back together with messed up hair.
Actually this looks very, very bad.

"You!" she spat, her eyes widening like dinner plates.
"Founda gun," Italian man shouted from the other room.
Oh my god Debbie got it all wrong when she reassured me they weren't in the mafia.
Time to go.

Snatched my bag and shoes from the counter and bolted passed her, pushed her aside and ran through the front door into the safety of the open air. I can hear her screaming at me to come back and explain why I was with her husband and I'm not sure if she is running after me but her voice is awfully loud and I'm sure I can feel her wrath getting closer. Oh god she really meant it when she said she was going to come after me. Not sure where I am running to but must find people fast. Think I have dropped one of my shoes but I'm really, really happy I'm in bare feet as speed is the only thing that's going to save me now. I can see rows and rows of olive trees ahead and make a beeline for it.

I turn around to see crazy lady running after me, she has something in her hand and if I'm not mistaken it looks like some kind of weapon.

Oh my god I'm going to die.

Running through rows and rows of trees I have lost all sense of direction and even though my heart is racing and my lungs feel like they are sandpaper against my ribcage I can't stop now.

I ran into a fresh row of olive trees and at the end of the row I can make out who I think may be Slade and Steel. So I must be in row 5! Thanking my lucky stars I head towards them.

"Where you a going?" Italian man said as he stepped out from behind a tree scaring the bejeezes out of me and causing me to let out an involuntary yelp as I side step him in one smooth move that would definitely land me a spot in any of the AFL teams if the talent scouts had been present.

Oh my god he is holding what appears to be a rifle!

"My wify she a wanna talk to you," he yelled.

Panic sets in and I start screaming as I bolt even faster down the row towards Slade and Steel.

This is not how I envisioned I was going to die. Shot in a mafia style execution by an insecure wife who claims I am having relations with her husband because he lured me into tasting his olive oil.

Slade and Steel appear clearly in my line of vision and Mary is also there. She swings the camera around to me as I approach them at the speed of sound.

"Oh here she comes," I hear her say to Slade and Steel as they are watching me approach. Slade is holding the scroll that delivered the romantic message, looking like he is waiting with bated breath for the surprise that is mentioned in the message.

The sound of a rifle being shot echoes through the air.

Oh my god they are shooting at me.

"Ruuunnnn!!!!" I scream as I bolt passed the three of them as Mary follows my actions with the camera.

I quickly turn to see if they are complying with my hysterical instructions but they are just standing there looking puzzled. Italian man and his wife however are not standing still looking puzzled; in fact they are both now giving chase yelling at me to stop while demonstrating they are holding weapons of destruction in their hands by waving them around. Oh god I need to find my way to the car park and fast.

Trying to fumble in my bag for my phone to call Matt and tell him to get the van running as I need to make a quick getaway and running for my life at the same time is proving a challenge. I glance behind me again to now see Italian man and his wife have been joined in chase by Steel, Slade and Mary still holding the video camera.

Turning into a fresh row of trees I can see the pressing shed at the end of the row, which means the van is parked not far from there. Fumbling with my phone in hand I duck behind a leafy olive tree slowing briefly to ring, I don't dare stop completely as it's easier to start running again when your feet haven't stopped moving.

I quickly pressed the appropriate number on my phone, my hand visibly shaking the whole time.

My god my lungs are hurting and I'm having trouble catching my breath, if running for my life doesn't make me slimmer or fitter then I don't know what will.

I can feel a presence behind me; I spun around and let out an involuntary yelp.

"Oh bloody hell, you scared the living daylights out of me."

"You okay? Do you need to go to the toilet or something?'" asked Bear as he, Jamie, Jake and Brendon look at me as if I am some kind of fruit loop.

But knowing they are here I feel so much better, safety in numbers and all that.

"No," I wheezed trying to catch my breath while I continued to jog on the spot, "I just need to…"

"Yo," came the voice on the other end of the phone.

"Matt quick go to the van and start it up, don't ask questions just do it, it's a matter of life and death. I'm on my way."

Quickly hanging up and throwing my phone back into my bag I turn back to inform the group that we all need to get back to the van and fast, when Italian man stepped out from the trees behind me.

"She a over here," he called back to his wife.

Another scream escaped my mouth as I turned to run, thank god my feet were already moving.

Another faint gunshot rings out and this time my scream is enough to peel the bark from the olive trees.

"Ruunnnnn!!!!" I screamed again as I bolted through the group, scattering them like bowling pins as I made a beeline for the van.

I just hope bloody Matt has taken me seriously and is waiting to make a getaway.

Running for what seems to be an eternity and my lungs are screaming at me to stop before they end up in my month but up ahead I can see the faint outline of the van. My legs seem to find a second wind upon seeing a vision of safety before me and I look behind me to see if I'm still being chased.

Italian man, Slade, Steel, Mary, Jamie, Bear, Jake, and Brendon are all in hot pursuit like I'm Forrest Gump running for no reason at all and they are my followers. Problem is, on closer inspection, well as much as you can see when you are running one way while your head is pivoted in another direction, I cannot see Italian man's wife! I'm hoping her lungs are also trying to explode out of her chest and she has stopped for a rest.

Argh!

Stopped dead as I connected with something and now have hit the ground backwards.

Oh no.

"Why are you a running you silly girl," said Italian's man wife as she towered over me holding something in her hand.

Oh god.

"Don't kill me," I begged as I curled up in a fetal position with my arm over my eyes so I don't see what fate will deliver me.

"Oh you a stop a her," said Italian man's voice, as I can hear the thunder of a dozen feet coming to a halt behind him.

"Don't hurt me," I begged again, almost hysterical, "I wasn't having relations with your husband I swear, I didn't even know we were coming here today."

"What's going on here?" said a voice that can only be Daniel's.

Oh thank god he is here; I recognise his trouser's legs as I raise my eyes slightly and I reach out and grip his leg.

"They are coming after me," I wailed, "tell them to back off or you will call the police."

"After you?" said Daniel with a puzzled expression.

"Yes after me, 'cause she thinks I'm after her husband because he feeds me olive oil," I said bravely but still slightly hysterically while continuing to grip on to Daniel's leg.

I look up and everyone is staring at me, except Mary who still has the camera rolling and stuck in close proximity of my face.

Italian man and his wife look at each other in utter astonishment.

"Lisa is everything okay?" asked Daniel in annoyance as he tries to shake my grip from his leg.

"No she a crazy lady," snapped Italian man, "she need doctor, fast."

"So is this Lisa?" came a female voice behind me.

I look up to see a lady standing next to Daniel holding a notebook and pen in her hand who I'm very much betting is the lady from the local paper that Daniel had texted me about earlier.

"Yes this is Lisa," Daniel sighed.

Oh shit here comes Matt.

"Lisa, Damo and me have had the van running for five fucken minutes, my head hurts, and what life and death situation are you talking about?"

Facebook Status Update.

Lisa Collins.

List of things I hate: Insecure foreign people who think I'm after their husbands.

Misunderstandings.

Cameras.

15

Urgent CWA meeting in back of town hall.

Okay maybe someone *should* kill me now.

"Oh that's the funniest thing I have ever seen," screeched Mrs Crankshaw with tears of laughter falling down her cheeks as Mary is taking great pleasure in showing footage of my small misunderstanding in the olive groves to the members of the CWA as I sit at the official committee table pretending not to care.

Okay, okay, so how was I meant to know that a 'gun' in an orchard is the device used to scare off the birds. And the only reason they were chasing me was because I had left half the contents of my handbag behind when I bolted, and the 'weapon' I thought crazy Italian lady had in her hand happened to be my shoe that I dropped in my hasty getaway, plus the only reason Italian man wanted me to stop running was because he was concerned I had a concussion.

Daniel was concerned I was creating unnecessary drama for the newspaper interview and after apologising to a very amused looking reporter she agreed to come back to do the interview at a more convenient time.

Bear was concerned that if I was trying to be killed then why wasn't there any half naked mud wrestling involved?

Mary was concerned she didn't have enough battery charge in the camera to capture all my antics.

And as for the rest of them, including a very worried Slade and Steel, well let's not go there.

But it's so unfair because when we were leaving, Italian man's wife gave me a secret 'I'm still going to kill you' glare which no-one believes and now I have been officially banned from ever entering the premises of 'Oliva Garden' again.

Millie said it's probably for the best.

Not that I care, place is cursed with crazy people.

Didn't feel like talking to anyone after my ordeal so while the rest of them went to the pub to watch the footy, I spent the afternoon in my bedroom feeling sorry for myself while Monty also sat beside me and sulked, I think he must have got in Millie's way again. But I am starting to think the universe is playing one big joke on me, I mean I'm sure I haven't put it on my list that I want to be chased by crazy people while I'm on my way to a secret date. Jake was so sweet though, he texted me a couple of times and asked if I was okay and said he believed me about the crazy lady as he had heard she was a sandwich short of a picnic and did I want to come over?

And if I didn't have to attend this damn meeting I'd be there in a flash.

Fran is laughing so hard her whole body is vibrating from the force of it as they all continue to hoot over my little episode. Right that's it.

"Okay, order, order!!" I said in my president's voice that is reserved for unruly meetings like this.

Mrs Crankshaw called an urgent meeting with the CWA members this afternoon. Everyone is here. Very unusual to have such a meeting like this at short notice as normally the members are so bound by their daily routine that any sudden change to their ritual would mean upsets to bowel movements or sleeping patterns; so it must be serious.

Betty has taken the advice of her grandson and brought herself a scooter to get around on which is now parked up proudly at the back of the hall after many efforts from members to get it up the rickety steps. Betty didn't want to leave it outside in fear it may be stolen due to the key being permanently in the ignition so there is low risk of her losing it.

Must be a senior moment thing.

Laughter slowly dying down as Mrs Crankshaw responded to my request. Wiping the tears from her eyes she stood up and cleared her throat.

"Yes… ahem, hello all, thanks for coming at such short notice but we have an urgent matter to attend to."

Expressions of concern on faces all round.

"Well as you know our beloved hall has seen many years of good service to us all."

Murmurs of agreement.

"And it's fair to say the building isn't all in great condition."

Seems to be a difference of opinion about this.

"Well as many of you are aware the local council own the hall but the CWA is responsible for this part of the building which has been our headquarters for nearly 100 years now."

Impressed murmurs this time.

"Well sadly I received a letter from the local council today."

Total silence as Mrs Crankshaw opens the letter she has in her hand and puts on her reading glasses.

This better be good, not only am I missing out on another evening with Jake, I'm also missing an episode of Home and Away.

"Okay dears, it reads:

Dear CWA Taromeo Branch

Our records show that in 1914 an agreement between the Taromeo District Council and the Country Woman's Association in relation to the use of the back room and kitchen facilities located at the Taromeo and District Community Hall was signed. The time period of the lease was 100 years from the date of signature.

It has come to our attention this lease is due to expire.

In accordance with the Health and Safety Act it is required that inspections of public buildings be done to ensure maintenance and safety standards are met to the H&S Act. An inspection was carried out by a credited building inspector. Please see summary below:

- Asbestos found in ceiling of building.

- Termite damage to main structure.

- Plumbing to be of a poor standard and not up to current regulation requirements for public use.

- No fire exit exists and main door is inappropriate and unsafe if such an event was to occur.

Based on the above findings it is in our interests to condemn this building rather than repair it. The building will not be replaced.

Taromeo Regional Council would like to take this opportunity to congratulate the CWA Taromeo Branch on its up and coming 100 years of service to the community. We wish you all the best in finding a new venue to carry on this valuable community service.

Notice of termination of lease is attached."

Mrs Crankshaw removes her glasses and sighs.

"So it seems my dears, it's the end of an era for us."

Sad mumbles all round.

Okay yes it's sad, but it's not the end of the world. God I hope there isn't a fire tonight, I mean I knew the building was a bit old but not on the verge of being unsafe to sneeze in. Maybe we'd better move this outside.

"So anyway," Mrs Crankshaw said, "this building will no longer exist from next month."

Silence all around.

Okay I'm waiting for her to get to the point.

Oh maybe that was the point.

Better ask.

"So, your point being?"

"That we may have to terminate Lisa," snapped Mrs Crankshaw all choked up with emotion, "terminate I tell you!"

Woah! Mrs Crankshaw has been doing that a lot lately. I mean she's always been snappy but for months now she has been getting round like she has the weight of the world on her shoulders.

Mind you rumours are flying around town at the moment about her and Max being in dire straits financially, which could be taking its toll. I mean not that I believe it's true but it must be exhausting being talked about all day.

"Okay calm down, so terminate as in…?"

"What she is trying to say Lisa," said Maggie beside me trying to explain before Mrs Crankshaw has another mini meltdown. "Is that the end of the building will mean the end of the CWA."

"Well it doesn't have to be," I scoffed, "I mean it's only a building, we can find another place."

"Well that's what we're here to vote on," said Betty, "is it worth pursuing another lease or do we close our division of the association?"

Really, is that what we're here for? You know as the president you would think I would need to know these things.

"Details were in the email we sent out earlier," said Maggie reading my thoughts and handing out printed copies.

I wanted to tell her I don't have time to sit all day and wait for emails; I have a dating show to run.

A wave of depression came over me at the thought of the dating show. I mean it's not like it's going well. And unless I come up with a new strategy I just want to throw in the towel. Maybe this wasn't such a good idea, after all let's face it, time is not on my side, I only have three more days to produce the dating show and find the perfect man.

But then again I'm not sure if it is about finding the perfect man any more, it seems to be more like showing Brendon how things are done in this part of the world, and if I was honest with myself, apart from Jake, none of them are really turning me on. Not that I have had a chance to get to know any of them really but it's not due to lack of effort on my part. And it's not like Jake is a contender, he's just there for decoration. Ohh didn't feel good when I said that, maybe he is more than just a hot presence in my life.

Okay confused now.

"Lisa?"

"Hmmmm?"

Snapped out of my thoughts to see all attention is on me.

"Tch, daydreaming again," Mrs Crankshaw scoffed, "are you going to call in a vote?"

Oh I'm up.

"Err yes Mrs Crankshaw good point, okay umm, first of all is there any discussion on this before we put it to a vote?"

"Lisa we just did that, weren't you listening?" Mrs Crankshaw tutted again.

"She's probably dreaming about all those hotties she has following her at the moment," Betty said.

Sniggers all round.

Except Mrs Crankshaw who looks annoyed, this isn't like her; normally she is the one stirring at any chance to have a laugh at my expense. Hmm she really must be upset about this.

To be honest if they cancel the CWA tomorrow then that would mean I have more time for my up-and-coming romance so maybe it's a good thing. After all if I do get a man and have babies, with work and the B&B I'm not going to have time for community stuff.

"Righto so we have done that, well okay so everyone's all good with it, then we will errrr, carry on with this vote."

"Lisa," interrupted Maggie, coming to my rescue, "we just had a discussion on whether we find a new venue or close this division of the CWA."

"Ohhh okay…" not sure what the protocol of calling a vote as official as this is, but I'm sure if I use the right words I can wing it. I clear my throat.

"Ahem, attention, the chair now moves a motion to vote, now um… hands up who would like to pursue another venue?"

Hmmm only one person, who happens to be Maggie.

"And a show of hands for the other," I continue.

"You can't say 'other' Lisa you have to say the words to make it official," said Mrs Crankshaw sounding like she is fighting back tears.

In fact all of them look sullen.

"Okay," I pressed on a bit confused with what is going on here, "hands up those who wish to close this division of the CWA?"

Show of reluctant hands all around.

"Well then, vote carried. I move a motion that the group, no… sorry, CWA, I mean *Taromeo Division* of the CWA will then be terminated from um… next month, can I get a seconder for this?"

Jeez I'm getting good at this, think even Mrs Crankshaw is impressed. Hmm okay maybe not, as now the room has burst into hysterical sobbing.

Oh god they are even hugging and I still don't have a seconder to my motion. Mrs Crankshaw is sobbing uncontrollably. I mean did she even take in my official words. I don't get what's going on here. I thought this is what they wanted. God I'm going to have to get to the bottom of this.

Grr now I'm really going to miss all of Home and Away.

"Excuse me, excuse me," I said standing and clapping my hands so I can be heard over the noise of the wailing and sobbing. All eyes turn to me as they dab their eyes and blow their noses. I take my seat again.

"If you are all upset about closing then why did you vote for closure?"

"Because it just seems an easier option," said Mrs Crankshaw.

"Easier option than what?" I asked confused, "finding another building for headquarters, I mean pff do we really need a building? We can have our meetings anywhere, in fact the local pub now caters for community meetings and you could always have it at the B&B, Sid loves making coffee."

"Yes Lisa," said Gloria, who was sitting on the other side of Maggie, "I hear what you are saying but our books are dry, there is no money in the kitty. And by giving up the venue it means we don't have a current license or kitchen facilities to handle food for fundraising, it's compulsory nowadays and you know the CWA has been built on the reputation that we share our kitchen skills and recipes, it just doesn't seem right without it."

Is this what the big fuss is all about? For some reason I feel a control need rising, not sure where it's coming from but it's like someone flicked the power switch in me. I mean they are just going to give up on 100 years of community service all because they don't have a license or facilities to handle food.

Oh god why oh why do I have to care, whatever happened to care factor zero?

I'm really going to get home late tonight.

Groaning I stood from my chair again.

"So that's it then," I said in my leadership voice that is only reserved for like… well, never, "you're just going to let a simple thing like a bloody food license and a kitchen get in the way of 100 years of bloody community service?"

"Lisa, language!" scolded Mrs Crankshaw.

"Have we or have we not had successful fundraisers in the past?" I continued, ignoring Mrs Crankshaw's scolding.

Slight murmurs of agreement all round.

"Have we or have we not pulled through when Pamela Horton used us to siphon funds?"

Disapproving agreement all round.

"Did we give up making jam when there were whispers of homeware tampering going on?"

Quiet comments of 'no we didn't'.

"Have we or have we not pulled through by selling adult products to raise the finances when Betty here needed her breasts removed?"

Murmurs of hope this time.

Running with the adrenalin that is building in my veins I jump on the table to drive my message home. I look down to see Mary with the video camera rolling again.

"Did we or did we not pull through when we were being investigated for selling cannabis in our eye pillows?"

A series of 'yes's' from below as Betty adjusts her hearing aid.

"And are we banding together TO CONTINUE TO FEED A BUS-LOAD OF YOUNG MEN NOW THEY'RE IN TOWN?!"

Chants of 'hell yes' all round.

"So are we going to let an empty bank account get in our way?!"

"Hell no!"

"Are we going to let a silly thing such as a food license and lack of kitchen get in the way of our fundraising?"

"Hell no!"

"And are we going to be defeated?!"

"No we are not!"

I can see the excitement in their eyes and even Fran has dropped her knitting to get amongst it, in fact I haven't seen them more lively since… well again, never.

Now I know how Martin Luther King felt when he delivered the greatest speech of all time. If there wasn't a risk of this table flipping or standing on Maggie's fingers I'd be pacing it right now.

"And who are we?"

"The CWA."

"And what does that stand for?"

"Chicks With Attitude," shouted Betty, driving her fist into the air.

"So are we going to terminate?!"

"Hell no!"

Sounds of applause ring through the little room and I don't think we need to do a revote. I turned to Gloria to see if she has recorded the original vote in the minutes but in a defiant act she tears the sheet of paper from her notebook and rips it in half, causing more applause and cheers all round.

Even Mrs Crankshaw who is always a stickler for the rules of the association is cheering and whooping.

Seeing the new enthusiasm in the room has snapped me out of my gloomy mood, if a little thing like no money and no venue doesn't stop a group of four old women, two middle aged women, and me, from continuing on handing down a community service, then why let a simple thing like no dates stop me from producing a dating show. All I have to do is come up with a different strategy, I mean did I quit when Millie said a move to the country is bad, no. Did I quit when Millie said starting a wedding planning business by making up fake clients was bad, no. Did I quit when Millie said a petting zoo was not a good idea, no. Did I quit when Millie tried to tell me a dating show wasn't a good idea due to me being desperate for a man, no.

Actually when you say it like that it sounds like the problem here is Millie.

But after all I have come a long way since leaving the city three years ago. I'm not that impulsive girl who gives up at the drop of a hat, in fact I think maybe I have found my true self, maybe I will be a filmmaker, get my voice heard, showcase myself to the world, maybe I don't need a man.

Who am I kidding; of course I need a man.

Sounds of cheers and applause are starting to waiver and I just don't want to lose the moment.

"So what are we going to do about it?!" I said throwing my arms in the air.

Stunned silence suddenly fills the room.

"Well I don't know dear," said Betty in a quiet puzzled voice, "we haven't really thought about it."

16

Day 3, 5.30am.

Yes 5.30am.

Yes I'm walking down the road.

Yes I have been at Jake's… again.

There I said it.

But this time we didn't spend the night playing scrabble.

Well it wasn't entirely my fault; after the CWA meeting where it was decided everyone was to go home and think about a fundraising plan to get us back on our feet before another meeting was to be held the next day, I was feeling so empowered I was going to spend the evening planning another strategy for continuing the coup on Brendon's production until I steered the car into my driveway and Jake was parked there waiting for me.

I couldn't let Millie see him; in fact I was horrified he was there. Didn't he realise the danger he put himself in? Not to mention the explaining I would have to do if she discovered he was here, but luckily for Jake, Millie and Sid had gone into the city to see Sid's aunty (which is also Millie's biological aunty but Millie doesn't like me to mention that).

Jake said he just called around to see how I was and knew that I was on my way home (he's not telepathic or anything it's because Mrs Crankshaw phoned and told him the good news about the CWA) and he brought a bottle of wine, so what else was I meant to do? I mean he brought wine. So I parked my car, ran inside to make out I'm in bed asleep, locked the bedroom door from the inside again so Millie doesn't come barging in, jumped out window into Jake's ute and well… let's just say after a little wine, okay, a lot of wine…

Fine. I got drunk and ended up sleeping with Jake.

There it's out now.

Also so hungover now.

And I was expecting to feel all regretful but in fact I don't, I feel just fine about it, must be my new sense of empowerment.

Jake wanted me to stay and have breakfast but I just cannot bring myself to deal with both Millie and Matt if they found out where I have been for the past three nights so I think I'll just keep this to myself.

Unless it gets serious… oh my god what if the father of my babies will be Jake Crankshaw? I mean he would make beautiful babies and he has really changed. I would like to say we spent all night talking and making love but I drunk so much wine that after a very blurred conversation and a quick round of sex, I fell asleep. But all the same it was a great night.

And Millie and Matt will just have to suck it up, in fact I don't really care what they think, after all it was Millie who let him on the pretend 'dating show', what was she expecting me to do with him, ignore him?

But all the same I'm not going to tell them yet.

Getting closer to the house and a sense of déjà vu is happening, no surprises there as my footprints from yesterday are embedded in the dirt and it's like following a trail of breadcrumbs home, I just hope that… oh no, I was afraid of this.

"Lisa!" called Jamie waving frantically as I approached the fence.

"Fancy seeing you here again, I was hoping you would arrive," said Jamie like an excited kid, as I struggled through the fence, my head pounding with every movement. "I was so inspired by your meditation yesterday, it lifted me to a higher level, you really are a great teacher," he beamed.

You know I really should go out with Jamie, after all he is the only one of the group (well okay besides Jake) that didn't think the small misunderstanding in the olive groves yesterday was anything out of the ordinary, in fact it inspired him, or so his text message said later that day.

But I won't go out with Jamie because he has long matted hair and I can only imagine what is living in there.

"Yeah no worries," I mumbled as I picked up my bag containing my phone and unused condoms and dragged my tired carcass towards the house, stumbling on the uneven terrain of the cow paddock. Not really into meditation today so I'm just going to tell Jamie that enough thanks has been given and I'm going to sneak into bed and give thanks in my sleep. But now Jamie has seen me. I should have just gone around the normal way to the house, you know up the driveway, but still cannot risk Millie seeing me.

Wait a moment.

"Jamie how do you get here every morning?" I asked, "I mean don't you stay with the others at Daniel's place?"

"Oh yes," he said, "but Sid is kind enough to come and get me every morning, after all Sid has to agree with me that meditation is sooo important to everyone's wellbeing even though he doesn't have much time for it any more. So he offered to pick me up seeing as he goes into town every morning at 5am anyway."

Oh shit that's right I forgot Sid often goes into town to catch the markets and get fresh milk and bread. Which means Millie is sometimes up at that time…

"I am glad you're here," said Jamie, "I did ask Millie to see if you are awake, she banged on the door a few times but it's obvious now you were already here. Just love your enthusiasm Lisa."

… yep and just as I suspected, there is Millie, standing on the porch looking my way and even though there is a fair amount of distance between us, the look of suspicion on her face is enough, and what makes it worse is she looks like she has settled in for the show. I'm so pleased my phone is out of battery otherwise she would be texting her displeasure.

Bugger and damn, I was hoping to avoid this, especially now I have a hangover, but I'll have to go along with this meditation facade. Millie is no fool, so hoping it'll give me enough time to come up with a valid reason why for the third time in three days I have ended up in a cow paddock at 5.30 in the morning when my bedroom door is locked from the inside.

Thank god it's just Jamie and I, oh and by the looks of Sid jogging for the fence line, Sid as well. I don't know if I could've faced all the other men at this hour of the morning especially after spending the night with Jake, it kinda puts the game on a new level.

And when I say 'new level' I mean I'm not really interested in anyone else any more.

"I'm here," panted Sid, "have I missed anything?"

Hopefully meditation won't last long because I think I'm going to throw up.

"No we haven't started yet mate," beamed Jamie, "Lisa here was about to start."

"Okay, Mother, Mother hear our voice," I chanted in a non-interested voice.

"We haven't done our breathing yet," interrupts Jamie.

"Fine, deep breath then," I continued in my drone voice that is reserved for moments when I just don't want to be here. I glanced towards the house while sounds of inhaling and exhaling are coming from Jamie and Sid and yep bloody Millie is still standing there. Why is it that she can sense the bloody moment something is going on, in fact if I didn't know any better I'd swear she stalks me day and night.

And I have really got to start to not give a rats what Millie thinks, after all it's my life, I can see whomever I like whenever I like and if I want to climb out my bedroom window to do so, I will. But if she does make it her business and asks me where I was this morning I'll just tell her I have taken up early morning walking.

I mean, what is she, my mother?

My god this fresh air and empty stomach is not doing me any good at all, really really want to throw up.

Think I should give meditation a miss, hmmm but feeling Millie's eyes on me it might just be better to avoid questions and get this over with.

"Lisa?"

"Oh yeah right, okay, breathing over. Mother, Mother hear our voice," I mumbled waving one arm around in mid air, "hear our thanks and all that."

"No Lisa it's not like that," said Sid squinting in the distance towards the road. "Hey is that your parent's Winnebago coming down the road?"

"What?"

Please tell me Sid has early morning-itis and cannot see straight.

Oh shit, that does look very much like parents.

But what are they doing here?

Bloody Millie, I bet she rung them to tell on me the minute she suspected I was up to something and they have driven at high speed to make sure they get here in time so as not to miss making my life even more complicated.

Okay maybe Millie didn't do that but some heads-up on their arrival would be nice. Unless it's not them and it's some lost tourist in a similar Winnebago.

Please don't turn into here, please don't turn into here.

Oh bugger, shit, damn.

5.52am.

Yes my parents are here.

"Lisa what were you doing out in the cow paddock if you have the flu?" Mum growled as Sid is throwing hot water on the timber porch to rid it of the vomit I just expelled from my mouth, while Dad is looking sideways at Jamie and praying he is not my latest boyfriend.

"I haven't got the flu," I groaned, but feeling slightly better now the excess alcohol has been removed from my system.

Running towards the house in a blind panic after seeing parents turn up unexpectedly wasn't good for churning stomach, but I was trying to get to parents before Millie did and filled them in on things happening here, like bus-load of men and dating show. But instead of offering a welcoming greeting to parents, they arrived on porch to witness daughter emptying contents of the night before all over the polished timber while Millie is trying to offer comfort and not start hurling herself.

"I must have eaten something bad," I groaned again.

"Well you look terrible."

Yep Mum's here.

"You're not feeling well and you still turned up to give thanks to the earth?" asked Jamie looking concerned, "oh Lisa you are such a giving person."

"Yes she just gave all over the porch," joked Sid.

"Give thanks to whom?" Mum asked in her polite voice with a hint of sarcasm in the tone, you know the one.

"The earth and all it has to offer Mrs Collins. Can I call you Mrs Collins?" Jamie said, taking Mum's hand while Dad has a discreet fit at the sight of some long haired lout laying hands on Mum. "Lisa is an earth child and I am honoured to participate in her morning ritual of giving thanks. She has inspired many men in her teachings to appreciate the planet that gives us life and energy."

Millie is sniggering behind her hand.

"Lisa has a ritual?" Mum asks puzzled and looking uncomfortable as Jamie continues to hold her hand.

Is that all Mum heard, 'ritual', nothing about many men?

"May I just say it's a pleasure to meet the mother of such a special woman," Jamie continued, "I hope your stay here is a pleasant one," Jamie said releasing Mum's hand.

"And you are?" Dad asks as he folds his arms across his chest.

"Think a cup of tea may be the go," Millie said coming to my rescue before I die with embarrassment and she explodes with laughter.

"Sounds great," said Jamie following Millie into the house.

"Oh yes let me have a cuddle of my little darling Amy," Mum said forgetting the scene that just happened for the opportunity to have a cuddle with Amy.

So that just leaves me and Dad and a great heap of awkwardness.

6.54am, breakfast table.

Someone kill me now.

"Lisa get your head off the table!" Mum growled as Sid brings another round of coffee to the table.

So far I have managed to avoid filling Mum and Dad in on what has been happening here due to a showing of their recent snaps from Queensland. Dad took the opportunity to show how advanced he is in the technology department by showing the holiday pictures off on his new *tablet*.

Dad is still weary of Jamie who is sitting beside Mum getting enthused about the holiday snaps. Honestly you would think Mum and Dad brought pictures back from Mars by the way he is acting. Occasionally Mum and Dad flick glances at me waiting for me to explain who Jamie is and I have to say how proud I am of Millie because it's now been 62 minutes since parents arrival and so far she hasn't mentioned anything about the dating show, or in her case, the tourism documentary; or my little episode at the olive groves, or the fact we are entertaining a bus-load of men at the moment.

So it may be that we can get through parent's visit without revealing any information about daughter's life. Which brings me to my next question.

"So what brings your um, surprise visit?" I asked in my voice that sounds like I'm pleased they are here; but I'm not really.

Okay Mum has pursed her lips, this is going to be bad.

Dad puts down the tablet while Mum retrieves her purse from the floor beating Jamie to it as he almost falls out of his chair to help retrieve it for her.

"Well this!" Mum said puzzled as she pulls out a piece of paper revealing the advert that Brendon had placed for the dating show. "We thought nothing of it at first, actually to be honest I thought it was a better idea than those a lot of reality shows on television, so it got me thinking it may be a good thing for Joan's oldest boy, you know Joan that used to live across the road from Ray and Linda down in Adelaide? No you probably won't remember dear you were only nine when we stayed at Linda and Ray's. Anyway Joan's son has been having a hard time with the girls apparently and he is a bit partial to country life according to Linda so I logged on to the site to find out how you go about nominating someone and Linda too thought it was a splendid idea when I rang her to have a chat, but I was a bit surprised when the girl on the website looked very much like you."

Okay think I'll just place my head back down on the table, it's much nicer down here.

"So anyway, I commented to your father about the remarkable resemblance and on closer inspection we started to think it was you, so then we thought you must have taken up modeling or something which was very likely since you work with a photographer…"

Argh! *In partnership* with a photographer, *in partnership*, not *working with*. Which part of *'Cannon and Collins. Photography, Event Planning and Supplies'* do they not get!?

"So anyway your father looked a bit closer and saw it was indeed Daniel's logo on the website and then it occurred to us that *'The Country Girl Wants a Husband'* was indeed you."

"So we were a bit concerned poppet you may have gotten yourself into something that could potentially be harmful," Dad added.

"No, I'm fine," I mumbled from behind my mop of hair which had fallen around my face as my forehead remains planted on the kitchen table.

"So it wasn't you then?" asked Mum.

"Looks awfully like you," said Dad holding up the tablet so everyone can see.

"Does look very much like her Mr Collins," commented Jamie "but maybe it is just someone who looks similar,

I believe everyone has a lookalike out there, maybe you have found Lisa's."

"Yes I think you could be right there," says Mum squinting at the image on the website, "this lady seems to have more of an orange tinge to her hair."

"It *is* me," I sighed from the depths of my kitchen table top.

"So what are you doing advertising yourself on the internet?" asks Dad.

"What happened to your hair?" Mum asks, "did you do that on purpose?"

"Is this something to do with myface?" Dad commented, "all those 'selfies' you youngins put up?"

"No," I mumbled, "it's meant to be a website promoting a dating program that was meant to be filmed here."

"I'm on a dating show?!" Jamie exclaimed.

"Who is making this film?" Dad asks.

"Lisa get your head off the table and talk to your father please!" growled Mum.

I could really do with Millie's input right about now but for the first time in the history of our friendship she has decided it is *not* the time to voice her opinion.

Raised my head from the table to explain just as Brendon entered the kitchen, yep right on cue like in the movies, think I'll put my head back down again.

8.50am, back in blissful territory of bedroom.

Had to climb back through the window again so really must come up with a different strategy of sneaking out of the house unnoticed if I'm going to continue to see Jake.

After polite exchanges of good mornings all round from Brendon to my parents, I introduced them and explained that Brendon was here to do a 'promotional documentary' of the area and further explained that we did come up with the idea of *'The Country Girl Wants a Husband'*, hence the advert, but due to lack of applications we had to rethink the whole idea and came up with the mystery bus tour to promote the area, so are now playing host to a bunch of miners from out west for a week.

So Mum and Dad are now satisfied and think it was a splendid idea of Brendon's to produce a country show about the area rather than a 'tarted up version of The Farmer Wants a Wife' (Dad's words) and after I endured a 20 minute hug session from Jamie about 'accepting myself after rejection and inviting the realm of love back into my life' I have now escaped to my bedroom to get ready for the day's events while Mum and Dad are outside setting up the Winnebago for a week long stay.

Cannot stop thinking about Jake.

Not that I can remember a hell of a lot from last night but feel very, very empowered today.

Must have been the sex.

I really don't want to go anywhere today except my bed as am feeling very tired but the prospect of seeing Jake again is very alluring, even though I won't be able to talk to him because of Matt's presence, so I'll just have to suck it up, put my wellness hat on and get dressed. Right after I lie on my bed for a while.

Not sure how long I have been blissfully lying here as trying hard not to nod off. I'm seriously thinking of not attending and just texting Jake and telling him to also pull a sickie so he can sneak in though the bedroom window and lay here with me, when the universe must have heard my plan and sent Millie in.

"Hey guess what?" she said gingerly knocking at my slightly ajar door. "The tour of the cheese factory at Robinson has been postponed until tomorrow as they double booked, so you're off the tour bus for now."

Yay.

Well no wonder, the universe heard my plan and they didn't want me to vomit all over the cheese. I mean today of all days when I'm hungover and have a weak stomach I could have ended up in a cheese factory smelling fermented cheese.

"Thought you would be pleased given your current state," she said hearing my relief from under the cover, "the men are pleased as well as the cricket is on today."

"But that's miles away Millie," I said confused, "isn't this suppose to be about the local area?"

"Yes but we're scheduled to go to the Crankshaw farm and watch the milking so thought it may be a good idea to show them where the milk goes to from this area," said Millie placing her hand on my forehead to check if I have a temperature.

"Oh so it is self inflicted," she commented.

"Tour of cheese factory and milking at Crankshaw's farm, gee I bet the tourists are going to want to flock here," I said in my sarcastic voice from the depths of my bed covers.

"It's actually more of a documentary about social interaction in the bush than a tourist promotion Lisa," reminded Millie, "and you cannot say you're not having fun, after all they are a great bunch of guys and they seem to be enjoying themselves."

"Yeah only 'cause they are getting free food and accommodation, would have been better if it was a dating show," I mumbled.

Millie rolled her eyes.

"So we are due to move out at 3pm this afternoon to watch the milking at Crankshaw's farm," she said, making her way towards the door.

Boo.

But yay for having the rest of the morning to lie here. I waited for Millie to exit the room before I checked my phone to see if Jake has texted me.

And he hasn't. The bastard.

But then gently reminded myself there's a big possibility he's sleeping himself as he too endured a big night so he's off the hook for now. I have also just realised Millie hasn't questioned or made any reference to the fact she caught me in a cow paddock at 5.30am for the third morning in a row, so I'm a little afraid of that, you know calm before the storm and all that.

Set my alarm for this afternoon so as not to miss the big tour of extracting milk from cow's boobies. And now for morning of blissful sleep.

I'll just check again to see if Jake has texted me first. Still nothing, must be worn out.

Okay, sleep now.

Ohhh phones ringing, must be Jake.

"Jake," I said in my sexy but cute voice.

"Who? No dear it's me, Betty."

Oh god what does she want? "I'm sleeping."

"I've had a bit of an epiphany."

"About??"

"About a fundraising idea to get the CWA on track."

Groan.

"After your little speech last night about not giving up, I got really revved up and motivated. I've been thinking about it all night dear."

"Betty couldn't it have waited until later, we're having another meeting tonight remember?"

"Lisa I won't remember what it is tonight that's why I have to tell you now, that's why it's called an epiphany."

"Okay," I sighed, "let me hear it."

"I propose we do a lemonade stand."

Oh god.

"The thought came to me just this morning actually as I was waiting for the post office to open," Betty continued, "I needed some more postage stamps as I used the last one up sending a birthday card to my nephew in England, he is 41 now, married to a lovely woman; anyway I got there early before opening so I'd miss the crowd and as I was sitting outside waiting I watched as the regular buses that have the men in them, pull up to use the public toilets, some fine looking men on those buses, well dressed for mine workers."

Please, please be going somewhere with this.

"… and I thought to myself dear, they must be thirsty, coming all that way and they have a long journey ahead of them, and they only have a ten minute stop, not enough time to wander around the shops, so I was thinking if we set up a lemonade stand maybe even offering cups of tea for a gold coin donation outside the bus stop, we may pull in a bit of money dear and it's offering a fine service at the same time."

Okay in other circumstances it would sound like a fabulous idea but given the fact I'm lying in bed wanting to sleep it just sounds like hard work.

I rolled over on to my back and rubbed my brow.

"That's great Betty, well done; it's noted, now if you would excuse me…"

"Actually 'here for all your services' should be our new motto," said Betty getting enthusiastic, "do you think the others would agree if I made up a banner?"

"Yes brilliant," I mumbled from the depths of my tired throat, "banner, brilliant. Now if you will excuse me…"

"Shall I phone Mrs Crankshaw and let her know?" Betty asked.

"Yes I think you should," I said, winding up the conversation.

"Okay dear I'll see you tonight."

"Yes, yes, goodbye."

Checked phone in small glimmer of hope that Jake may have texted me during that period of conversation but nothing on the screen.

Okay not to panic I'm sure he's just sleeping.

Placed phone down again and went back to grabbing bed covers in preparation for blissful uninterrupted sleep.

"Hey sleepyhead," Brendon said entering the room in a chirpy manner. "Don't mind me I'm just here to get some comments about how the week is going," he said removing the clothes that are littering the only chair in my room and sitting down. "I'm taking advantage of this morning's cancelation and doing some interviews, but when you're ready," he said playing around with the buttons on his camera.

What is wrong with people, do I look like I'm ready for an interview?

Ohhh text message just came through. And it's from Jake.

'good morning sexy, r u ready to run away with me?'

Oh my god is he serious or just being funny?

I don't know how to reply to that, there is no smiley face or xx after it, sort of sounds like a rhetorical question.

Brendon is still fiddling with something on his camera waiting for the opportunity from me to give him something worth filming but I'm just going to ignore him for now,

I mean my future all depends on how I reply to this text message, I don't have time for distractions.

I'm going through a million scenarios in my head when Matt abruptly enters the room.

"Oh good, you're awake," he said as he heads towards my closet and starts raking through my clothes.

"Matt what are you doing!?"

"Picking sumfing for you to wear on your lunch date wif Damo."

"Pardon?" I spluttered, "what lunch date?"

"Well he's getting fucked off wif waiting so I told him he can have his date wif you today, he's taking you out for lunch."

"I thought you said you don't want to date young men?" asked Brendon puzzled.

"I don't," I sighed, slightly panicked as Matt is throwing clothes at me from my wardrobe, "Matt I cannot go on a date today I have the flu."

"Not wot Millie said and we had a deal remember."

"Deal?" asked Brendon as he all of a sudden stops fiddling with whatever was hindering his camera and starts filming.

"Yeah Damo wants a date wif Lisa 'cause he couldn't apply to the dumb arse dating fing 'cause Lisa is ageist."

"Oh my god Matt that doesn't even make sense."

And another text message has come through from Jake, it reads, 'well?'

He *was* expecting a reply. Talk about pressure.

"You could wear this," Matt continues, taking a summer patterned dress from its hanger.

I cannot cope with this; really need to answer Jake… god phone's ringing.

"Hello," I said with urgency.

"Lisa luv, it's Betty, Fran is with me she popped in for a cuppa on her way to pick up her prescription, her carpal tunnel is getting worse poor thing, anyway she is just giving me a hand with the banner and we are in a bit of pickle as we have two slogans here but are not sure which one to choose so 'here for all your services' or 'CWA for all your service needs'. Which one is better dear?"

Grrrr haven't got time for this.

"The second one," I said quickly, aware that another text message has arrived on my phone, before abruptly hanging up.

"Nah too flowery," said Matt throwing yet another dress onto the already clothes strewn bed.

'I'm waiting', Jake's text message reads. Oh god I don't know what to say.

Oh god another text message; 'well?'

"Who's on da phone?" Matt pressed, stopping his activity briefly to put his hand on his hip demanding an answer like my mother.

"No-one!" I said irritably as I send a 'yes' back to Jake before he sends another message.

I am not going to get out of this date and Brendon is looking utterly confused with the prospect of me going out on a date with Damo, so in order to get Matt off my back I'm just going to have to get this over with and let Matt know in advance that it will be the worse 60 minutes of my life.

Date with Damo.

Why does Brendon insist on coming?

Okay he didn't exactly tag along with me, but he is also in the local café where Damo has taken me for our lunch date. And I'm sooo mortified because everyone knows me and I can see the girls behind the counter already whispering and pointing.

Didn't get a reply from Jake after I sent him my 'yes' to his question about running away, so I'm a bit worried, I mean what if he's freaking out and packing his bags for a quick escape *from* me, or took me seriously and is now in my bedroom packing my bags for a quick joint getaway.

Best not to think about that at the moment.

Actually on second thought, Brendon must have followed me here because even in a small town like this it's still not that small a world that the amateur film guy who is making a documentary on social interaction would happen to be in the same place with his main subject who was out on a forced date with local youth half her age. Hmmmm.

Matt is also parked across the street, he thinks I cannot see him but if he truly wants to play detective then why the hell he would arrive in the same van that has been transporting us all week is beyond me.

"Thanks for coming out with me" said Damo in an awkward voice as our coffees are delivered by a smirking waitress who happens to hang out in the same circles as Damo and Matt. "I just felt a bit, well you know, since that night I didn't want you to think that I didn't appreciate it, or you for that matter," he quickly said.

Okay confused but just want this over with so I'll run with it.

Damo has made a bit of an effort today, he has pulled his jeans up just passed his hips and swapped his black skull tee-shirt for a nice grey one.

"Oh that's fine," I scoffed, "you know onwards and upwards."

On god I've just spied Betty on the grassy knoll across the road, hope she doesn't see me.

"Well this is the reason I wanted to take you out today," continued Damo, running with a little confidence he suddenly found hidden deep down, "I just need to know where I stand so I can move on. I know it was my first time so I guess it's only natural I cannot stop thinking of you."

Fran and Mary are also there with Betty and they look like they are setting up tables on the grassy area outside the public amenities.

"First time for what?" I said turning back to Damo just as our toasted sandwiches arrive, bought by the same smirking young waitress. Not sure what he is going on about but he did say something about first time. I don't want to turn him down before I finish lunch as I am a bit peckish and it would be a little awkward for him, I mean it's kinda sweet he made an effort. And away from Matt, Damo seems, well normal, so I'll just keep conversation up at the moment.

Also I think Matt is timing our date, so a quick getaway may be out of the question.

Oh Betty's convinced John from the Parks Committee to help her with a shade gazebo. Wonder what she is up to.

"You know... my first time," said Damo looking slightly awkward.

"First time?" I asked again puzzled, before finally getting what Damo was trying to say without saying it, "ohhh first time," I said nodding in a knowing way.

Brendon is sitting at a table in the corner looking down at his camera screen which is pointing in our direction.

Hmmmm.

"Yeah, I hope this is not making you awkward?" asked Damo.

"About your first time?" I smiled trying to ease his awkwardness, "no not at all, everyone has a first time. I remember what mine was like," I said taking a bite of my sandwich, "cringe at the thought now."

Drifting back to the memory of the first time I had sex with David Masey in his bedroom while his parents watched 'Night Rider' in the next room. I can still hear the theme music in my ears some times when sex is mentioned.

"Well I just wanted you to know that even though I like you a lot and it would be cool to have a girlfriend like you, I wouldn't expect a relationship just 'cause we, you know..."

Okay now Maggie has arrived across the road and it looks like some debate is going on amongst the four of them.

Definitely looks like a CWA thing and god I hope they don't see me, as then they will rope me into their little debate which I haven't got time for at the moment. Better start moving this date with Damo along a bit quicker so I can get out of here before they spot me.

"So Damo do you have a job?" I asked turning my attention back to him, interrupting whatever he was saying.

"Um yeah, I'm a goldfish breeder," he said sounding slightly annoyed.

"Really! I didn't know there was such a thing; I mean is that a real job?"

"Look Lisa I think you're being a bit rude," he continued, "I've been trying to clear the air between us and you seem to be avoiding the question."

Shit, sudden outburst of assertiveness from stoner Damo, he obviously hasn't had his morning bong.

"Sorry," I apologised "it's just that well you and I both know Damo it's not going to work with us," I soothed, "after all I'm twice your age and…"

"That's what I've been trying to say," said Damo irritably, "yes I like you heaps, you're a cool chick and thanks for being my first but we don't need to go out just 'cause we done it."

"Your first!?" I spluttered.

"Yeah."

"As in first date?"

"No, as in first… you know."

"Virginity?" I spluttered, my eyes involuntary widening like frisbees.

"Yeah."

"You're blaming me?" I said tying hard not to raise my voice, well aware that the rumours have already started around town that I am dating a variety of men including stoner Damo.

"Um, you were there," he said looking slightly embarrassed, "don't you remember?"

"I was there when your virginity was taken, are you trying to be funny, why would I want to see such a thing?"

"You took it," said Damo looking mortified, "oh god you must have been more out-of-it than I thought," he said, burying his head in his hands.

"When did this happen?" I cried, my chest hurting from trying to keep calm and not scream.

"The night we went to the Ute Muster Ball, we ended up back at Daniel's and you were upset about having no-one 'cause Daniel just told you he was gay and you were feeling bad that you were turning 40 so to make you feel better I told you that I'm still a virgin at 20 and how vulnerable and out of place I felt about it. And that's when you suggested that we could... well you know. I know you did it 'cause you felt sorry for me but that's okay."

"39!" I reminded him, "I turned 39 not 40! But I woke up in Daniel's bed?" I said, slightly stunned from what I had just heard.

Actually come to think of it I shouldn't be that stunned, it's not the first time I have had relations with a youth and not remembered it.

Oh my god, there are words for people like me!

"Yeah, we didn't want Matt to catch us so you jumped into Daniel's bed, Daniel didn't mind, he slept on the couch."

Memories of discovering discarded condoms packets in Daniel rubbish bin comes flooding back and I compose myself.

"I'm pleased we had this conversation," I said, "and I'm pleased we used, you know… condoms," I said in my lowest of low voices trying not bring up images in my head.

Okay Damo's suddenly looking embarrassed and uncomfortable at the same time.

"What now?" I sighed.

"Um… we didn't," he said in his lowest voice, "Matt and Daniel used them to make water bombs and they used them all up. I wasn't going to do it," he said quickly, "honest, but you said it was fine as I was a virgin and you hadn't slept with anyone since Rick a year ago and well… you said you were protected with some white light, I duno what that is, but modern medicine changes all the time."

"I what?" I spluttered, "um Damo I'm not protected in *that* way," I squawked, "I meant… oh lord knows what I meant."

"Yeah but you still wanted to do it," said Damo sheepishly.

Oh god, so I went and had unprotected sex with Damo while I was drunk and had orange hair.

That's it!

From next week I'm giving up alcohol and booking myself in for counseling.

17

"Look Damo I appreciate you telling me all this and I am sooo sorry if I took your… you know. I hope it was just as special … wait a minute…" glancing out the window to the crowd across the street which has again caught my eye, I can see Betty standing up on a wooden crate belting out some speech through a loudspeaker while the buses that house the miners pull up in front. I cannot make out the banner which she has strewn above the gazebo which was shading some trestle tables laden with…

Oh bloody hell.

Abruptly got up, excusing myself from Damo in a rushed manner. Clearly Betty and the CWA team decided to go ahead and have the bloody lemonade stand anyway, I mean it has to go passed the other members before this happens and have the appropriate council permits.

Strutting across the street towards them I can feel both Damo and Brendon following me, which confirms my suspicions that Brendon didn't just 'happen to be there'; also confirms that Matt is stalking me because he spots me heading out of the café and ducks out of sight.

Bus-load of men now are all lined up at the CWA stall fishing in their pockets while Betty continues to yell through her loudspeaker.

"What are you doing?" I hissed at Mary who was handing over a paper cup full of slightly yellow liquid.

"The lemonade stand," said Mary puzzled, "we had it on good authority the bus will be here shortly so well, we thought no time like the present."

"Yes but don't we all need to vote first?" I said as Matt casually rocks up beside Damo as if he has just arrived on the scene while Brendon is filming everything. Honestly that guy so needs a lesson in film making.

"But dear, Betty told me you okayed it?" said Mary looking slightly alarmed and upset.

"Are we allowed to do this?" I asked rubbing my brow, "I mean what about a food license and do we have insurance?"

"Shhh," said Mary putting her finger up to her lips in an irritable manner, "we cannot find the insurance certificate and well Mrs Crankshaw normally handles the legal side of things."

"So where is Mrs Crankshaw?" I asked, taking in the line of men and wishing it was *this* bus-load of men that ended up on my pretend non-existent dating show.

"Well that's the thing dear," Mary said lowering her voice and taking me by the arm, leading me away from the table as the sound of coins hitting the money tin ring through the air. "Well we didn't have time to make any lemonade but Fran remembered that we had some bottles of lemon squash left over from our eye-pillow fundraiser last year."

Okay not liking where this is going as we're barely five minutes into doing business and already the phrase 'fresh lemonade' is falsely advertised.

"And so we didn't have time to phone the Crankshaw's so we all jumped in my car..."

"Yes, yes, and?"

"Well when we got to Max and Barb's place, well... there seemed to be a small array of activity going on, very secretive, and Barbara got quite cranky with us arriving unannounced; it was like they were getting prepared to move?"

"Move," I scoffed, "move where?"

"Well there was a small removal van parked there, getting loaded so I guess..."

"What!"

"We did ask Mrs Crankshaw, I mean Barb, what was going on but she seemed a little snappy and didn't really say. Lisa? Lisa where are you going?"

No time to stand and chit-chat,

Mary just said there was a removal van at the Crankshaw's, which only means one thing and that is Jake is leaving, with or without me. Ran to my car at super high speed and quickly unlocked the door and jumped in, about to put car in gear when Brendon jumped in the back seat with his video camera. About to protest about his rude way of hitching a ride but haven't got the time for a debate so told him abruptly to shut the fucken door, and sped off towards the Crankshaw's.

Frantically trying to call Jake but he's not answering his phone. I'm so worried that he is just going to disappear out of my life again, and I cannot make head nor tail of what he wants from me. Although he did text this morning and ask if I wanted to run away with him but really I thought he was just playing around and if he was serious then why hadn't he been in contact with me to tell me he has booked a removal van, I haven't got any messages from him on my phone. Unless he saw me in town with Damo? Oh my god that's it, Jake has heard rumours about my date with stoner Damo in the café, has got upset and hired a removal van and is running away all by himself. Those counter bitches, wait till I see them, spreading rumours like that.

"So where are we going?" piped up Brendon from the back seat trying to steady his video camera and hang on for dear life.

"Going to catch the love of my life before he leaves me again," I cried anxiously negotiating a sharp corner at high speed.

"Oh," said Brendon shrugging slightly, "and what about them?" he asked, pointing to the rearview mirror as the white rest home van driven by Matt, and accompanied by Damo, appear in my line of vision also negotiating the corner at high speed.

"Them? God knows."

My phone starts to ring and I quickly pick it up and look at the display screen in the hope it is Jake but it's not Jake, it's Millie calling.

"Haven't got time for this Millie," I screamed at my ringing phone as I turned into the Crankshaw's road at high speed, it appears I have lost Matt and Damo, which is just as well, don't need Matt's judgment right now, pff, obviously my Toyota can outrun the van any day.

My foot flattens on the accelerator involuntarily as I spy the Crankshaw home up ahead; it appears to be deserted and there is no removal van there. Oh no, it looks like he has gone already, why, why does this happen to me?

Reached the homestead and jumped out of the car as soon as it came to a halt.

Panic set in as I realised the caravan is gone and so is Jake's ute. Bolted into the house with Brendon in hot pursuit, burst through the door and started yelling for Jake. There doesn't seem to be anyone here and the place looks a little empty, in fact, apart from the furniture it looks bare.

Ran back outside and tried to use my supersonic eyes to see if any vehicle is down by the shed but I can't see anything. I spied the old quad bike sitting under the rusted old tin shed. Ah-huh.

"Jump on," I yelled to Brendon, he quickly does so and we speed off towards the milking shed. If Jake has ran off then Max will be able to tell me where he has gone, I can't let him do this to me a second time, I just can't.

Drove at high speed on quad bike as Brendon grips tighter trying to balance his camera on his knee. Hit mud puddle and now Brendon is cursing about mud on his lens but honestly, what does he expect if he wants to join crazed woman on quad bike going at high speed through muddy farm. He is bound to get a little mud somewhere.

Arrived at cow shed and jumped off bike in unladylike manner. Ran into the cow shed but again total silence and no-one to be seen, not even a vehicle in sight, in fact the whole place feels deserted and empty.

Dropping to my knees in despair I cannot believe universe has done this to me, why oh why have they taken Jake away from me for a second time? I mean I'm not a bad person, I have a range of rescued animals, I was even nice to Pamela Horton and she was having an affair with my boyfriend.

"What is going on?" asked Brendon as I continue to kneel on the concrete floor of the cow shed with my head in my hands.

"It's Jake!" I wailed, "he's gone, gone I tell you."

"Gone where?" Brendon asked puzzled.

"I don't know!" I wailed, "that's the problem, he is just gone!"

"Who's gone?" asked Jake, appearing behind me causing me to yelp in fright.

Oh my god he is here.

"What are you doing on the floor?" Jake asks amused, holding what appears to be a fuel container in one hand and a dodgy extension cord over his arm, looking at Brendon with an amused look of confusion while Brendon responds with a shrug.

"Oh never mind," I said pulling myself to my feet and wiping the tears of hysteria from my face, "um, just a misunderstanding."

"You're early," Jake said without question, throwing the cord onto the milking turntable and placing the fuel container on the floor,

"Millie just rang, Matt is on his way with the rest of them shortly. I was just about to grab the quad and meet up with Uncle Max who is bringing the herd up," Jake said dusting off his hands, "but the bike appears to be misplaced," he said with a grin.

"Oh yeah well… errr didn't want to get my car dirty."

Jake grins at me over his shoulder as he exits the shed and kicks the bike into gear to go met up with Max.

Okay now I feel officially silly. I mean yes I have been in situations before that were a little bit silly but this is a lot silly. How could I believe for one second that Jake was going to run off again or that he had heard any rumours about my date with Damo, I mean pfff, there is no sign of a moving van anywhere or that anyone has moved out, except Jake's caravan has gone. But Jake hasn't, so that doesn't explain anything. Really, really must get out of my head.

"So you going to tell me what that was about?" asked Brendon looking into the lens of his camera again.

"Pfff, no!"

4 boring hours later.

Thank god it's all over.

I mean Bear, Paul, Darcy, Captain Sweatpants, Slade and Steel, in fact everyone apart from Jamie who decided to stay behind with Mum and help her with her crochet stitches, found it interesting and fascinating, but I have seen this before so therefore I don't find it interesting and fascinating and if it wasn't for the fact that Jake was there demonstrating and providing me with eye candy, I would in fact be asleep.

But I did notice some very odd behaviour around the farm and it seems like something is not quite right, cannot put my finger on it. Max is acting all coy and secretive which is unlike him and Mrs Crankshaw was looking both solemn and nervous when I saw her from afar, I didn't dare go and speak to her, maybe she found out about what the CWA are doing and is worried about the consequences.

At one stage I slipped out of the shed to get some fresh air and also to check out Jake's ute as I swear I saw boxes stacked up in the back seat. Couldn't get close enough to see what type of boxes as Matt was watching me like a hawk since we were at the Crankshaw farm and had a deal for me not to go near Jake. Plus he's texting me every two minutes about my date with Damo.

Obviously Damo didn't tell Matt about the virginity stealing.

Cringe at the thought of how I could have been so, well, giving. I must have been so desperate that night to pour my heart out to yet another youth who in turn poured his deepest secret out to me, which resulted in pity sex on both counts.

I really must learn not to be such a sensitive person.

But now it's over all I want to do is be with Jake, I had to go with the traffic flow towards the van while Jake got further and further away from me as I was herded into the van like a cow into a stock truck. Brendon borrowed my car to go back and help Millie set up as apparently we are having something called a traditional 'camp oven dinner' tonight, some guy is coming out to cook and prepare beforehand and talk to us about early farm implements and how they were used in the olden days.

Hmm, not sure what I should wear to that. But I think it's safe to say anything slightly modern and hip is out of the question.

But back in the van the atmosphere is buzzing and alive and as Bear pointed out, he has never seen so many tits in one room, which of course led to hoots of laughter from everyone except me who rolled my eyes and continued to look out the window like high and mighty ladylike person.

Well I just cannot be bothered with it all.

Keep checking my phone to see if Jake has texted, but nothing.

I was kinda hoping I would have had the opportunity to stay behind but opportunity didn't present itself so I think I'll just text him a friendly message and ask him if he's coming tonight.

Hmm on second thought I don't want him to think I was pushing anything.

"Sup?" Damo said sporting his newly found confidence with me after our little date of revelations, "didn't get a chance to say cheers for this morning," he continued, "so we good?"

"Yep, we're fine," I said, still not able to look him in the eye.

"That's good," he said, "water under the bridge now."

"Yep," I sighed as a wave of depression comes over me. This week hadn't really turned out as I expected, and it's fair to say operation 'produce dating show Lisa's way' has now been replaced by operation 'get back together with Jake'. And I don't even think that is working out too well.

But back home and despite Damo's attempts at the 'friends' conversation, there is no way it will ever be un-awkward. Man why couldn't it go back to the way it was when I knew nothing of my drunken behaviour and all was well in the world.

Was hoping for some peace but there is a flurry of activity around here once again and I really just want to go back to Jake.

Bear, Paul, Slade and Steel, Darcy and Captain Sweatpants are out at the fire pit that Sid made earlier with the stones he found in the back paddock. It really looks good with the manicured lawn, the seats Sid made out of old sleepers that had been sitting in the old abattoir, and the stack of firewood beside it. I did notice Brendon has been out shooting photos with his camera so Millie must have asked him to take some for the new brochure she is putting together.

It is such a beautiful evening as the sun sets and I must say the atmosphere here is so relaxed. Sid is busy stoking up the fire pit and chatting with the man that has come out to provide us with the camp food this evening, while Millie and Daniel are chatting happily with the men. Matt and Damo are filling eskies up with ice and drinks, Jamie and Mum are doing a crossword puzzle and sharing a glass of ginger beer, and Dad, well Dad looks like he wants to tear Jamie to shreds.

But it is so nice here and I know sometimes I should start to appreciate my surroundings more.

Well I would appreciate it more if Jake was here.

I haven't heard from him for a while and am fighting the urge to message him and ask if he is coming down to join in on the get together, but after last night it's kind of shifted things between us again so I think I should leave it for another hour at least; you know I don't want him to think I am too keen. And judging from his friendly reaction this afternoon I can safely say no rumours about my date with Damo have reached him yet.

Decided to join others around the fire so I grabbed a beer from the cooler and sat down next to Darcy; since Darcy and I have had a sorta date then it's safe to sit by him.
And besides he is one of the few who doesn't think I am mad. Since the little 'misunderstanding' in the olive groves if I was to sit next to Slade or Steel they would discreetly get up and not so discreetly, run.

Brendon has been in my face with his camera, since… well since the 'olive grove situation'. Every time I try to sit and have a conversation he is there. So annoying.
So I'm just not going to talk to anyone. Oh bugger, Mum and Dad have joined us, followed by Jamie.

Well I'll just sit here in total silence in the hope I am left alone, just not in the mood for talking tonight, I feel like a wave of depression has just hit today and it's not even that time of the month.

In fact the only thing cheering me up right now is what seems to be Jamie's obsession with my mother. He doesn't seem to have left her side since meeting her, he has even pitched a tent outside the Winnebago, so funny. Mum is actually leaving me alone for a change, and Dad's too busy keeping an eye on the Jamie situation to worry about what I'm up to.

Staring at the embers of the fire pit while humourous and relaxed chit chat is going on around me I find myself reflecting back on the past week, it was only five days ago I was sooo excited and had high hopes of finding Mr Right from a bus-load of men, not to mention the possibility of stardom by producing a country dating show. Now five days on I am sitting around a campfire with bus-load of men you couldn't pay me to be with, nosy parents, one annoying man with a camera and a local youth whose virginity I stole; only to be obsessing about the ex boyfriend down the road.

Welcome to my sad life.

But all the same, slapped a false grin on my face during dinner, which I have to say was simply delicious, slapped an even falser grin on while listening to camp oven man's rant about farm implements and even falser still when Captain Sweatpants attempted a get-to-know-ya conversation before giving up when he realised we have nothing to talk about.

I miss Jake and I'm soo annoyed he is not here. I keep looking at my phone every five minutes willing it to beep a message, but still nothing.

I wandered into the kitchen to make a cup of tea, as I decided alcohol just leads to promiscuous behaviour, just as Millie was heating Amy's bottle up in preparation for getting her down for the night.

"Oh good just the person I wanted to see, need to talk with you," she said looking passed my shoulder at Brendon who seemed to have followed me into the kitchen unnoticed, his camera in hand as usual.

"Oh sorry," he said after he realised Millie was giving him a 'fuck off this is a private conversation' look. Which means it's a serious conversation she wants to have with me because Millie isn't all about privacy usually.

Millie waited until Brendon backed away before continuing. "Lisa I'm not going to sugarcoat it," she said as she removed Amy's bottle from the microwave and poured a bit of milk on her wrist before popping it back in, "are you seeing toss-pot Jake Crankshaw again?"

Oh god here it comes.

"Who told you that?" I asked, avoiding the question, "was it Matt? The little shit."

"Wasn't anyone," said Millie, "I have eyes, I'm not stupid. Meditation in a cow paddock is not your thing Lisa, neither is 5.30am, didn't take long to figure out where you had been."

Don't know what to say as if I tell Millie I am seeing him then she will judge the situation before it even has time to begin, I mean I'm not even sure if I am 'officially' seeing Jake. But if I tell her I'm not and Jake and I end up getting married and having babies then what?

It's a no win either way.

"Lisa?"

"Just a little bit," I said in a quiet voice hoping it will make the delivery sound better. Also the answer is a compromise, it's telling Millie I am but not in a full on way.

Millie responded with a loud huff as she fetches Amy's bottle out of the microwave again.

"And you haven't learned?" she said, seeming satisfied with the temperature.

I went to say something else but Millie just shook her head and proceeded to exit the room, "whatever, it's your life," she sighed, "just hope you know what you're doing."

"I do know what I am doing," I said to the back of Millie as she leaves.

Well I do, in fact just the thought of him is making me pine even more, I checked my phone again but no messages.

I wander back outside to a waiting Matt. He is still watching me like a hawk, even questioned where I was going when I got up to go to the toilet. Don't know why he cares whether or not I'm seeing Jake, I know he doesn't like the guy but as smart as Matt thinks he is, in a couple of days the men will be gone but Jake will still be here and Matt's threat to tell Millie about me trying to blackmail him will have no merit any more and Millie now knows anyway. So he can watch me for all it's worth but it's not preventing me from seeing Jake. I just have to be a little more secretive about it that's all.

Rejoined the group, who seem relaxed and happy and Dad has even taken his eyes off Jamie for a bit to feed Amy. Brendon has the camera pointed in my direction again and I swear to god he will end up wearing it if he doesn't find something else to film.

"Lisa dear," said Betty pulling me from my thoughts of how I will deal with Brendon and his camera, as she made herself comfortable in a chair with her scooter helmet in her hands.

What! When did she get here?

"Got the strangest requests today at the lemonade stand," she said after nodding a polite greeting to Mum beside her, "well of course it all went well like we thought it would, we made close to two hundred dollars but we have had a lot of enquires about what other services we offer. So I figured we may have to do some scones, maybe Fran can put her magic fingers to work again and offer some neck pillows or something. Although, maybe any sort of pillows are not such a hot idea as I think we have to show them to the local police first, you know dear, to prove the stuffing is not illegal."

"Whatever you think," I sighed trying to steer conversation away from… well trying to end conversation really.

"Lisa?" said Jamie, gently tapping me on the arm and giving Betty's shoulder a quick greeting pat, "when you have finished I would like to converse with you in private," he beamed.

Oh god what does he want to talk about? If it's about meditation I swear to god I'll scream.

"I'll wait," said Betty giving Jamie's hand a quick squeeze in response to his greeting touch, "you two go and have a little talk, I'll just grab a cup of tea."

Jamie gently takes my hand as I drag myself out of the chair in a huff, grabbing my phone as he leads me away from the group. Matt and Millie stare with their eyebrows raised at the sight of Jamie holding my hand leading me away from the circle that surrounds the fire.

He gently lowers me to sit on the edge of the porch steps while I glance at my phone to see if Jake has messaged in the last 40 seconds.

He strokes my hand in total silence like he is pondering something; wish he would get on with whatever he has to say as I really want to get back to my own space.

"Lisa," he begins gently, "ever since I arrived here I feel I have been drawn to you and I feel I was sent here to put right the wrongdoings of the past."

Oh bloody hell, here it comes, Jamie and his spiritual revelations. Not that there is anything wrong with that but I am far more spiritual when I am on my own and no-one is bothering me about *their* spiritual stuff.

"I sense you are truly sad, and feel you are missing something."

Yes, Jake and my own space I said in my head, of course not out loud, my eyes looking everywhere but at his.

Wait, is that Brendon lurking in the shadows with his camera?

"I feel this," he continued, "because I feel we are connected, and even though we haven't known each other for a long time, in fact we have known each other in a previous time, your mother's presence confirms this."

"My mother's presence?" I exclaimed suddenly, diverting my attention away from the lurking shadows, god what has my mother said now?

"Yes your mother and I also have a past life," he beamed, "we are all connected."

Typical, my mother has to be involved in everything.

"Does my mother know this?" I asked in a sarcastic tone, "I mean if Dad finds out…" I said trying to be funny because I'm bored with this conversation and don't really care if Jamie and I are connected in a past life or not, it's this life I'm more interested in and I'm not interested in Jamie.

Oh my god that *is* Brendon lurking in the shadows with his camera. What the hell is he up to?

"Your mother and I had an unfinished life together in medieval times," Jamie continued in a sad tone, "it was such a horrible end," he said shaking his head in despair.

Maybe Brendon is filming Jamie's theoretical performance, 'cause I swear he thinks he is playing a role in a play by the way he dramatises everything.

"Of course I cannot make it right with your mother," he said with regret, "but I can offer something that will fulfill both your needs," he said with all brightness, "so what I am about to offer is from my heart, a gift I want to give you."

"Yes?" I said wanting so much to get this over with.

"Lisa," he begins with an unnecessary pause while he squeezes my hand even more, "I know how much you want to have a baby and Matt tells me your unhappiness is due to your biological clock ticking away. Your soul mate has not yet arrived to give you what you desire at this time so Lisa I want to offer you my seed."

"P... pardon?" I spluttered.

"It would be my honour," he continued like it's no big deal he just offered to father my child, "your mother expressed to me how she would love a grandchild of her own so this is my way of helping you both and making right with the past."

I can hear Brendon sniggering in the shadows and I am beyond speechless, I mean what do you say to an offer like that?

No. You say no.

"There you are!" said Matt suddenly making an appearance out of nowhere looking like he is super pissed off about something.

"So you *are* shagging Jake Crankshaw," exclaimed Matt, "Millie told me all about it."

Well cat's out of the bag now.

"How could you do it wif that idiot?" Matt carried on, "you don't know where he has been apart from my mum and you said you would never go there again Lisa. And what about poor Damo, you went on a date wif him, how would he feel if he had known you were shagging Jake while going on a date with him?"

"Matt, that's none of your business," I said through gritted teeth as I can feel Jamie release his grip from my hand.

Well I guess Jamie's offer of his seed is off the table.

Matt is ranting on and I really want to run away as I can't deal with this, Jamie is now asking if this is true and has assured me Jake is not my soul mate as he feels in his heart it's not him.

Great, now Millie is here wanting to know what is going on.

And here comes Mum.

I really just want to disappear to Jake's as amongst all this chaos and lecturing all I want is him, which proves he must be my soul mate, I don't care that I haven't heard from him or the fact he may want to be left alone, I will go to him.

Right after I figure out how to get to my car without a thousand questions on where I am going.

And get to the house for my car keys and bag.

Okay need universe to provide me with a means of escape.

Over Jamie's shoulder I spied Betty's scooter parked up against the hedge, and I know she always has the key in the ignition.

"What's that?!" I exclaimed, pointing to the sky; as everyone turns to look at the sky I made a beeline towards Betty's scooter, pushing passed Brendon and his camera in my desperate haste for escape.

On the back of Betty's scooter negotiating gravel road at high speed.
I can sense some headlights behind me in the distance and I am aware that I am on an old person's motorised scooter on a country road without a high-vis vest or helmet, so safety is not the best; but I am grateful to the universe for providing me with a mode of transport to escape offers of babies and lectures about current boyfriends. And what I have decided to do is confront Jake and ask him straight out where I stand. I mean it's obvious I still have feelings for him and the crazy thing is, I thought I never did have feelings for him since I spent over a year in a relationship with his twin brother.

I now realise the reason I was so attracted to Rick was because he was a replacement for Jake and the reason I didn't love Rick was because he didn't have Jake's personality.

Man oh man, if I had known riding a scooter down a country road at night would bring out revelations about one's self, I would have stolen one and taken it for a ride much earlier.

The car behind me is getting closer as I stay to the edge of the road trying hard to keep the scooter from wobbling as I signal for the car to go around me, but it doesn't, it is going to insist on sitting up my bum.

As I approach Jake's I can see a faint glow of light coming from the Crankshaw's farm. It's lighting up the night sky like an orb of orange glow, in fact from here it looks like someone is burning a big bonfire, although the way this car is sitting up my bum it could be the reflection from the car headlights.

Concentrating very hard on keeping the scooter from sliding off the edge of the road while continuing to signal the car behind me to go around is proving difficult and the amount of concentration required is doing my head in. Also thoughts of the car behind me being straight out of the movie 'Wolf Creek' is not helping. I can see the Crankshaw's mail box approaching, and breathe a sigh of relief I have made it to my destination without being hijacked by the car behind me.

I carefully head down the driveway so as not to fall into one of the many ruts and holes caused by the weather and cows, I'm thinking it may be faster to ditch the scooter and run from here.

Okay not an option as car behind me has also turned into Crankshaw's driveway.

Now it's beeping its horn at me! Okay *now* it wants to go around.

Turning my head around to abuse car in road rage style tone, I see Matt behind the wheel.

He is heading down the rutty driveway with his head out the side window while Brendon is in the front seat with camera in hand.

And Matt is yelling something at me.

And I bet it's about Jake.

"I can see whomever I like!" I yelled back at him while keeping the wobbly scooter steady, "I don't care if he slept with your mum, I love him!"

"No, look!" Matt yelled pointing up ahead while Brendon drops the camera from his face and goes pale white all of a sudden.

Oh no!

I stop the scooter dead as my jaw drops and Matt pulls up beside me in the car.

"I'll call triple 0," Brendon says reaching for his phone.

The Crankshaw's farm is on fire.

Not just the farm house but the dairy unit as well. And it looks like it has been burning for a long time as it's well ablaze.

The orange glow of the fire stretches for miles into the night sky and the heat from the blaze this close is intense.

Panic sets in as I tried to run towards the inferno to see if Mrs Crankshaw and Max are in there and of course Jake as well but Matt dive tackles me before I could reach the house.

"It's too far gone," he yelled, "you're going to get yourself killed."

I can hear the faint sounds of fire engines coming towards the house and as I look around, there doesn't seem to be any sign of Jake's ute near the house, or the farm bike he was on the last time I had seen him. But the bile rose in my throat at the thought of where Mrs Crankshaw and Max could be.

Millie and Sid have also now arrived, along with some of the men, as they pile out of the car, their jaws dropping with disbelief. I feel helpless and tears of panic are rolling down my cheeks. Matt continues to hang on to me in case I run towards the fire again and the sirens of the emergency crew are getting louder.

"This is why I haven't heard from Jake," I cried to Matt. "He could be trapped in the fire," I wailed as Millie approaches and Matt releases his hold on me.

Matt and Sid jump in the vehicles to move them out of the way to let the approaching fire trucks through. The sight of the fire crew brings sudden relief to me and even though I am trying to block out the image of the possibility that the Crankshaw's may still be inside the burning house, I know Jake is okay, I know this because even through my tears of panic he has appeared to me.

Oh my god Jake really has just appeared in my line of vision.

Oh thank god he is alive!

"You're alive!" I exclaimed as I threw myself at him, Jake gave me a half hearted hug but his eyes the whole time were pinned on the burning inferno in front of him.

"Oh my!" exclaimed Mrs Crankshaw as we all turned around to see her clutching her heart as she and Max climb out of Jake's ute that had pulled up behind us.

Everyone breathes a sigh of relief and Millie leaves me to go and comfort Mrs Crankshaw who has moved to the front of the vehicle still clutching at her chest while Max remains standing at the car door. Mrs Crankshaw looks a little stunned while Max has the strangest look on his face, not a look of shock or disbelief, but more of sadness.

Jake looks like he is not fazed at all, in fact his face is unreadable as he continues to stare at the fiery blaze in front of him.

18

5.28am.

Walking home from what used to be Jake's place, the skin on my face filthy dirty from soot. I'm so tired and I can still taste the smoke in my mouth.

Well not walking all the way, I got Matt to drop me off down the road a bit; I need to clear my head before returning to the chaos and emotion that has ended up at home as everyone gathers at the B&B.

It wasn't a nice sight as daylight broke to reveal the true extent of the damage. The homestead and dairy unit stood empty, nothing but charcoal frames remained. Luckily Max and Jake had moved the cows down to the back grazing fields after the last milking so all the stock were clear of the fire. Millie, myself, Matt and Brendon volunteered to herd them to the neighbouring property this morning so they could get milked.

Matt took Max and Mrs Crankshaw back to the B&B while Sid rode Betty's scooter back to the house. Jake remained to assist the police with their investigations.

"Remind me again why we are walking?" asks Millie as she strolls beside me, equally as tired and grubby as a result of the smoke and playing dairy farmer.

"Because I need time to clear my head," I said, "and besides I think my lungs may need the fresh air."

"Roger that," said Millie in a quiet voice.

We walk in silence for a while, the scuff of gravel beneath our moving feet the only sound between us. I didn't get a chance to speak with Jake, to be honest it wouldn't surprise me if it never registered to him I was there, he seem so entranced in the fire, it was beyond spooky. Mrs Crankshaw and Max seemed a little aloof and withdrawn. I guess shock affects everyone in different ways.

"Hey?" said Millie suddenly breaking the silence, "you don't think he did it do you?"

"Who?"

"Jake. You don't think he would have started the fire do you?"

"What? As in accidentally?"

"No, as in deliberately," she said in a quiet voice, pausing to look at me.

"Millie!" I spluttered, stopping dead on the spot and turning towards her, "that's an awful thing to say, you better be careful, that's my future boyfriend you're accusing!" I crinkle my nose in disgust and continue walking.

"Well the police are saying it's suspected arson," said Millie catching up with me, "and come on Lisa don't you think it's a little suspicious that Jake shows up out of the blue after selling his share of the family farm and embezzling CWA funds to run off with a married woman? Who he then discarded like an old rag anyway, leaving her high and dry in a mental health unit; and all of a sudden he is the model citizen, a standup all round nice guy and by magic what's left of the family farm, including Rick's share has suddenly caught fire."

"Millie that's not fair," I scolded, "Jake may have made a lot of mistakes but arson is not something he would be capable of, he's not like that."

"How do you know he's not capable?" pressed Millie, "you said that last time and looked what happened."

"Yeah well this time he is different Millie."

"Different how?"

"Just different, I cannot explain it," I snapped walking faster to get away from her taunts, my face burning red, because I have to admit the thought did cross my mind. Millie is right, Jake shows up and this happens. Does seem a little odd, but another part of me is saying Jake wouldn't do it, and no I can't explain how he's different, I believe he has changed for the better. But in light of everything it's going to take some hard work by Jake and myself to convince Millie and everyone else.

We continued to walk towards the familiar letter box which signals home and I can see Jamie in the cow paddock, looks like he is with Sid.

"I did warn you not to get sucked in Lisa," said Millie her voice softening a bit, "just be careful."

Oh great, now Jamie has spotted us.

"He didn't do it Millie," I said quietly before turning back to a frantic Jamie who is now running towards us.

"Oh my earth children," said Jamie embracing us both, "my heart has been hurting all night for those poor people and cows, I hope you are okay."

"We're fine," said Millie in a bright voice pulling away from Jamie's embrace, "but Lisa here may need a meditation with the cows," she said, continuing towards the front entrance, "she seems to have lost her way," she added in a sarcastic tone.

"No time," Jamie tutted sadly as I shot a glare at Millie, "the police want to speak with Lisa."

"Me?" I exclaimed.

"Yes, apparently Betty had reported her scooter stolen and they want to talk with you."

Sitting at kitchen table with police.

Okay so after a couple of cups of tea and witnessing my apology to a very mad Betty, all charges of theft of an old person's scooter have now been dropped.

But now I am being interviewed about the fire.

Not that there is anything I can help them with, the police have interviewed everyone that was there at the last milking including bus-load of men, but no-one saw anything out of the ordinary.

"So it was just you and Brendon that arrived at the farm first?" asked the police officer. The same police officer that was here when I discovered the dope in the ceiling; the same police officer that attended the church after Larry my ghost friend alerted them to the dead body under the stairwell on the day of Matt and Neroli's wedding; and the same police officer that interviewed the members of the CWA after the scandal when we sold eye pillows filled with marijuana.

So it's understandable he is looking at me as if to say 'you again'. Well in fact he did say that, I just wish he hadn't said it in front of Mum and Dad, as by the look they are giving me I will face another interrogation after he leaves.

"And when you arrived at the farm did you notice anything different?"

I said no but my head was saying yes, I mean I did notice Jake's caravan was gone.

"So after you arrived at the Crankshaw's farm what did you do?"

"I went inside to look for Jake," I said, "but there didn't appear to be anyone home."

Well I ran inside screaming his name but we can leave out all the dramatics.

"So then you left the farm?"

"Um no I then took... I mean *borrowed,* the farm bike to go down to the milking shed to look for someone."

"So you borrowed the farm bike?"

"Yes."

"Whom did you ask to borrow the farm's bike?"

"Um... no-one."

"So you just took it?"

"No I borrowed it."

The police officer raised his brow and scribbled something down on his paper before continuing.

"So Edsgard went with you?"

"Brendon? Yes that's right."

"And when you arrived at the milking shed did you see anything unusual?"

"Um, no, no-one was there."

"So no-one was around the milking shed at that time?"

"Oh, not when I first got there but then Jake arrived and told us the others from the tour group were on their way."

"And again Ms Collins you didn't see anything out of the ordinary?"

"No," I shook my head.

Okay, except for Jake carrying a fuel tin and dodgy extension lead, plus his ute was full of boxes.

"Okay well that's all Miss Collins, and I don't have to tell you the drill as I'm sure you already know but if you do remember anything else that may help us please let us know."

I got up to leave the table as Brendon was waiting to talk to the officer. Instead of exiting through the living room where everyone was gathered I exited through the back door in the hope I can make it to the shower before anyone stops to talk to me.

Alas no such luck.

"You okay?" asked Daniel as I tiptoed around to the bathroom and smacked straight into Daniel coming the other way. It's weird as I haven't really spent any time with Daniel since the whole gay thing, I mean for the past twelve months he has done nothing but consume my head and in the past week he seems a million miles away.

"Yeah fine," I scoffed, "you know, police always make me nervous," I joked.

"So anyone take your fancy?" said Daniel.

"What ya mean?"

"From the potential dates we set up for you," he said rolling his eyes in a friendly way.

"Oh… that."

God that seems a million miles away as well.

"Okay then," said Daniel sensing my disinterest, "some woman are just so hard to please," he sighed in a joking way.

"Well did you want to come and say goodbye? Matt is just about to take the guys to the main bus in town."

"What? Are they leaving already? They still have two more days here don't they?"

"They did have but the mine wants them to back earlier."

Daniel gives my chin a quick friendly squeeze as he skips off whistling a tune as he goes. He is in a good mood despite everything, unless he has been under a rock, did he not hear about what just happened to the Crankshaw's? Well again, I guess shock affects everyone differently.

Matt went home for a shower and change of clothes which meant the bus-load of men are not quite going yet, which means I also have time for a quick shower.

As the water trickles down my back I cannot help but feel sad they are going, and I also feel like it's a lost opportunity. Which is strange as I didn't like any of them, certainly none of them took an interest in me or me in them, so really it was a complete waste of time. In fact I feel like the whole week has been one big circus, don't know where Angela the tarot reader was coming from when she said I will have to choose. I mean let's face it, out of the men the universe supplied me, none are even close to being my type and the one I did like is suspected of arson.

Woah, where did that come from? I mean no-one is accusing anyone of anything yet, so why do I have it in the back of my mind that Jake burnt down the farm?

Maybe it was the fact that Jake was holding a fuel can and dodgy electrical cord and the fire department said they suspect the dairy shed had a faulty cord running from it that sparked some fuel which ignited.

Doesn't explain how the house went up, one accident yes, but two…??

And the more I think about it, where did that caravan go? I'm sure Mrs Crankshaw said something about they are going to stay in the caravan, which means it wasn't damaged in any way. I mean it seems a bit unusual it wasn't there on the night of the fire.

... and arson, I mean who else can it be? It's not like the Crankshaw's have any enemies.

Hmmm but then again there are rumours about them being in financial trouble, maybe they have gambling debts or something underground they have been hiding, oh my god, it *is* possible Jake did it.

All of a sudden even though the water is warm, my body has gone cold, and there is only one thing I need to do and that is to confront Jake and ask him outright! If he does confess and said he did it then well, that's it, him and I are finished for sure; and if he says he didn't do it, will I spend the rest of my life wondering if he did?

Nah of course not, I'd accept the answer.

Shutting off the water I dry myself off and reach for the phone.

No message from Jake so I text him and ask if he is okay and does he want to come up for dinner.

There, that's sending a silent message to say 'I don't care if you are being accused of arson, I'm here for you'.

"Lisa you in there?" came a voice with a knock at the door.

Sounds like Dad.

"Um yes?"

"I need to speak with you about your, ahem, 'friend'."

"Which one," I asked, drying off my legs.

"The hippie looking one," said Dad in a stern voice.

Groaning, I slipped on my shorts and top and opened the door.

"For the record Dad, he is not my friend," I said as I continued to towel dry my head, "so what about him?"

"He needs to go," said Dad in a stern voice, "he is annoying your mother and me; he seems to think he is a long lost lover, I don't think he's right in the head."

"Oh Dad, he's fine, he's a new age man, that's what his beliefs are, he wouldn't hurt a fly."

"Sounds like a can short of a six-pack. You invited him here; you need to ask him to leave as my patience with him is wearing very thin."

"Don't worry Dad he'll be gone soon, very soon in fact, the tour group is leaving today."

"No dear they have already left, and your hippy friend has chosen to stay here, he said his journey is not complete."

What the…?

Pushing passed Dad I ran to the living room. What does he mean bus-load of men have already left? I didn't even get a chance to say goodbye.

Entered the living room to find Millie collecting some plates. Yep bus-load of men that were littering the place not 12 minutes earlier, have gone.

"Are they gone?" I ask Millie feeling deflated.

"Yep," she said breathing a sigh, "Matt has just dropped them off at the main bus in town. It's been a great week apart from this morning don't you think?"

Okay now I feel really deflated.

"Um don't you think?" said Millie again in her voice which can only mean 'if you don't agree I will rip your head off'.

"Yes great week," I mumbled, trying to hide the fact I feel let down, okay so I didn't like any of them but now they are gone…

"Brendon's just packing up as well," said Millie pulling me from my thoughts.

"Brendon is leaving?" I repeated in disbelief.

"Well what did you think, he was going to stay forever?" said Millie puzzled, "he said he will work on the tourism video then put it together for us as a package, so that's exciting, but may take a while. The police have seized his camera for now as he took footage of the Crankshaw farm on fire. Still cannot believe it."

"Where are Mrs Crankshaw and Max?" I asked, "are they still here?"

"No they have gone to Max's sisters in town; Jake came and got them before.

The new caravan they brought is around there so they are going to live in that while the insurance is sorted out, luckily Jake decided to move the caravan aye, otherwise it would have gone up in smoke as well."

Jake was here and he didn't even come in and say hello? Now I really feel deflated.

Typical. I take a shower for a brief moment and everything happens.

I know Millie was taking a dig at Jake so I just glare at her as she continues to tidy up. But I'm sure Jake said the caravan was in town getting repairs done which means he has lied about it, not that I would admit that to Millie. I am certain deep down Jake didn't do it.

Millie hasn't spoken to the police yet and I am praying she doesn't because knowing her she won't come out and say anything exactly but Millie possesses this talent of saying something without actually saying anything, so I know in a roundabout way she will plant a seed in the police's head that Jake did it.

But why didn't Jake come in and say hello? I mean okay he has a lot on his plate at the moment but I'm supposed to be his girlfriend, aren't I?

Brendon's entrance pulls me from my depressed thoughts; he looks a little odd without his camera. He places his bags down as Millie approaches him for a farewell hug. Sid also comes through with Amy in his arms to say goodbye; this is all happening too fast for me, as quick as everyone arrived they go again and I feel like I am standing on a ledge with nothing in front of me. Sid, Millie and Brendon continue to chatter lightly about the past week and Brendon is thanking them for their hospitality. Finally after another embrace from Millie, Brendon turns to me.

"Thank you Lisa," he says giving me a half hearted embrace, "I have had so much fun this week."

"Hmm," I said not feeling his comment.

"Shame things have ended like they have but I shall be in touch soon with the tourism film, I think you're going to like it," he said in a singsong voice.

Hmm don't think so, I said in my head, not out loud of course, only because I don't feel like talking full stop.

"Thanks for everything," I mumbled as I withdrew from his embrace, mumbled something about a safe trip and left the room before I burst into tears.

Now I'm back in my bedroom under the sanctuary of my bedcovers sulking like a child that has been denied ice cream but I am so tired and my stomach has been doing flip-flops for days now.

I feel like I have reached an all time low and I'm starting to regret the fact I didn't insist we do a dating show; I should have insisted that I go on proper dates with the men, in fact I should have insisted I choose the men. Then I wouldn't be under the covers of my bed with a facial expression like a hound dog, I would be with my new man making plans for marriage and babies.

I'm meant to be at the shop today but cannot face it, think I might text Daniel and tell him I'm sick.

Oh my god, which reminds me I haven't even checked my phone to see if Jake has answered my text, jeez, I'm slipping.

Quickly deflated again when I saw no such message has been replied to. Flicked a text to Daniel letting him know I won't be coming into the shop today due to up-and-coming pmt symptoms which is code for feeling naff so piss off world.

Pulled covers over my head again and slumped down into the softness of my bed to feel sorry for myself, hadn't been sulking for even five minutes when phone started to ring.

Grr, probably Daniel.

No, it's Betty, not answering it.

Let phone ring and lay there listening to the beep as my phone informs me I have a missed call.

I could go on and on in my head about what I should have done, or analyse why I get drunk and sleep with youths, or why I am sooo attracted to Jake who is not only a thief and adulterer but also a suspected arsonist, okay so he's not suspected yet, well not by police, only by Millie so that shouldn't count; but instead I am choosing to forget anything ever happened and sleep for a week.

Oh phone is ringing.

Oh bloody hell it's Betty again. Not going to let it ring again just going to decline call.

Should really turn my phone off but thinking is not such a good idea since Jake may want to call me. Okay now where was I? Oh yes, sleeping for a week.

"Lisa?" called Millie barging into my bedroom like a barging bossy person, "phone for you, it's Betty."

Grrr, feel the slight thud on the bed as Millie throws the phone on to the covers and leaves hastily. I fling back the sheets, laying on my back for a second contemplating if I should talk to her or not.

"Lisa… Lisa… hello… hello?" comes Betty's voice through the line as the phone lies in the middle of the bed.

Grrr.

"Yes, yes I'm here," I said picking up the phone.

"I tried your mobile twice and left a message, are we coming to you or are you going to the shop today dear? Because we can come there if it suits."

"Coming for what?"

"Urgent CWA meeting. Everyone is here, we're just waiting for you."

"When did this meeting get called?" I asked irritably, "I haven't had any notice."

"Of course you wouldn't have had any notice, we only just called you."

'Urgent' CWA meeting in the shop of Cannon and Collins. Photography, Event Planning and Supplies.

Okay I *now* know why I get drunk and sleep with youths.

"I thought you were sick?" asked Daniel as I slumped down into my chair behind my desk. I answered him with a wave of my hand as Betty stood up.

"Okay dears I called this urgent meeting because as you all know our dear friend and long standing member lost everything last night in a fire."

I only just noticed Mrs Crankshaw is the only one not here.

"Well I was just speaking with her and Max this morning and as I was offering words of comfort I reminded her that the insurance will give her the new house she was always wanting, you know to give her a bit of light at the end of the tunnel, and well," Betty paused for a moment breathing a sad sigh, "it turns out they were not insured."

Everybody lets out a slight gasp, even Daniel who was sitting behind his desk pretending not to hear, almost choked as he took a sip of his coffee.

"How can they not be insured?" Maggie began, sounding slightly outraged, "how can you run a farm and not be insured, that's a bit irresponsible."

Murmurs of agreement.

"Well that's the other sad part," said Betty, "they had to let the insurance lapse because they couldn't afford to renew it; the farm financial status has been grim for some time apparently."

"But they just brought a new caravan," said Mary, "surely it couldn't have been that bad."

"The caravan was brought by Jake, that's why Jake has come back, to help them out of their debt."

I'm suddenly more alert at the sound of Jake's name, and more still, of the fact he came back to help, god why isn't Millie here to hear this?

"Well so he should," said Maggie in a self righteous tone, "after all he caused this in the first place."

I so wanted to defend Jake against Maggie's comment but I let it go.

I glanced over at Daniel to see him picking up his phone, I know his ears have been flapping throughout this meeting, well it's not his fault his desk is just on the other side of the room, he cannot help but be thrust into the middle of an old people's meeting but I bet you anything he is about to ring Rick and ask him if it's true.

And if it is true, which I have no doubt it is, then why didn't Rick help out? Obviously it's Jake that has come back to save things, I mean Rick hasn't been near the place for months. Just goes to show who the true hero is after all.

Man, why isn't Millie here!

Should have recorded it.

"So anyway that's the story," sighed Betty continuing, "but even if they were insured, at this stage the police are suspecting arson so if they prove it the insurance wouldn't pay out unless they prove the suspect is not related and it was a random act."

"Arson," said Mary in disbelief.

"Well what else could it be?" said Maggie, "unusual that both the milking shed and house went up, let's face it they are nowhere near each other, no fire jumps from building to building that far away, sounds like arson to me."

"But who would want to do such a thing?" Mary said, "the Crankshaw's have been upstanding citizens of the community for years, they don't seem the type to have enemies."

"No *they* don't," said Maggie with her eyebrows slightly raised, "but other family members might."

No-one said anything to that, they didn't have to, they all nodded to each other in a wink wink, nudge nudge way. I folded my arms across my chest in defense of Jake, how dare they. Just because he made a mistake doesn't mean he has to wear that label for life. After all he was the one who came back to help them out of their financial troubles, they quickly forget that don't they.

Bugger it, I am going to say something and put these biddies in their place. Went to open my mouth when Daniel interrupted, "ladies I think we should just settle down for a moment," he said getting out from his chair and moving to lean against the front of his desk, "no-one has been arrested and charged with anything yet so I think we better rein in the accusations don't you think?"

God I love Daniel.

So do the rest of the CWA ladies by the way they look at him all swoony like, I wonder if they know he is gay?

"We are not accusing anyone," said Maggie, "we are simply suggesting if it was arson, then there would only be one person warped and twisted enough to want to do such harm to them."

"That's the same as accusing ladies," Daniel smirked.

Right that's it. I stood up abruptly.

"Listen, just because people make mistakes in the past doesn't mean they should be labeled for life!" I exclaimed, "Daniel is right, we should not be judging or 'suggesting' anyone did anything until it is proven in a court of law!"

"Oh come on now Lisa, even you know how bitter and twisted Pamela can be," scoffed Maggie, sounding slightly offended with my outburst.

"Pamela?"

Okay yeah, that's fair enough, I think I'll sit back down now, I mean the woman is nuts, I wouldn't put it passed her.

"Well if you ask me," said Betty, "she's capable of it, she's been resentful about Jake for a long time now."

"Is she still on her medication?" asked Mary.

"She refuses to take it," whispered Fran, "she reckons there is nothing wrong with her."

"Oh pff, as if," said Betty.

"Ladies!" said Daniel in a stern but amused way, "you're getting off track here, you cannot honestly tell me you called a meeting just to speculate on things."

"No of course not," Betty scoffed, "we're not that sort of people."

Daniel rolled his eyes slightly with a little smile on his face before going back to his business.

"I called you all here because as you know the lemonade stand is a bit of a hit right now but at the moment we don't really have any other cause for doing it other than to get funds back into the CWA account and get us moving again, so this morning I decided to make this," Betty said holding up a sign that says: *'Rebuilding Udders One Glass at a Time'*, accompanied by a picture of a cow and a glass of lemonade.

Oh god.

Daniel is still sporting the same amused face as he walks out of the shop with his phone in his hand; yep I think he is off to call Rick.

"And underneath I have the story of who the Crankshaw's are and what happened; okay maybe we won't raise enough money to rebuild the house but we may be able to contribute something," said Betty.

"I think it's brilliant," said Maggie, "what a wonderful idea Betty."

Murmurs of agreement all round.

"Lisa?"

I didn't answer as I suddenly spotted Jake across the street coming out of the hardware store. He still hasn't answered my text and to be honest he looks terrible.

Okay I cannot stand this silence any longer, I really need to go and talk to him, he cannot lead me on like this and then suddenly not speak to me, it's only been 24 hours but it feels like days.

"Yeah whatever you like," I said running from the shop, passed Daniel, to try and catch Jake before he drives off. I quickly crossed the street at a half-running, half-walking pace. Jake spots me coming towards him and he looks a little surprised. Sporting a 'great to see you' smile on my face which automatically came over me, I quickened my pace and walked towards him. But all of a sudden I stopped dead.

His expression was hard as his eyes bored into me; I could feel a cold stab going into my stomach. His glance was only brief but it was enough to send me the message; he doesn't care about me at all and he certainly doesn't want me to talk to him.

Jake got into his ute and drove off without looking at me again and I am left standing in the middle of the street feeling like the whole world just came to an end.

19

Next morning (I think).

It must be, because the birds are chirping and there is a slight misty dew covering the tree branches outside my window. I must have slept like a log.

After being snubbed by Jake in the street and pulled from the middle of the road by Daniel to save me from almost getting ran over, I drove straight home in a daze and crawled into bed. I know all the affirmation posts you read on Facebook tell you to think positive and how your thoughts project the outcomes and tomorrow is a new day and blah, blah, blah, but I think they can all go and get naffed! There is nothing positive about being rejected by the one you love not once but twice. Okay so he didn't reject me as such, but ever since we slept together he hasn't even talked to me properly.

And yes I am aware that in-between times his aunties' farm was burnt to the ground but that's no reason to snub me on the street.

I feel so rested and even though I feel deflated things aren't as bad as they seemed.

Brendon is now gone and even though I may have missed an opportunity, I have decided I will make my own opportunities, which currently is to make a casserole and take it around to Mrs Crankshaw, that way I can not only do a good deed but also get to see Jake in an indirect way and then he will talk to me and realise he does want to be with me and make babies after all and then all will be right with the world. Also better get my butt to work since I skipped yesterday.

Quickly texted Daniel and told him I'm feeling better and will be into work today. I better get up and get this casserole done beforehand so I can drop it in before I go to work.

About to get out of bed when I got a text back from Daniel reminding me there is no need to come in as it's Saturday, followed by a 'glad you're feeling better'.

Saturday? Pff, no it's Thursday.

Text Daniel back and told him so as I crawled out of bed. My body is so stiff but I do feel really rested.

Phone started to ring and a quick glance at it reveals it is Daniel. I keep forgetting how much Daniel despises texting.

"Lisa it's Saturday," he said when I answered it.

"No it's Thursday, check your calendar," I said in a teasing way as I rummaged through my messy closet for something to wear. God Matt was the last one in here I wish he had put stuff back on their hangers properly.

"No Lisa I need you to listen to me, first of all, it's Saturday, you have been asleep since Wednesday. Millie got a bit concerned and phoned the doctor but he suggested that maybe the shock of the recent events had worn you out so we let you sleep on."

"I've been asleep?" I repeated.

"Yes, so it's Saturday and no need to come into work but Lisa there is something else you should know…"

Quickly hang up and check the date on my phone, yep it is indeed Saturday. I bolted to the kitchen. Oh my god I have been asleep for two days, do people not realise how much I would miss in two days?

Everything. Lots can happen in two days. I really must get this casserole done and get to Jake's immediately, oh my god two days, they must think I don't care about him, I mean them, or something. Quickly retrieve frozen meat from the freezer and throw it in the microwave to defrost. Where are the blasted carrots?

"Oh you're awake," exclaimed Millie as I frantically search the pantry for ingredients, "what are you doing?"

"Two days! You let me sleep for two days!" I screech at Millie.

"Well the doctor suggested I don't wake you," snapped Millie, "what did you want me to do?"

"Wake me Millie; wake me up. Now I have to make this damn casserole!" I yelled at her.

"Okay, okay, calm down, do you need some help?"

"Just go," I whispered to her in a dramatic way pointing to the door.

"Well before I go," said Millie, unfazed by my outburst, "just thought you should know I was going to wake you anyway as Brendon is on his way up here and wants to see you, he mentioned something about an opportunity you may be interested in," she said before departing.

Don't really care about Brendon and his false opportunities; I have a casserole to make.

My phone rang again and I answer it while grabbing the last onion from the onion bin.

"Hello," I answered in hasty panic trying to find the blasted casserole dish.

"Lisa dear it's Betty, just thought you would like to know we have some great news."

"That's great Betty but I'm in the middle of something here."

"Well the lemonade stand went really well and even though Mrs Crankshaw and Max insisted we don't do it for them, we went ahead and did it anyway."

"That's great Betty; tell me more later, right now I have to go."

"… so we have raised two thousand dollars. Well one thousand eight hundred and seventy five but Maggie's husband said he will pitch in the remainder one hundred and twenty five dollars."

"Hang on, eighteen hundred and seventy five dollars in two days?" I paused from my frantic cooking mission, "how did you manage to make that much money out of selling lemonade in such a short time?"

"Well dear we didn't *exactly* just sell just lemonade, we kinda had to branch out in other areas, in fact it's a little embarrassing and we really don't think it's for the faint-hearted person to know about and there is some concern as Fran seems to think it may be illegal but..."

"Okay, okay, forget it. I don't want to know Betty, look I am having a wee cooking crisis so I have to go..."

"Well before you do dear we have invited the Crankshaw's down to the park this morning to present them with the cheque, we thought it be appropriate to do this the same time as the mining bus gets in since well they were, I mean are, our biggest customer. So if you could make it that would be great. Sorry it's such short notice but the bus will be here soon and Jake said he will try and convince Max and Barb to go down for a bit of surprise."

Jake?

"Betty when did you say this was happening?"

"In about 20 minutes dear but we know you have been a bit under the weather so..."

"Be right there!"

Ditched casserole and ran towards bedroom to change hideous clothes. This is my opportunity to see Jake in an amicable environment. I threw on my safe dress and headed for the bathroom, the good thing about this safe dress is it doesn't require a lot of makeup and can also get away with wild hair. Ditching toothbrush I grabbed keys and headed off towards the door.

"Where are you going?" said Millie as I hastily pushed passed her toward the car, "Brendon will be here soon."

"Park in town," I called back to her, "will explain later, no time to lose."

Started car and headed towards town, phone rang again and I thought it would have been Millie cursing me for leaving the kitchen in a mess but it's Daniel again. I let it go to voice mail as I frantically drove into town. Passing the charred remains of the Crankshaw farm, I cannot help but feel a stab of pain for them both, all that hard work over the years and this is how it ends. And Maggie's right, there cannot be any other explanation for the fire other than arson, two separate buildings alight at the same time is definitely no accident and now it's been suggested that the only enemy the Crankshaw's had is Pamela Horton. After all Jake had sold his share of the farm to developers so he could have enough money for him and Pamela, who was married at the time, to run away.

Only Jake left without her, taking the money with him, leaving her behind after the affair had been exposed with no money and her marriage in ruins, it's no wonder she had a mental breakdown and ended up in care. I guess it's kind of plausible she could have done it. I'm kinda relieved because it's pointed suspicion away from Jake. Even though this theory has only come about from chatting in my office with a bunch of CWA ladies, but I'm sure the police have a handle on it.

Arrived in town to see a crowd gathering at the lemonade stand. I listened to my voice message from Daniel as I climbed out the car and made my way towards the marquee. Daniel's message said he needed to tell me he found out something interesting about the Crankshaw's that he thought was odd and if I was interested to call him back. Daniel says that all the time, 'if I'm interested', I'm not one to gossip but...

The mining bus has just pulled up and across the street I can see Mrs Crankshaw and Max arriving in Jake's shiny ute, driven by Jake, with equally shiny caravan hitched behind it. They must be on their way to the farm to set up the caravan for living quarters.

"Lisa," Daniel said appearing beside me, "I've been trying to call you."

"Yes I got your voice message," I said, "but I haven't got time, I'm here to present this fundraising cheque to the Crankshaw's."

"Well keep this to yourself," he said scratching his head, "but I phoned Rick to see how he was, he's not in town at the moment, he's away working but is making plans to come back. Of course naturally he is a bit shocked but I bought up the insurance dilemma and what Barb had told Betty 'cause Rick told me in confidence a while back about the financial trouble they were in. And I'm sure he mentioned that to keep the creditors out of it as they didn't want any paper trail of their troubles on record, both Rick and Jake had been footing the bills, along with the insurance, which Rick had renewed and paid in full months ago."

"So… what you are saying is the Crankshaw's are insured?"

"Yes, very much so."

"So why would Mrs Crankshaw tell Betty they weren't?" I whispered to Daniel.

"You got me," he mumbled back, "attention maybe."

"But the Crankshaw's are refusing any charity handouts," I said, "well according to Betty they are. Jake had to convince them to come down here today and accept a cheque from the CWA."

"Is that what this is about?" Daniel asks slightly alarmed as he scans the rather large crowd that has just gathered.

"Lisa, you ready?" Betty asked, appearing at my side and tugging on my arm, "come on they are waiting."

She leads me to a makeshift podium and thrusts the bank cheque into my hand. I spied Jake lingering in the back of the crowd; his face was one of neutral expression. Maggie leads Mrs Crankshaw and a red faced Max towards the stand, the bus-load of miners were still purchasing drinks with looks of curiosity on their faces as they try and work out what is going on.

Max and Mrs Crankshaw don't look happy; in fact they both look like someone has done them an injustice. Or maybe the fact they lied about their insurance and are now about to accept a charity cheque is eating away at their conscience.

"Lisa!" Betty hissed beside me as I pulled myself from my thoughts to a waiting silent crowd.

Oh okay I just realised I didn't prepare a speech, shit, I'm just going to have to make it up as I go along which is a bad idea.

I clear my throat.

"Hello ladies and gentleman, and bus-load of men; we are gathered here today to um, I mean we are gathered today for a great cause."

Looking out into the sea of faces I see Angela the tarot reader and a few from my old meditation group.

Okay not to worry, just picture them naked.

"The cause being one of great tragedy and loss."

Oh just spied Mum and Dad, eww quick don't picture them naked, abort, abort.

"Well you see there was a fire and one of the great pillars of our community lost everything in this fire."

I focus on Jake again and standing behind Jake with a very official looking man, is Brendon and his camera.

Honestly that man really needs to get a hobby.

Also just realised I don't think I had a pee this morning after two day of sleeping, I'm surprised I've gone this long.

"So with the power invested in me I would like to..."

Okay shouldn't have thought about pee, am desperate now.

"Lisa!" Betty hissed beside me, "don't forget to mention the CWA."

"Pardon?" I hissed back.

"The CWA, you know?" as she pointed discreetly to the lemonade stand.

Oh right of course.

"Ahem as I was saying, with the power invested in me by the CWA, I would like to present this cheque for two thousand dollars to Max and Barbara Crankshaw from the fundraising efforts of the Country Woman's Institute Taromeo branch lemonade stand to put towards the rebuilding of their dairy farm," phew.

Sounds of applause ring out as I signal them to come forward and claim their cheque in a hasty manner as I really really need to pee now. Both Mrs Crankshaw and Max look embarrassed as they gingerly take the cheque from my hand pausing briefly to get their photo taken by Mary.

"Now remember, there are refreshments available," I continued running with my sense of importance, "so don't forget with your small donation you could be helping the next great cause, our motto after all is 'The CWA, here for all your needs'. Max, Barbara, is there anything you would like to say?"

"Lisa get down from there," Mum hissed as her and Dad, followed by Jamie, appeared, "the police are here and you're embarrassing yourself with your shuffling and jiggling, do you need the loo or something?"

"Great speech," Jamie said, "so enlightening."

"What is going on here?" asked the police officer, accompanied by his colleague, "we weren't informed of an event taking place today."

"Oh well no, you wouldn't have been you see because it was kind of a spur of the moment thing. We had a small fundraiser for Max and Barbara Crankshaw, so we were just handing them the cheque from our fundraising efforts."

"And where are the Crankshaw's?" the second officer asked, "we just need to confirm this."

"Oh they are here," I said turning around in time to see Max and Barbara walking quickly though the crowd towards Jake's ute as fast as Mrs Crankshaw's chubby legs will go. Jake catches up with the pair from the side line and also starts quickly towards the ute.

Oh shit, Jake's leaving and I didn't get a chance to talk to him, again.

"Oh no you don't!" I yelled as I also took off to catch Jake before he makes it to the ute. My small outburst attracts attention and now everyone pauses to watch what the big chase is all about. Max is the first one to reach the truck as he jumps in the driver's seat and starts the engine.

"Quickly my darling!" he shouts to Mrs Crankshaw who hastily opens the passenger door and jumps in as Max quickly does a u-turn, almost toppling the hitched caravan in his attempt to make a hasty exit. Jake now reaches the ute but I stop dead in my tracks because instead of Max stopping the ute to let Jake in the back, he speeds off just as Jake reaches for the door handle.

What the...?

"So long!" Mrs Crankshaw yells out the window, waving the cheque at the stunned crowd, "farming suckkksss," she yelled as the ute and caravan disappear down the road leaving the onlookers, not to mention Jake, stunned.

"Okay Ms Collins, whose lemonade stand is this and does it have a permit?" the policeman asks.

20

The crowd has now dispersed and the bus transporting the miners has gone, apart from Brendon who is still here with his annoying camera. Everyone has gone back to their lives and forgotten what just happened except for me.

And Betty, Fran and Mary.

And of course Jake.

Jake never said a lot after that, I let him use my phone so he could call his mobile which was left in the runaway ute but as suspected, Mrs Crankshaw and Max did not pick up. Daniel offered him a ride round to Rick's place which Jake accepted.

And even though not much was said between us I can definitely say with confidence the silent treatment he was giving me was not because of something I had done, he's just got a lot on his plate at the moment.

"Ms Collins? Please answer the question."

Oh god.

"It's Betty's, Betty's lemonade stand. But you see Barbara Crankshaw was meant to arrange the permit."

"And let me guess, it got lost in a fire?" the officer said in an unjustified sarcastic tone.

"Uh uh," I nodded.

"Okay Ms Collins," he sighed, "you and the CWA have one week to apply for a new permit or the lemonade stand will be shut down, do you understand me?"

"Uh ha," I nodded as Betty and the girls give each other a silent high five behind the police officer's back.

Left them to it as I made my way to the car after sitting in the public toilets discarding two days worth of pee.

I cannot wait to get home and tell Millie before anyone else does. I cannot believe the Crankshaw's would just up and do a runner like that in front of everyone; in fact I give a slight giggle at the thought of it. But as funny as it sounds, were they the ones that burnt down their farm? From what just happened, they must have had a bigger plan, you don't just do a runner on the spur of the moment. Do you?

Cannot wait to get home so I can sit with Millie and analyse it, and you never know, she may even apologise to me for doubting Jake in the first place.

Nah, Millie doesn't apologise.

"Lisa wait up!" said Brendon as he runs toward me with a camera in his hand.

Oh that's right I forgot he was here, quick don't turn around just pretend you didn't see him.

"Lisa I need to talk to you about something right now."

Quick get in the car.

He probably wants to talk to me about the stupid tourism video, well I'm over it. If he wants to talk to me he can bloody well do so when it suits me, I mean has Brendon forgotten he gave me the impression of becoming a celebrity dating show hostess and then tricked me into making damper bread and being chased through olive groves by crazy Italian people?

And then he leaves the area with just a 'thanks for your time'. Well I haven't forgotten, so if Brendon wants to talk to me then he has to make an appointment.

"Lisa will you stop!" he said leaning in the window of the car just as I was about to start the engine, "I want you to meet someone," he said, signaling to the man wearing a crisp shirt and dress pants and sporting designer sunglasses to come over.

"Not interested," I said in a hoity tone, "I'm far too busy and important to meet people," I said, starting the engine.

"Lisa. This is Darryl Loft," Brendon said quickly, holding on to the car as if it was rolling backwards and he is trying to hold it still, "he is a television producer, he wants you to have your own reality tv show."

Facebook.

Lisa Collins.

About me:

Well after inviting a bus-load of men to appear on an amateur dating show in the hope of finding true love so I can get married and have babies only to discover it wasn't a dating show but a boring tourism documentary, I have now decided not to get married and have babies. Instead I am going to focus on my career as a television personality. I have just signed a contact with TAE (The Aussie Entertainment Network) for which I will be staring in my own reality television series. It's about a former city girl who moves to the country and starts her own business. I have a wonderful assistant and spiritual advisor to help me (Jamie) and am about to add a new business venture to 'Cannon and Collins. Photography, Event Planning and Supplies', it will now be 'Cannon and Collins. Photography, Event Planning and Dating Agency'. We still hire party supplies but cannot fit it into the title. Check out our page on Facebook.

21

6 weeks later.

3.45pm, sitting in doctors room.

Yes I'm at the doctors but all is fine, just getting a checkup as think I'm coming down with a flu and cannot afford to be sick now I have my new career as a television celebrity about to start.

And it's soo exciting I have hardly slept a wink. I have decided I would make a better aunty than mother and I don't need a man now I am a celebrity career woman. Millie got so jealous when I told her (in a nice way). She said it was about time I got my own show since drama seems to follow me everywhere.

After Brendon got the call from the police station to collect his camera when they'd finished with viewing the footage for the enquiry into the Crankshaw fire, the policeman said it was the most entertaining amateur film he had ever seen, so much so that the police station held an impromptu movie night and most of them hadn't had such a good laugh in years.

Hmmmm.

But anyway with that in mind, Brendon decided to take a chance and show the film to the producer from the new television network and well…

And the good part is I don't have to do much, just be me and carry on what I normally do with a camera crew behind me and get paid for it, how cool is that! It's going to be so much more fun now I have set up a dating agency. Daniel wasn't keen to begin with but when I read him the statistics of country dating and said we could capitalise on this by him offering glamour shots of clients and me getting more and more events in the way of weddings and engagement parties, he finally started to see it from a business point of view and not a 'Lisa wants a date' point of view.

It took some convincing on my part that I am completely over men and the dating scene and from now on will just be a dating adviser.

I was a bit worried when Brendon first introduced me to Darryl Loft and the idea was pitched to me about 'tales from the lemonade stand', that's the title of the show.

I didn't know why they wanted to do a reality television series about my life, I mean it's not like it's very interesting but as Brendon pointed out, for the first couple of episodes they will use some of the footage from what they already have, you know the Ute Muster Ball, when the bus-load of men came to town, when we discovered the Crankshaw farm burning, that sort of thing, so I guess it'll be entertaining. And he assured me people love this stuff so I'll just have to trust it's all going to work out.

And since the idea began, my ghost friend Larry has shown up again so I know it's meant to be, even though putting up with Larry is going to be hard; I mean just the other day he tangled Fran up in Brendon's microphone cord and she got such a fright her incontinence problem came back so I know having him around may be a bit of a challenge, but all the same, I'm pleased he's back.

Mum and Dad however are a bit worried as they think my imaginary friend from childhood is back and are under the opinion I may need to slow down a little, but I told them not to worry as I haven't seen my imaginary friend Bono the walking walrus since I was nine and I don't need a break, I'm doing just fine.

They left two days ago to go gem hunting in Winton. Thank goodness. Although Jamie has been whinging for Mum ever since, hope he shuts up soon he is driving me crazy.

Matt is desperately trying to jump on my stardom, he has declared himself my self-appointed body guard and chauffeur but of course only in-between his real job as an apprentice mechanic.

He has even written out his own contract for me to sign which I haven't read yet but according to Damo one of the conditions is that he is to be supplied with a Holden SS Commodore (red) and he must be in all film shots and gets to wear a mafia style suit.

Hmm we will see.

Jake is still around and we talk occasionally but the spark is not there any more, not sure when it died, but that's okay because if it was meant to be it would have been.

Jake and Rick got a postcard from the Crankshaw's a couple of weeks ago saying they are not really sorry for taking off like that, they were so sick of the daily struggle of the farm and are now enjoying retirement and both boys can quote 'go suck eggs'.

The police still want to speak to them about the fire and investigations into the arson are ongoing. So far the suspects are: Jake (not likely), Mr and Mrs Crankshaw (possibility), and Pamela Horton (most likely).

We have a sweepstake board up at the new CWA headquarters about who started the fire and my money is on Pamela.

Yes the CWA has new headquarters after the members proudly purchased the old Scout building on Jacob Street from the profits of the lemonade stand.

It's great, a bit old but it has a full working kitchen and toilet facilities; and since Brendon filmed footage of the lemonade stand it has now became a bit of an icon in the town.

The local community Beautification Society even got together and made it into a permanent structure for the many buses that stop in the town before heading out west to the mines. We sell all sorts of things from there, mainly souvenirs and that sort of thing, but Fran and Betty still get slightly nervous when the police are either mentioned or nearby so best I stay out of it, the less I know the better.

Maybe it was the bus-load of men, or the fact Jake came back into my life, or the fact I have discovered I have a habit of getting drunk and sleeping with youths, whatever it was, it made me realise that none of those things could ever fill me with happiness.

Happiness comes from within and I don't need a man or babies to fulfill that. I just need to be happy. And for the first time since I turned 39, I can honestly say I am looking forward to turning 40.

Lisa Collins, celebrity television star and successful business woman.

"Okay Lisa I have your results," said the doctor, coming back into the room, "well you haven't got an infection, nor does it appear you have a virus."

"Oh that's great," I said retrieving my bag from the floor.

"But you do have a condition that will slow you down for the next eight to nine months."

"Pardon?"

"Lisa, you are in fact... pregnant."

end*